GW00458676

Morecambe Bay Trilogy 1

Book 1 - Left For Dead

Book 2 - Circle of Lies

Book 3 - Truth Be Told

Morecambe Bay Trilogy 2

Book 4 - Trust Me Once

Book 5 - Fall From Grace

Book 6 - Bound By Blood

Morecambe Bay Trilogy 3

Book 7 - First To Die

Book 8 - Nothing To Lose

Book 9 - Last To Tell

Note: The Morecambe Bay trilogies are best read in the order shown above.

Don't Tell Meg Trilogy

Features DCI Kate Summers and Steven Terry.

Book 1 - Don't Tell Meg

Book 2 - The Murder Place

Book 3 - The Forgotten Children

Standalone Thrillers

Dead of Night

One Last Chance

No More Secrets

So Many Lies

Two Years After

Friends Who Lie

Now You See Her

TRUST ME ONCE

MORECAMBE BAY TRILOGY 2

PAUL J. TEAGUE

PROLOGUE

12:01 am January 1st, 2000

Tiffany heard the waves first, crashing in the darkness. They hadn't roused her though; it must have been the incessant crackling of fireworks sounding overhead, as persistent as gunfire.

She leaned forward and felt the seat belt pressing into her chest. Why was she strapped into a car? The last thing she remembered was leaving the village hall. The community celebration was in full flow, she'd made her excuses and left early.

She was still in her dress, but her vision was blurred and her head was pounding. Had she got slightly drunk? Nobody could blame her if she had. It was a new millennium, no less, a once in a lifetime opportunity to wave goodbye to one century and usher in another. There'd been so much hype surrounding it, Tiffany had almost had enough of the celebration before it began, but as the date neared, she'd steeled herself. She would most likely be dead by the time the next century came around, so she should make the most of it, for the children's sake as much as anything.

They were far too young to understand the significance of the celebrations, but she would take a photograph of them with a date stamp on it. If they were lucky enough to enjoy good health and good fortune, with medical advances at least one of them ought to live long enough to see in the 22nd century, if there was still a world available to live in by that date. If she had anything to do with it, there would be. The new wind farm would be just the beginning of things.

She moved her hand to her forehead, searching for a wound. Her head was thudding furiously, worse than any migraine. Tiffany figured she must have fallen or banged her head somehow. The pain was excruciating, and a sick sensation lingered in the pit of her stomach. What had happened? She started with what was in front of her. It was a car; the people carrier she'd wanted because it was big enough to fit three child seats in the back, each with a suitable seat belt. There was no way she was squeezing three young children into anything less.

A plastic Smurf toy was attached to the dashboard, confiscated after Jane was found with it in her mouth. She'd screamed when Tiffany had taken it away from her, so the compromise was that it rode with them in the front. It was Papa Smurf, but Jane always said it was Grandpa. The least she could do was to allow Jane to see the thing that reminded her of him. If only real life were as simple as the Smurfs; perhaps things wouldn't be so bad if Grandpa had managed to hang on a little longer until things were sorted out properly.

Tiffany scanned the area in front of her. What a state the car was in. The discarded snack packets and juice cartons stuffed into the glove compartment and down the sides of the doors made it an extension of their living space, a continuation of family mayhem on four wheels. The car tax disc holder was peeling away from the window. She reached out, feeling a sudden urge to smooth it down, but was once again tugged back by the seat belt.

Why was she in the passenger seat? She always drove the people carrier when the kids were in it. When it was just the two of them, David drove them in the run-around; that had been the deal since he'd got a ticket for speeding. She was appalled that Callie had been in the back of the vehicle at the time.

'She loved it; she was laughing her head off,' David had protested. It was the last time he'd ventured a defence when it came to putting any of the kids in danger. He'd learnt his lesson fast and well.

Tiffany felt around for her phone. It wasn't tucked under her leg, where she usually put it, uncomfortable though it was.

For a moment she wondered if she was in the middle of a gun battle, then realised it was the fireworks whizzing and crackling in the sky. Her eyes began to focus on the spectacular colourful flashes to her side and over the sea. At the sound of cheering and jollity to her left, she tried to pull herself up to get a better view of her surroundings.

To her right was the new RNLI boathouse. They still called it new, even though it had been there for a couple of years. If she strained her neck to the left, she could make out the sides of the now dilapidated Midland Hotel, its plain walls beautifully tinted by the explosive colours of the fireworks. Quite a crowd had gathered along the promenade, all in high spirits, many of them loud and drunk.

It was only then that Tiffany noticed the car was

running. The engine was so quiet she could barely hear it amid the constant fireworks. What the hell was she doing parked at the slipway by the lifeboat station, with the car engine on? Her mind sharpened, alert to everything that was wrong about this situation. They were supposed to be meeting at the village hall, yet this was Morecambe, and she had no reason to be there. She'd never felt as sick as this.

Then she realised. The smoke wasn't coming from hundreds of fireworks shooting into the sky. It was inside the car, surrounding her, stealing away her consciousness moment by moment. She tried to reach for the door catch, but she was paralysed by fear as the fumes enveloped her.

Filled with panic, Tiffany scanned the space. At her side, a tube was hanging through a narrow gap at the top of the rear window. Something had been stuffed into the gap; it was one of Callie's bibs. Her body stiffened as the survival instinct finally kicked in. She hadn't done this to herself, surely? Rowan was a difficult baby, and she'd felt down at times, but nothing bordering on serious depression. Why couldn't she move to save herself? She was fading, the fumes overcoming her like a predator in the darkness.

She struggled to keep her eyes open, then forced herself to turn as she thought of the children. Were any of them in the car with her? There was a small chance that she'd done this unspeakable act to herself, but never, never would she do this to her children. Their seats were empty, abandoned, toys and juice cups discarded as if they'd unclipped themselves and walked away. But they were too young for that. Rowan was a baby; only Callie could walk, and Jane insisted on crawling everywhere, adamant that walking was not for the likes of her. Where were they?

The rage inside her was smothered by the blanket of

thickening fumes as she felt herself drifting away, unable to move.

As she finally gave up the struggle to keep her eyes open, she heard a click at her right-hand side. A fresh rush of cold midnight air swept into the car, reviving her momentarily. She was aware of a voice, a young female voice, recognisable. Who was it? They were in a state of panic, out of their depth. Then there was silence.

After what seemed like an age, Tiffany realised the engine was no longer running. The door next to her opened, and somebody reached across to unbuckle the seat belt. The fresh air swept through her like an elixir, but she vomited as she was released and dragged out of the car. Her rescuer laid her gently on the concrete slipway, apologising profusely, as if it was her fault.

'Oh God, I was too late. I'm so sorry, Tiffany. I'm so sorry I didn't get here in time.'

She was crying with frustration, desperate to help, but fretting as if she'd failed.

'I've called an ambulance, Tiffany. You'll be all right. I've got to go now, or they'll know it was me. I'm so sorry I was too late.'

As the freezing air forced its way into Tiffany's exhausted lungs, her brain started to function again. The voice was Kate Allan's. What was she doing here? Ah, she was a young constable, with every reason to be there on the eve of a new millennium. She could see Kate running off, looking around her as if she feared she might be spotted. But she was in civilian clothing, with no sign of the police uniform of which she was so proud.

What about the children? Where was David? Tiffany felt a rush of adrenaline shoot through her body as she realised something terrible must have happened. As the fireworks continued to explode in an array of colour overhead, and the cheers from the hotel became more charged with excitement at the new millennium, her head slumped to the side, giving her a view of the waves lapping around the concrete of the slipway. Bobbing about in the water was Rowan's teddy bear, the insistent waves carrying it slowly but surely out into the bay.

CHAPTER ONE

Charlotte switched off the audio on her smartphone, removed her earbuds and grimaced at Nigel.

'I'm beginning to wish I hadn't taken the shorthand module; I'm struggling to get my speed up.'

Nigel laughed and took a swig of the coffee that Charlotte had made ten minutes previously.

'The problem is,' he said after swallowing a mouthful, 'you can't use video or audio recorders in court, so it's always a handy skill to have up your sleeve. I rarely use it these days, but I'm always grateful that I can do it when I need to make notes at speed. Anyway, you made the decision to put the glamour of running the Lakes View Guest House behind you, to try out this lucrative journalistic life.'

He snorted at his own comment.

'That's not exactly true; I'm still managing the guest house with Will. Piper and Agnieszka have stepped in to help, to let me do this. I'm just glad to have the chance of a career change. Another one. It's working well for everybody, I could hardly look a gift horse in the mouth, could I?'

Charlotte moved her arm around, still aware of some

discomfort where she'd dislocated it. Running the guest house had proved too physical for her in the aftermath of her injuries. The more sedentary pace of a distance learning course in journalism, with two days' work experience along-side Nigel, was the ideal prescription for recovery.

The phone rang at Nigel's side.

'There's the Batphone,' he said with a smile. 'Who knows what our next assignment could be? A missing dog? A vandalised park bench? Get the Batmobile ready, Charlotte, Morecambe needs us!'

She laughed out loud, then silenced herself as Nigel lifted the receiver. It had been a sleepy six months working at his side, but after the excitement of the previous year, it suited them both. Most of the time the town plodded along at a slow and steady pace, and that was fine by Charlotte. She'd already experienced enough excitement in the resort to last a lifetime.

Nigel's tone altered suddenly. For a moment, Charlotte considered returning to her shorthand, but there was something about the way he'd just changed gear that told her this was something more than a routine call.

With rising impatience, she listened to his non-committal responses, which gave nothing away but were packed with so much promise.

'Yes... Irwin? No, I wasn't on the paper then. No... No... Really?'

He clicked his mouse and pulled up Google to run a search.

'Yes, it's all over Google. I can't believe I never heard about it. OK, when will it be? Yes. OK. Great. Speak later.'

Charlotte was fit to burst.

'What was that about?' she asked, hardly able to contain her curiosity.

'One moment,' Nigel replied.

'This is incredible,' he said, more to himself than Charlotte.

Charlotte looked at him, waiting for his response. At last he stopped his interrogation of Google and turned his chair towards her.

'This is a great story. That was my contact at the police station tipping me off. We can't report anything yet, but he's given us the nod so we can get working in the background. Did you ever read about the Irwin case?'

'Irwin? No, never heard of him,' Charlotte replied, entranced by the intrigue of the call.

'Not him, a whole family. There were five of them. Husband, wife and three children under the age of five years old. Four of them disappeared into thin air.'

'What, here in Morecambe? How do you do that?'

'Who knows? The wife survived, but the other four family members were thought to have died, probably drowned at sea.'

'Were they in a boat?' Charlotte asked, keen to get to the nub of this story.

'No, this bit will surprise you. Are you OK to speak about what happened before? I don't want to bring too many bad memories flooding back.'

'Nigel, it's fine. Tell me.'

'You know the slipway beside the RNLI building on the sea front?'

'How could I forget it after what happened with me and Olli?'

'That's why I checked. Their family car was found there, but the husband and kids had vanished and the wife was lying beside the vehicle. It looked like some kind of suicide attempt. The kids' toys were found out at sea. No bodies were recovered, and no one ever saw the other family members again, so they were presumed dead.'

'What about the wife?'

'She didn't have a clue what had happened. She lost her mind afterwards, apparently.'

'How recent is this?' Charlotte asked.

'Well, that's the thing. It happened over twenty years ago, on the night of the new millennium.'

Charlotte thought back to that night. It was before Lucia was born and she was pregnant with Olli. She remembered because she and Will had spent the evening in Accident & Emergency getting the baby checked out, in among the New Year revellers who'd peaked too soon and had already had too much to drink. They were in Bristol at the time and the maternity leave had given her a welcome break from teaching, even if the price was a difficult pregnancy and prolonged morning sickness.

'That was a long time ago,' she said. 'I didn't have a grey hair on my head back then and every bit of my body was at least one inch higher.'

Nigel laughed.

'Why are you getting a call about something that happened years ago? Surely it's done and dusted?'

'That's what the police thought, but there's been a new development this morning. The details are still sketchy, so we can't run a story yet, but I'm going to send you out to do some digging, if you're happy for me to drag you kicking and screaming from your shorthand?'

'It's a terrible blow, but like the professional I am, I'll work through the trauma.'

Charlotte liked the irreverent atmosphere which went with the job. The journalists had to cover harrowing stories in between the humdrum matters such as lost pets and cancelled events. The relaxed atmosphere was refreshing after so many years of watching her tongue in school staff rooms.

'So, are you ever going to tell me what happened?' she asked, warming to the prospect of some news story research to sink her teeth into.

'Morecambe police found a body at the slipway in the early hours of this morning.'

'Dead?'

'No, they thought they'd found a drunk at first, but it was a young woman; they reckon she's in her early twenties. She's in a coma at Lancaster Infirmary.'

'OK, that's an interesting news story, but what does it have to do with that family – the Irwins, isn't that what you said?'

'This is all conjecture at the moment. DC Metcalfe shouldn't have tipped me off, but we know each other through our kids, so he drips information to me from time to time. You have to stay tight-lipped on this one, Charlotte; we can't report it officially until we can confirm the facts. But if what DC Metcalfe says is correct, this could be a sensational news story for the paper.'

Charlotte's right hand was already reaching for her notebook and pen. When Nigel got excited about a news story, she knew she was in for a treat. It was a chance to escape the dullness of the distance learning course and get her hands dirty with some proper reporting.

'Remember, they thought the Irwin kids and the husband were dead,' said Nigel. 'And that was twenty years ago. Well, the woman who turned up this morning is the same age as one of the Irwin children would be now.'

'That's a stretch, isn't it?' Charlotte asked, her hopes of it being a great news story fading fast.

'Under normal circumstances, yes. But she was found with an old news cutting in her pocket from the year 2000. It told the full story of their disappearance.'

'That's still not much to go on, is it?'

'No, but here's the thing. Police records show that Callie Irwin had a pronounced birthmark above her right eye. Guess what this woman has?'

'You're kidding?'

'No, and it gets better. Callie Irwin would be twenty-three years old now, and she had auburn hair as a toddler. Guess what DC Metcalfe told me about this woman? As well as the birthmark, her estimated age is 22-26, and she has auburn hair. Oh, and she was wearing the wedding ring reported missing when the mother was found over twenty years ago.'

CHAPTER TWO

Charlotte felt a stirring of excitement as she walked along the street towards the resort's library. She would never have admitted it to Will or the kids, but she missed the adrenaline rush of being in the heat of the fire. She didn't crave the terrible danger they'd been exposed to last year; it was just that life in the guest house had quickly become routine and she'd grown frustrated by the restrictions on her movement while her body recovered. The weekend's charity event would finally put all those concerns about her physical wellbeing behind her.

Will thought she was crazy, but the specialist at the hospital had pronounced her leg to be up to it at long last, so when Abi suggested making the tandem parachute jump at a local airfield, she'd jumped at the chance. She craved the rush of fear and excitement as much as her wish to support Abi's Down's Syndrome work. Life had felt flat for her and she'd been happy when Piper and Agnieszka had finally taken up her offer of regular employment.

She could sense that they might uncover a remarkable scoop. Although she'd never considered herself potential journalist material before, it turned out she had a good nose for it. She was grateful Will had indulged her by letting her follow her dream.

'As long as you sort out the day-to-day management of the business, it's up to you how you arrange the staffing.'

'The team at The Bay View Weekly doesn't start the day until ten o'clock,' Charlotte had replied, elated at such a warm response. 'I can make sure we're clear for breakfast then head up to the office. I promise, it'll all run like clockwork.'

And so it had, even though Will was constantly fishing to find out what she was up to. She had to allow him that. The lives of all four of them had been in jeopardy, so he was entitled to be jittery. Nigel's view that events like they'd experienced only ever happened once in a blue moon had helped to settle the matter for good. She was a trainee journalist, with her husband's blessing.

The library was a familiar fixture in Charlotte's life now, although it had been some time since she'd come across Jon Rogers, the local history expert who worked there. She'd begun to build a rapport with him; he had certainly helped her on more than one occasion in the past. She stopped in the entrance area, wondering if he might have retired. He was one of those gnarled, grey-haired men who appeared to have been born middle-aged yet never seemed to retire. On a previous occasion when they'd chatted, he'd alluded to retirement, unsure as to who would replace him when he left. The man was a walking encyclopedia, his mind packed with every bit of knowledge that existed about Morecambe's past.

She asked a library assistant about Jon, and they went to find him. Even the staff didn't seem to know where he lived;

it was almost as if he'd made his home in some den among the archive documents and dusty artefacts.

He surprised her by approaching from behind.

'Charlotte Grayson!' he said, causing her to jump and drop her notebook.

'Hello Jon, it's good to see you again. I'm delighted you haven't retired yet.'

She bent down to pick up her pad and could feel her face flushing at the embarrassment of being so jumpy.

Jon lowered his voice. 'I was worried about you. I read what happened in the newspaper, but I'm delighted to see you here again. You were the talk of the town for a while. And there was me thinking you and your family came to Morecambe to enjoy the quiet life.'

Charlotte laughed.

'We did come for a slower pace of life, but it appears to have eluded us so far.'

'So how can I help you this time? I must admit, whenever you turn up at the library, it's always with something a little out of the ordinary. I hope you're not going to ask me about a local building or anything as humdrum as that.'

'As if I would ask the library's local history expert anything about local history,' she said with a grin. 'I'm working at the newspaper now, training to be a journalist—'

'Well, you do seem to have a knack for ending up in the middle of breaking news stories,' Jon teased her.

'This one doesn't involve me, you'll be happy to hear. But it is remarkably interesting. What do you know about the Irwin family? This goes back to the turn of the century, by the way.'

'Eighteenth or nineteenth century?' Jon replied.

Charlotte was about to answer when she realised he was teasing her again.

'I remember those events very well, Charlotte. I was there. Not actually where it happened, but at an event close to The Midland, just along the promenade. I was questioned briefly by the police, as were all the attendees at the event, but our minds were elsewhere. Imagine how thrilling it was for me as a local historian to live a life that's spanned two centuries; I was beside myself with excitement.'

'It's the sort of event you remember all your life,' Charlotte agreed. 'Like what you were doing when the Twin Towers collapsed and where you were when Challenger exploded. Some things stay with you.'

'I take it you know what happened?' Jon asked, suddenly serious. 'It was a terrible case. I felt so sorry for the mother, even though she was a suspect for some time afterwards. The police couldn't prove anything; it was a series of bizarre events. Three children and a husband vanished, just like that. No trace of them anywhere, no sign of a fight or a struggle. And the mother – what was her name? I can't recall it now...'

'Tiffany Irwin,' Charlotte offered.

'That's right; she was known as Tiff locally. There was a lot of intrigue around the land owned by her deceased parents and a fallout with her brother. It was a bit of a mess, I recall. But nothing ever stuck; four of them disappeared from the face of the earth and poor old Tiff had a complete mental breakdown. It was all incredibly sad. Why are you asking about it so many years after? Is it an anniversary or something?'

Charlotte was tempted to reveal all the details of the police tip-off, but she contained herself and gave Jon a non-committal reply.

'Can I use the microfiche machines and copy some newspaper cuttings from around that time? We're interested in digging a little deeper and running a background feature on what happened.'

'Sure,' said Jon. He started to turn away, then paused and looked at her.

'There's something I need to mention, because I know you haven't been living here for very long. You can't report on the Irwin family without mentioning the other people who went missing around then. At least one of the families still lives locally, and I'm sure they'd be upset if you didn't mention them.'

'You mean more people disappeared like the Irwins? On the same night?'

'Not the same night, but within a short space of time. Fortunately, events like that don't happen often. The police put it down to the start of a brand new century and all the anxiety and worry surrounding it. But it was strange, that's for sure. They weren't thought to be linked. But one of them always struck me as being very unusual.'

CHAPTER THREE

Charlotte cursed the microfiche as she struggled to manoeuvre the plastic sheets. They held a tremendous number of scanned newspaper pages, and it was as much as she could do to resist being diverted by the other news stories that had dominated in Morecambe in the first week of a new millennium.

The big frustration of the day appeared to be that many local businesses had paid considerable sums of money to consultants to protect their equipment from the so-called Millennium Bug, yet come the big day, the expected Armageddon had not arrived. Charlotte remembered it well; she'd steered clear of most of it, thanks to her maternity leave.

It took no time at all to locate the news story about the Irwin family; The Bay View Weekly had gone to town with it for the first four weeks of the year.

Vanished! Three Children, One Husband, One Live-In Nanny ... And A Wife Who Remembers Nothing.

The headline was accusatory, and the following week's was just as bad:

Tragedy In The Bay. Local Mother Makes Memory Loss Claim.

Charlotte read how the police had searched the area several times. Some soft toys belonging to the children were found in the mouth of the bay, but there'd been no sign of the father, David, nor any eyewitness accounts, sightings or leads.

The second week of news coverage saved a small space on the front page for another headline.

Second Person Goes Missing In Bay Area.

This was a lady called Morgan Utworth, who'd disappeared from the resort. The article explained how police were not linking the two cases, but they had still investigated to check for similarities.

The third week's news softened the angle on Tiffany Irwin.

Tragic Family Mourned As Bay Area Unites In Sympathy.

Tiffany Irwin had taken part in a TV reconstruction, making a plea for anybody who knew anything about her family to reach out and speak in confidence to the police. It must have been a convincing performance, because the paper suggested the father might have been responsible for taking the children in some misguided suicide. By the time of the fourth week of coverage at the end of January 2000, the newspaper had an exclusive.

Revealed! Two More Missing In Millennium Week. Tragic Family Links Investigated.

By now, Charlotte was completely absorbed. As ever, Jon Rogers had proved his local knowledge was unassailable. The article explained how the details of the other disappearances had been suppressed because of the ongoing investigation surrounding the Irwin family. There was another woman called Joanne Taylor, and a young man, Brett Allan. Brett's car had been found abandoned at nearby Sunderland Point, and Joanne Taylor never returned home one night.

It was an extraordinary number of people to go missing in such a short time, but as Charlotte scanned the more feature-based content from the inside pages of the newspaper, a psychologist from the university revealed that it was not entirely unexpected, given the timing of the new millennium.

Charlotte worked through the microfiche film strips methodically, printing any pages which she thought might be useful. If this person who the police had found on the sea front was an Irwin, it would make national news and the newspaper would be right at the heart of it, supplying information to the broadsheets and possibly even at an international level. This was the perfect story for a trainee reporter keen to make an early impact in the profession. Hopefully it wouldn't require Charlotte to use any shorthand.

She leaned back in her chair and stretched out her arms and legs. One drawback of helping with the guests in the mornings was that she still had to get up early to join Isla, Agnieszka or Piper, whoever was on shift, to get the busy breakfast sittings out of the way. She found herself flagging by midday, but always rallied after a lunch break, a short walk along the sea front and a drink of black coffee. It was fast becoming her hot drink of choice since working with Nigel in the newsroom. She decided to take an early lunch and texted Lucia to see if she was in the mood to join her for a bite to eat. She tapped out her text message.

Are you around? Fancy lunch? I'm buying.

To her surprise, Lucia got straight back to her.

I'm in the library doing some studying. Are you at the office?

Since the events of the previous year, Lucia had struggled to settle down at school. Who could blame her, after being abducted twice then nearly losing her life at Heysham Port? She'd had difficulty adjusting to the normality of school, finding most of her friends' trivial conversations infuriating. When she'd asked to be home schooled, Will and Charlotte agreed.

It had been simple enough to deregister her from school and sign up to an organisation called Education Otherwise. They'd purchased four distance learning packages from reputable providers online, and the rest was up to Lucia. She managed her own timetable, worked when she felt like it, used the library and internet as her primary resources, and every now and then would jump on a train and visit some museum or art gallery as part of her learning.

She'd matured immensely since leaving school, met some other local home schooled kids who seemed to have much more about them than her previous school friends, and appeared to have got her life back on track. It was like gaining an adult daughter, and their relationship had improved radically of late. If Lucia emerged from it with four 'A' levels and a university place, then all the better.

Charlotte collected her printed papers, thanked Jon for his help and jotted down his telephone number in case she had any further questions. It didn't take long to find Lucia at a quiet desk at the rear of the library. She was typing away furiously on her laptop as she made notes from a textbook, which looked like it would cost a small fortune to buy.

'Surprise!' she said, delighted to see her daughter so engrossed. Lucia had never settled in school after the move to Morecambe.

Within ten minutes, they were at a nearby café, tucking into hot drinks and well-filled paninis dripping with melted cheese.

'How's your day been?' Charlotte asked. There was a time, not that long ago, when she'd have feared the answer.

'Great, thanks Mum. I love this arrangement. I got 94% in my latest psychology assignment. It's been so good getting to know Jenna. I'm glad they gave me permission to speak to her.'

'Well, you know what I thought about that at the time. I'm not sure you'll ever appreciate how hard it was to let you visit someone who schemed to abduct you—'

Lucia cut her short.

'Yes, but her relationships with men have been terrible. It was just the latest in a pattern of poor choices. She sees that now; when they finally release her properly from prison, she'll be able to make a good stab at getting her life back on track. She's so grateful to you for helping Piper. Despite everything that happened, she still thinks you did the right thing.'

Charlotte wasn't so sure. But the ties of her old friend-ship with Jenna hadn't been completely severed by the trauma of the incident, and she was grateful that life was getting better for her at last. She was in an open prison now and would be free again soon. Then she and Piper could begin to repair their own damaged relationship. If she'd played a small part in that healing process, it had to be a good thing.

'I'm pleased things are going so well. You know how proud I am of you.'

'What are these, Mum? They look interesting.'

Lucia was examining the printouts which Charlotte had left on the far side of the table.

Charlotte explained the broad outline of the story, omitting the information passed on by Nigel's contact earlier that day.

'It says they were found at the slipway by the RNLI. I walked up that way this morning, on my way to the library. Something was going on, because a couple of police cars were parked there. It was taped off, as if they were searching the area.'

Charlotte knew she was a useless liar. Even while claiming ignorance, she could tell Lucia had seen straight through her.

'It wasn't a murder, was it? Wasn't that where you and Olli were rescued last year?'

Charlotte wondered if Lucia should be the one considering a career in journalism. She kept it vague, remembering Nigel had specifically asked her not to share the tip-off.

'Nobody died,' she said in as reassuring a voice as she could muster. 'I can't discuss it right now, but it'll be all over the paper this week.'

Lucia didn't appear to be listening. She was studying a photograph on one of the printouts.

'What is it?' Charlotte asked. 'Have you spotted something?'

'Yes, this photo,' Lucia replied. 'I recognised this police officer straight away. You can't miss her, but the name threw me.'

Charlotte leaned over to look.

'What a small world it is,' Lucia continued. 'She's referred to as PC Kate Allan in the newspaper article, but of course she's married now. The first officer on the scene when the family vanished was DCI Kate Summers. That was two decades ago; she looks a lot younger.'

Charlotte checked the photograph and the name. It made sense that DCI Summers had risen through the ranks of the local police force. Yet there she was, a rookie police constable, first on the scene in one of Morecambe's biggest missing persons investigations. Talk about bad pennies.

CHAPTER FOUR

Lucia was right. As Charlotte examined the printout closely, she was surprised she hadn't seen it herself while examining the images on the microfiche machine. There were two pictures of the police officer, a standard, formal police image and an informal photograph taken of the officers on the scene at the slipway in 2000 as the disappearances were being investigated. Her hair was in a short bob, no doubt for practicality, and she looked younger and more naïve. But it was definitely DCI Summers, the woman to whom Charlotte owed the lives of her family.

Although Charlotte's way of saving her family would never meet with police approval, it was the DCI's faith in her that had allowed her to get away with it. She had gone so far as to call Kate Summers a friend after the terrible events that had blighted their lives since they'd moved to the resort.

'I'll bet she's seen some things if she's been policing Morecambe for so long.'

Lucia's voice pulled Charlotte out of her distraction.

'When you know someone high up like that, you forget

they once had to do the dirty work,' she continued. 'I can't imagine DCI Summers ever having a first day on the job and not knowing what to do; she always acts like she was born a police officer.'

'I get the impression she prefers the practical side of the job,' Charlotte said, resolving to reach out to Kate. Maybe she would share a little more information about whether the person found on the slipway was one of the Irwin children. 'She seems to relish being out in the field; I've never heard her speaking as enthusiastically about the pen-pushing side of her job. Still, she's a useful contact, especially now I'm in journalism. I'll speak to her about this. I bet she can share some useful information. At the very least, hearing her memories will make a great feature for the newspaper.'

Once they'd finished their lunch and caught up with their plans for the weekend, Lucia stood up, ready to head back to the library.

'I'm so proud of how you've stepped up these past few months,' Charlotte said as she was leaving, venturing a rare emotional moment with her daughter. At one time Lucia would have thrown it back in her face.

'Thanks, Mum. I just decided it was time to get my act together. When you came to rescue me at the port, I could see how stupid I'd been. When I thought you'd fallen to your death, it made me realise what's most important in life. I was a little brat before; I'm sorry.'

Charlotte felt her eyes moistening, knowing full well her still-teenage daughter could only cope with so much mothering. She gave her a brief smile and waited until she'd left the café before allowing herself a few discreet tears. Although the physical wounds seemed to have healed, the emotional rawness was still there. Sometimes it would creep up from behind, a sudden wave of fear and anxiety, a shocking sense of how much danger they'd all been in. She was safe now, and so was her family. Life was good again.

Before settling the bill, Charlotte sent a text to DCI Summers. They hadn't communicated for some time, so it was better than interrupting her working day with a phone call out of the blue.

Can we speak about today's big news story? I see you were there as a young police officer. Would love to chat about your experiences for the newspaper. Charlotte.

She toyed with adding her surname, just in case DCI Summers had forgotten her among the array of names she no doubt held in her head. There was probably no need; after what they'd all been through, Kate Summers was unlikely ever to forget her.

The message went almost immediately. She got up from her table and walked over to pay the bill, hoping for a fast response to the text. It didn't come.

By the time Charlotte had got back to her desk at The Bay View Weekly's offices, she was agitated about the lack of a swift reply. Nigel seemed equally out of sorts.

'I've hit a wall of silence from the police; they're saying nothing about who they found. It's very frustrating. We have to commit to a front page, but there's nothing I'm confident to report on yet. Something's going on, and they're keeping tight-lipped about it.'

Charlotte handed over the two printed microfiche sheets with the photos of DCI Summers on them.

'Recognise anybody?' she said, smiling.

'Well I'm blowed!' Nigel exclaimed, a look of rekindled enthusiasm in his eyes. 'Who would have thought it – our old friend Kate Summers? It's so funny seeing her all serious and uniformed like that; she looks a lot more confident these days.'

'She must have been young in the year 2000... what do you reckon, early twenties? Not much older than Olli is now, I'd guess.'

'We should contact her and see if she'll talk—'

'Already done.'

'And?'

Charlotte looked at her phone.

'Nothing. She might be busy. Sometimes I have to curb my impatience; I just want people to get straight back to me.'

'I know the feeling,' Nigel said. 'One moment, I've just got an email response I've been waiting for.'

Not for the first time that day, Charlotte waited for Nigel to digest some incoming information sufficiently to share it with her.

'Good news!' he said, after what seemed like days. 'We've got a lead. Tiffany Irwin is still local. She's a resident at the Briar Bank Care Home. It's over Bare and Torrisholme way, I'm not entirely sure where.'

'What's Briar Bank? Surely she's not old enough to be in a care home?'

'It's not that kind of care facility. Briar Bank is for residential patients with mental health issues. They're deemed incapable of living unsupported. I'll forward this email to you – it's all explained in there.'

'Surely somebody of her age would recover from an incident like that?' Charlotte queried.

'What, losing three children, babies and all? And your husband? This newspaper article you've given me says it was a suspected suicide attempt on her part. Maybe she had a history of mental health issues dating way back.'

'The poor woman,' Charlotte said, as much to herself as Nigel. She thought back to when she had two babies of her own. She'd have done anything to protect them and keep them safe. Yet, however much she loved Olli and Lucia, even though they were young adults now, there had still been a time, if only for a moment, when the thought of taking her own life had occurred to her. She knew what a dark place you had to be in to even consider it, yet she'd been there and her two children were safe and sound. No wonder Tiffany Irwin was receiving psychiatric support. The thought of losing three tiny children and never knowing if they were dead or alive, with no clue about what might have happened to them, must have been insufferable.

Nigel was on the telephone already, running through his newspaper credentials with whoever he was speaking to. It was a good job everyone in the town thought well of the local newspaper. Nigel had once told her he'd spent a brief period on secondment at another publication which had zero credibility in the community it served. He'd recounted how hard it was to secure interviews; most people declined his requests, afraid of being misquoted or taken out of context. In its small, parochial way, working on The Bay View Weekly opened doors.

Nigel put the phone down and gave Charlotte a self-satisfied smile.

'And we're off!' he said. 'We can go to see the deputy manager at Briar Bank this afternoon. She's not promised anything, but if Tiffany Irwin gives her consent, we may be able to chat briefly. Whatever happens, a combination of an update on her and a re-hash of the event of January 1st 2000 will give us enough to work with for the front page. And they've promised us a press conference, at least, so even if it turns out to be nothing, we'll still have something to hang the story on. Can you follow-up with DCI

Summers? If we can land a chat with her, we'll be well away.'

'Sure,' Charlotte replied, picking up her phone and checking to see if she'd missed a text from Kate. There was still no reply. Irritated by Nigel's swift result with the care home, she dialled Kate's number. A more direct approach would flush her out. The phone rang several times, then went dead.

'Any joy?' Nigel asked, gathering together his things for the trip to Briar Bank.

'Nothing,' Charlotte replied, disappointed. 'I know she's a busy woman, but it's not as if we don't have past form. I'd expect her to text a reply, at least. Anybody would think she doesn't want to speak to me.'

nails were immaculately manicured, the nail varnish distinctive yet classy, and her clothing was so obviously expensive that she could have been a model in the Vogue magazine.

'Come into my office,' she said, not bothering to shake hands. As she turned her back on them to lead the way, Charlotte whispered to Nigel.

'I wish I'd put a nice dress on now. I look like I've just been blown in from the street.'

'You and me both,' he murmured. 'She's formidable. Best tread carefully.'

Zabrina's office looked out onto the gardens at the back, which were well-tended and extensive. Several patients were sitting at benches and taking the air.

'So how can I help you, Mr Davies?' Zabrina asked, once she'd settled herself in her impressive leather chair. 'Help yourself to a filter coffee if you'd like one,' she added, nodding to a small sink and worktop area to her side.

'I'm wondering if it would be possible to talk to Tiffany Irwin.'

Nigel cut to the chase. Charlotte reckoned Zabrina was the kind of woman who'd appreciate that.

'We have to be circumspect about the welfare of our clients,' Zabrina replied. 'Tiffany has confirmed she is happy to speak to you, but I will need to be assured beforehand that you won't cause her any distress. What is the nature of your visit?'

Charlotte scanned the room. There was a picture of Zabrina with a grey-haired, trim-bearded man who must be her husband or partner. They were holding hands in the picture, so she figured it was a reasonable assumption to make. She couldn't see any photographs of children which might have given clues about the family set-up. Zabrina obviously preferred classy artwork to family photos; the pictures on the walls didn't look like prints.

'We're keen to chat to Tiffany about her mental health experiences,' Nigel began.

Charlotte spun round to stare at him, then realised she was giving the game away. He was telling one of his journalistic white lies again. It made sense. Zabrina would be unlikely to give permission for him to rake up the very episode that resulted in Tiffany Irwin ending up here.

'There's so much interest in mental health issues these days, and we've heard Tiffany is an eloquent speaker and a long-term patient. We're planning to spotlight the excellent work you're doing here to show how beneficial it can be for patients.'

Zabrina might have been formidable, but like most people in positions of influence, the prospect of some flattery and a positive article in the newspaper was too much to resist.

'That sounds fine, Mr Davies. So long as you stick to your line of questioning, I see no reason to deny the visit. Be thankful that you telephoned me rather than my husband. He is much less forgiving of the local press.'

'You co-manage with your husband?' Charlotte asked.

'Yes, that's him in the photograph you've been looking at. We founded this facility twenty-five years ago, and it's been our life's work. His name is Quinton. He's not here at the moment, I'm afraid, otherwise I'd introduce you.'

Charlotte held back a snigger. Quinton and Zabrina were a couple who'd guaranteed their distinctiveness, if only because their names began with two of the least-used letters of the alphabet. They were a match made in heaven.

'I'll get Amanda to introduce you to Tiffany,' Zabrina

told them. 'Five minutes only, and photographs only with Amanda's and Tiffany's consent.'

Amanda picked them up from the reception area minutes later. Charlotte was pleased to see she had some warmth about her. She suspected Zabrina was all about income and profitability; empathy and compassion didn't appear to be high on her personal agenda.

'I'd be grateful if you could go gently with Tiff. She's usually quite steady, but she can sometimes become distressed. I'll let her know you've arrived. She's in room 102 at the end of the corridor.'

Amanda walked ahead, leaving Nigel and Charlotte a few seconds to exchange notes.

'Should we be doing this?' Charlotte asked. 'If she's fragile, I mean? I don't want her to get distressed.'

'We'll go gently, but how else do we get more details about her family?'

'You can come in now; Tiff's ready for you,' Amanda said, appearing from inside a room just ahead of them. As they entered, they could see it was sparse but the furnishings were of a high quality.

Tiffany Irwin was not at all what Charlotte was expecting. In the newspaper photograph, a single snap used repeatedly, she looked confident, happy, glowing and content. The photo in the old newspaper cuttings was over twenty years old, but given that Tiffany must now be in her forties, time hadn't been kind to her. Her eyes were empty, as if any hope had been extinguished a long time ago. Her hair was cut in a functional style, and her clothes were drab.

'Hello Tiffany,' Nigel said, taking the initiative.

'I'll be waiting outside,' Amanda said. 'Call if you need me. And please be brief.'

'Pleased to meet you,' Charlotte said, offering her hand

to shake Tiffany's. It was so limp that she didn't dare squeeze it, in case she crushed her fingers.

Before Nigel could ask his first question, Tiffany leaned forward in her chair, the first sign that she possessed sufficient energy to propel her body.

'You're here to ask me about the children, aren't you?'

Charlotte could tell Nigel was as surprised at the woman's directness as she was.

'Yes, we are,' Charlotte replied. 'Are you happy to discuss it?'

'Keep your voices low,' Tiffany warned. 'They don't like me talking about it. Why else would they keep me here on a cocktail of drugs?'

'What can you tell us about that night?' Nigel asked, softly. 'We're keen to hear your story.'

Charlotte could hear a male voice at the far end of the corridor, imposing and authoritative.

Tiffany's eyes filled with tears.

'I didn't try to kill myself; that much I can tell you. And I'm sure my children are still alive. I can sense it. A mother knows. My children did not die that night. I can't tell you what happened, however hard I try. I can't find my way through this haze of drugs to remember anything.'

The man they'd heard was outside the door now, speaking to Amanda. It sounded like she was in trouble.

'If you want to know what really happened, talk to that girl.'

'Which girl?' Nigel asked.

'Mr Davies?'

The man strode into the room, his face flushed with annoyance.

'My name is Quinton Madeley, the manager of this establishment. I insist that you terminate your interview with Ms Irwin immediately. Her health is not good enough at present. Please leave the building.'

Nigel and Charlotte both stood up. This man wasn't the type to respond to any appeals.

'Ask the young police officer,' Tiffany continued, regardless. 'She knows. She's the only one who can tell you what happened that night.'

CHAPTER SIX

Charlotte was preoccupied with the visit to Briar Bank Care Home the following morning. However hard she tried, she couldn't keep her mind on the job. She was thankful the ever-dependable Isla was on shift; Piper still required a lot of hand-holding on the days she was working. Charlotte chopped mushrooms and tomatoes, moving them to Isla's side by the cooker, reflecting on how things had taken such a sudden turn for the worse.

Quinton Madeley was an unpleasant, self-important, pompous man who was used to people jumping whenever he barked instructions. He wore too much gold for Charlotte's liking: a large, gaudy signet ring, a neck chain and a watch that looked so heavy it was a wonder he could lift his arm. She put it down to a poor and ill-informed attempt at exuding wealth. Zabrina carried it off much better. Charlotte wondered if she'd elevated him through their marriage. Perhaps the crown didn't fit so well.

'Your mind seems to be elsewhere this morning,' Isla remarked. It wouldn't be the first time. By now, Isla was accustomed to picking up the slack whenever Charlotte had other things on her mind. 'You're not worrying about your parachute jump on Sunday, are you? I've already told you it's too soon, whatever the doctor says. There's no shame in cancelling, you know.'

That wasn't uppermost in Charlotte's mind. She'd almost forgotten about Sunday's event.

'You've lived in the resort for years, Isla. Do you remember the Irwin family?'

Isla stopped laying slices of bacon on the griddle and looked up.

'You don't half pick the big events, Charlotte,' she said, her expression serious. 'Why has this come up?'

'It's something I'm researching for the newspaper. Do you remember it?'

'Anybody who lived in Morecambe at the time will remember it. I never knew them personally, but like most of the locals, they'd been into the guest house for a meal from time to time. I know a lot of people by sight. They seemed like a nice family. The last time they came here to eat, they had two young children. I think there was a third by the time...'

She seemed unsure about carrying on.

'I know they disappeared, Isla, and I also know it happened at the slipway where Olli and I were rescued. You don't have to tiptoe around what happened in the past. That's where it belongs now: in the past.'

'It was all over the nationals, not just the local newspaper. We had television and radio reporters descending on the town from all over the country. I do know someone who was involved, though.'

'The Irwins?' Charlotte asked.

'No, several other people went missing around the same time. The police seemed to make light of it. I have a friend who lives in Bare; she lost her daughter around then.'

'Really? One of those named in the newspapers? Who was it?'

'My friend is called Yasmin Utworth. Her daughter Morgan disappeared in January of the same year. It was terrible; it destroyed her marriage in the end. She's never been able to move on.'

Charlotte recognised the name from the newspaper archives.

'What happened?'

Any modicum of attention Charlotte had been giving the breakfast preparation was long gone.

'There's not much to tell. Morgan was a lovely girl. She left the house one day and never returned. That's it. The police couldn't work out if she was dead or if she'd just run away. It happened in the first week of January in 2000. It destroyed poor Yasmin. She still doesn't know if Morgan is alive. Her life has been on hold for over two decades. I have no idea how she carries on. At least I could grieve for my losses.'

Charlotte squeezed Isla's arm gently. There was so much loss and sadness all around her, yet people battled on when they had every reason to give up.

There was a cough at the door to the kitchen.

'Any chance of ordering breakfast?' a thin, sweaty man asked, leaning in as if he were entering forbidden territory.

'Oh, Mr Taylor, I'm so sorry. Please wait in the dining room and I'll be with you straight away.'

Charlotte gave Isla a look to show she wanted to talk more about Morgan Utworth, then wiped her hands and dashed out to attend to the guests.

She didn't get to finish the conversation with Isla due to

the sudden rush of breakfast guests and a distraction from Will before he left for work. With Agnieszka studying at the university where he worked, they'd all got to know each other well. Will accepted that Agnieszka had once been in the country illegally, working as an escort in the resort, but was now working hard to put that life behind her and forge a proper career for herself.

Will was ready early and waiting for Agnieszka to arrive so they could travel to the campus together. He was preoccupied with his phone.

'What's up?' Charlotte asked as she passed him in the hall, plates and cutlery stacked in both hands.

'Nothing,' he replied, in an evasive tone that suggested she'd caught him doing something.

'You're not surfing those dodgy adult websites again, are you?' Charlotte sidled up to him, whispering teasingly.

He was immediately defensive.

'No of course not. It's just a text. From a student. I wasn't expecting it this early in the day.'

Charlotte had loaded up the plates too heavily and needed to put them down, so she broke off the conversation to put them next to the sink. By the time she'd scraped the food into the slops bin and stacked them in the dishwasher, Agnieszka had arrived, late and out of breath, and they'd hastily said their goodbyes to rush for the bus. Isla, too, had to make a swift exit, as George had a hospital check-up in Lancaster.

Charlotte gave a groan of frustration at having to start a day this way, with unfinished business left hanging in the air. It was like the conversation at Briar Bank the day before. Nigel had tried to distract the objectionable Quinton Madeley while Charlotte had made a valiant attempt to sneak in a couple of extra questions with Tiffany Irwin. But

Tiffany had become anxious the moment she spotted Quinton, and the situation got out of hand.

'How was Kate involved?' Charlotte had asked Tiffany, as Nigel attempted to placate Quinton.

'She knows. She never spoke up. But she knows where my babies are. And him, that man! He keeps me in prison here—'

'I've told you to leave!' Quinton bellowed, pressing an alarm button on the unit which hung around his neck.

'You're getting worked up, Tiffany,' Quinton said, rushing towards her and taking her arm more roughly than Charlotte thought necessary.

'You too. Get out!' he yelled at Charlotte. 'If you don't leave immediately, I'll call the police.'

Two male nurses entered the room and sedated Tiffany. She struggled violently, desperate to release herself from Quinton's grasp.

Charlotte had felt sick when they left the building.

'Are they allowed to do that to patients?' she asked Nigel.

'If they become a danger to themselves or to the staff, I suppose it's par for the course,' Nigel replied. He also looked rattled by what he'd seen.

'Did Tiffany Irwin strike you as a woman who's a danger to herself or the staff?' Charlotte asked.

'No, she seemed wounded and desperately sad to me. I'd like to give that Quinton fella a punch in the face, though. What an obnoxious dick.'

'What do you think she meant? She was talking about Kate Allan, wasn't she? Or Kate Summers, as she is now. Kate was only a young policewoman then. She probably knew less about the case than she would nowadays as a DCI.'

'Have you got a reply from DCI Summers yet?'

The answer had been negative when she and Nigel had spoken the day before. Now, the morning after, it still hadn't changed. Charlotte had received a message delivery receipt for each of the numerous texts she'd sent DCI Summers. Each call had been cut off before it had even gone to voice mail.

Charlotte put the last of the dishes in the machine, added the powder and switched it on. As the blades whirred and the water sloshed about inside, she leaned against the worktop before returning to the dining lounge to set up the tables for the evening meal sitting. She worked through her list of priorities. Next time she saw Isla, she'd ask for the contact details of her friend, Yasmin, and see if she could arrange an interview. She needed to finish the conversation with Will too; she could see in his face that something was going on. If she didn't know better, she'd say he was keeping something from her.

Then there was DCI Summers, doing her best to avoid her. She was also perturbed at Tiffany's suggestion that somehow the detective knew something about the disappearance of the children. How was she involved, and why was she ignoring all the texts and calls?

Charlotte never finished setting the tables. She'd just sorted out her first appointment of the day. She would confront Kate Summers directly by visiting her at Morecambe Police Station.

CHAPTER SEVEN

As Charlotte turned away from the sea front at the bingo hall, heading in the general direction of the police station, she wondered if what she was intending to do was advisable. She and Will already had form with the local police, albeit largely as victims rather than perpetrators.

She was immensely grateful to DCI Summers, not only for her help with the family's previous problems, but more for her humanity and understanding. There were many occasions on which Kate Summers could have thrown the book at both Will and her, but she had cut them some slack. It was because of her that Charlotte could now make the walk to the police station without the need of a wheelchair, a stick or a taxi.

While she still suffered occasional aches and pains, she was determined to ditch the car as much as possible and put her body through its paces. She'd come so close to death that it had made her savour life much more keenly.

The salty smell of the persistent sea breeze was like an elixir to her; the simple act of walking such a distance was a miracle, and Charlotte was eager to appreciate every moment. Also, bizarrely, it was more uncomfortable for her to drive than to walk. Her physio had explained that twisting to reach for the seat belt would put a strain on the arm she'd dislocated. Since Will preferred to take the bus to Lancaster rather than sit in the interminable congestion of the city's one-way system, the car sat out in the back yard area much of the time, mainly used for trips to the cash and carry.

The police station was a concrete seventies construction, its harsh exterior totally at odds with the current drive to make the police more open and approachable. She paused outside the primary school in Poulton Square, which always seemed a cheerful place. Next door was an attractive church which she'd never made time to visit.

She walked on, stopping briefly for a moment's reflection before entering the police station. The last time she'd been there was after her release from hospital; Will had had to push her in a wheelchair. She shuddered at the memory of those events. Never again, she told herself.

The police officer on duty in reception recognised her. Once upon a time she would have found that a source of deep shame, but at least she wasn't on the list of Morecambe's most wanted. The usual array of posters adorned the walls, most of the faces seeking men who'd committed various crimes in the locality, plus the occasional woman. She thought of her friend Jenna from the holiday camp, so close to freedom now, and Piper and Agnieszka, former escorts working legitimately for the first time in their lives. Even Rex Emery, the former owner of their establishment all those years ago, was now a free man, having won his appeal against the conviction for crimes he did not commit.

She viewed the posters differently now. At one time she'd have cursed them all, dismissing them as criminals and nuisances, poisoning the local resort. Now she knew better than to condemn so quickly; they each had a story to tell. Sometimes life wasn't as black and white as it might seem, as she'd found out since relocating to Morecambe.

'Hello Mrs Grayson – Charlotte – it's nice to see you in better health now,' the officer said with a smile.

'It's even nicer not to be at the centre of a massive police investigation. I can't tell you how good it feels to be just passing by,' Charlotte replied, recognising PC Allie Taylor, a young officer. She couldn't have been much older than Kate Summers was in the newspaper cutting. It was strange to imagine the DCI as a rookie constable. She had the face of a woman who seemed to have been born knowing exactly what to do.

'I take it all is well? How can I help you today?'

'Is DCI Summers about? I've been trying to contact her for the past 24 hours, but she seems to be avoiding me.'

'That's unlike her,' PC Taylor said, reaching for the phone on the reception desk. 'I'll call her at her desk. I'm sure I saw her come in this morning.'

Charlotte examined the posters while she waited. One was urging residents to get their postcodes stamped on their bicycles. The eternal reminder to lock doors properly was also being pushed via a series of posters provided by a local primary school. Charlotte laughed to herself as she examined a picture of a police officer drawn by a child who was having problems grasping how to capture the human form with crayons. The officer, of indeterminable gender, had arms stretching out like a scarecrow's and legs which appeared to be made of jelly.

She turned her attention back to the activity at the reception desk as PC Taylor's tone suddenly changed. If you could draw a picture of how well PC Taylor was covering for DCI Summers, it would have been like that kid's picture. PC Taylor put the phone down.

'I'm sorry Mrs Grayson, I was mistaken. DCI Summers isn't in the office this morning.'

'I thought you'd seen her come in?'

'Well, it gets busy in here, so sometimes it's easy to lose track of the comings and goings.'

Charlotte wondered if she should push it further.

'Who were you speaking to on the phone? It sounded like she'd picked up.'

PC Taylor's face coloured just enough to confirm to Charlotte that she was giving her the run-around.

'Oh, it was another officer using her desk. We hot-desk a lot upstairs. Nobody gets a space of their own any more.'

'Is she avoiding me?' Charlotte asked bluntly.

This seemed to catch PC Taylor off guard. She looked like dealing with a constant flow of bad lads would be easier than chasing away a persistent Charlotte Grayson.

'Er, no, I mean... as I said, DCI Summers isn't in the office right now.'

She recovered herself.

'I can take a message and pass it on to her, when she's back in the office,' she added.

'Yes, please do.'

Charlotte passed on every form of contact she could think of; email, mobile phone, the switchboard phone at the newspaper and Nigel's phone number. When DCI Summers finally stuck her head above the parapet, she wanted to be ready. She was reluctant to walk away, but it was obvious she was beaten by a wall of silence. It only made her even more curious about DCI Summers' involvement in the Irwin family's case.

She wasn't due into the office until ten-thirty, so she

decided to kill some time checking out the church behind the primary school. The graveyard was green and flourishing, the graves well-kept and the church open. As she fumbled with the big, iron latch, she walked in noisily on a school assembly in full flow and embarrassed herself by apologising to the head teacher too loudly during what she only then realised was the Lord's Prayer. She and head teachers didn't seem to get on.

Charlotte left the church, wincing at her unwelcome intrusion. There was a small coffee shop in the square, so she went in for a hot drink and a bacon sandwich. The walk and the sea breeze had made her peckish.

Before long she was sitting at a window seat, nursing a cup of coffee, and enjoying a heavily buttered bacon sandwich. It tasted ten times better because she hadn't had to cook it.

She drew out her mobile phone and saw Nigel had sent her a text.

I'll pick you up this morning. Guest house? We have a job on.

She texted back. That was lucky; she could take longer with her coffee if she didn't have to walk back home.

I'm at the café on Poulton Square. Meet me there?

Nigel was swift to reply in agreement. Charlotte relaxed into her chair. It bought her twenty minutes or so, a welcome break at the beginning of the day. From where she was sitting, she had a clear view of the police station. A wave of indignation overcame her at the thought of Kate Summers avoiding her. She'd felt some connection between them after her own troubles, but maybe it had been just another police job to the DCI.

She picked up a national newspaper and flicked through the pages, grateful to have some time to catch up with the latest celebrity gossip and soap opera storylines. Five minutes later, a distinctive voice behind her attracted her attention.

'Can I have three bacon, two sausage and a vegetarian sandwich to take away please? Brown sauce on both sausage ones. Guess who got lumbered with this morning's breakfast run?'

Charlotte turned around, just to be certain. It was DCI Summers.

CHAPTER EIGHT

'Fancy meeting you here, DCI Summers.'

Charlotte put down her newspaper, got up from her seat and walked over to her. Kate had a look on her face as guilty as most of the clients she dealt with in her line of work. She was cornered, the full-width counter blocking her rear, and tables to the right and left preventing any attempt at escape. Charlotte had just landed her big fish on the hook, and the big fish hadn't even seen it coming.

'PC Taylor told me you weren't in the office when I called by.'

DCI Summers played it for time.

'Hello Charlotte, how nice to see you again, and without your stick too, I see. How lovely that you've recovered so well.'

Charlotte wasn't letting her off so easily. She said nothing and just looked into Kate's face, waiting for more.

'You know how it is with my job, in the office one moment and out the next. I got caught with getting the sandwiches this morning, and it's not even my turn.'

'I'm beginning to think you're avoiding me,' Charlotte said after another uncomfortable delay.

'It's not that, Charlotte. We have a couple of big cases on at the moment and I'm really busy—'

'So busy that you can't send out a less senior member of the team to collect the sausage sandwiches?'

Charlotte knew it was unfair, but she didn't like coming up empty-handed while she was gaining experience at the newspaper. While trying to prove herself, she'd hoped she could rely on DCI Summers to give her a helping hand.

'OK, I'm sorry, Charlotte. You've caught me red-handed. I don't want to talk to the press right now. This is newspaper business, isn't it? Nigel Davies told me about your career change. I'm surprised what happened to you hasn't put you off.'

'Yes, it's newspaper business and no, what happened last year didn't put me off. In fact, it's inspired me. It's a side of life I've never thought about, and I find it fascinating.'

'Fair enough,' Kate replied, checking on the progress of her order. She was caught for a few more minutes, while the lady serving started cooking a fresh batch of bacon. 'I must admit, it's why I find police work so absorbing. Sometimes, you can really get your teeth into some cases.'

As much as Charlotte enjoyed a good chit-chat, she wasn't going to let DCI Summers off the hook. They had a newspaper to fill and her prime source of information was standing directly in front of her.

'I need to talk to you about this woman they found on the slipway. What do you know about her?'

'It's not my case,' Kate answered. 'I only know what I hear in the office. You understand I can't share confidential information, don't you?'

'Of course. But there must be something you can tell me.'

'We haven't held a press conference yet; all the press outlets have the same information. Until we get an ID on this woman, we can't say any more.'

'But she's Callie Irwin, isn't she?' Charlotte pushed.

DCI Summers face turned even paler.

'We can't confirm anything yet. I assume you know the basics of the incident back in 2000? Callie was a baby, so there are no dental records and little health information. We'll only prove identity via DNA, and it takes time.'

'Yes, but what about the birthmark?'

'How did you find out about that?' Kate snapped.

Charlotte watched as her eyes flashed, getting a brief glimpse of the ferocity DCI Summers no doubt had to apply with her team every once in a while.

'I have my sources,' Charlotte smirked.

'Well, if I find out your source comes from Morecambe Police Station, they'll get an arse-kicking from me. That information was not on the basic press release, and I'd be grateful if you didn't repeat it. It will just lead to idle conjecture, which doesn't help in cases like this.'

'You seem to know a lot about the case, considering you're not assigned to it.'

Charlotte knew she was pushing her luck, but she couldn't help feeling DCI Summers was holding something back.

'I'm a member of the senior team, so of course I know about it. I'm just not working on it, that's all.'

She turned to watch the assistant who was placing her order into paper bags.

Kate would be able to leave soon; it was time to deliver

the body blow. Charlotte fumbled in her pocket and drew out a folded piece of paper.

'I'm surprised you're not in charge of this investigation,' Charlotte continued, nervous at what she was about to do. She liked DCI Summers a lot, and she had so much to thank her for. But this was business, and the detective was not being straight with her.

'Why?' Kate answered. 'Cases are assigned to us; this one didn't land on my desk.'

Charlotte unfolded the piece of paper to reveal the newspaper cutting taken from the microfiche at the library. She pointed to the photograph of the then Kate Allan standing on the sea front, next to the Irwins' vehicle.

'You were first on the scene according to my sources. You were Kate Allan then, before you married. But that's you, isn't it? You can't have been in the job long when this picture was taken.'

DCI Summers stepped back and her face reddened. Charlotte had never seen her like this, and it made her feel like a bully who'd just taken things a step too far.

'Here's your order!' the assistant said from behind the counter, placing a clutch of paper bags at Kate's side, the grease beginning to work its way through already. Kate gave the lady a ten-pound note.

'Keep the change,' she said, grasping the bags with one hand and turning to leave.

'I'm sorry if you feel I hijacked you,' Charlotte said, backing off a little. 'But there's something you're not telling me. You were there. What's going on?'

DCI Summers stopped mid-turn, took a moment to compose herself and looked directly into Charlotte's eyes.

'Don't push this, Charlotte, please. You and your family escaped with your lives when you got involved last time.

Please walk away from this one. Report what the police say at the press conferences and in their releases to the local press, but don't get involved. I like to think we're friends, after what we've been through?'

'Of course,' Charlotte answered.

'Well, listen to me as a friend, not as a police officer. Leave this one alone. Let Nigel Davies and his team handle it. I like you and your family, Charlotte, I do, and I don't want you to come to any harm. Walk away. I'm warning you. Just walk away.'

Kate held Charlotte's gaze for what seemed like forever. As she turned and marched towards the police station, Charlotte could see her shaking. A pang of guilt hit her for rattling the detective. She considered rushing after her but thought better of it. She would apologise later, though.

Charlotte returned to her seat. Her coffee was cold now, and she didn't feel like eating the last mouthful of bacon-packed bread that she'd left on her plate. Her phone showed a message notification. She always turned down the volume when in a public area, to avoid disturbing anyone, so she hadn't heard the call come in. She keyed in her pass code and accessed the voice message.

Hello Charlotte, it's Jon Rogers here from the library. After we spoke yesterday, I did a little more digging. Call by when you're passing next time; I've got some papers for you to collect. When Tiffany's parents died, the farmhouse was sold, but there was a big dispute over the land behind it. Tiffany has a brother called Fabian Armstrong. He lives in Blackpool these days. They fell out badly over the land. He's very involved with the fracking; he's quite a controversial character by all accounts. A wind farm was built on the land along the coastline, Heysham way. It's run by a company called Valdron Subramani. Anyway, it's all very interesting.

I've left a pile of papers for you at library reception; you can pick them up any time. OK, see you soon, bye.

Jon Rogers was God's gift to journalism. What the man didn't know about the local area wasn't worth knowing. This case with the Irwins was emitting a foul stench. Even if it wasn't Callie Irwin that they'd found on the slipway, it still merited more digging.

Nigel Davies drew up in the branded car and gave Charlotte a wave. She waved back at him to show she'd spotted him, then tidied her crockery so it would be easy for the lady in the café to clear up. Her phone vibrated as she was turning to leave. Half the world seemed to want to chat that day, even if Kate Summers did not. It was Will, with a brief message. This was how they ran their marriage most days, with much of their family life being organised via mobile devices.

Sorry to sound so mysterious, but we have to talk tonight. It's important. We've got a problem.

CHAPTER NINE

'We've got an interesting day ahead of us,' Nigel said, dispensing with the pleasantries as Charlotte got into the car.

'Sounds good,' she replied, thoughts of Will's text dominating her mind.

'We're heading for Lancaster Infirmary. I want to have a snoop around and see if we can get a few more details about our mystery person. The police are dragging their feet with this one, but we need a steer on their thinking before we commit to a front-page headline. I want to know if it's Callie Irwin or not; that fact makes or breaks our story.'

Charlotte barely registered what he'd said.

'Earth calling Charlotte Grayson. Do you read me?'

Nigel's jibe shook her out of her preoccupation.

'Sorry, Nigel. I was miles away.'

'Heavy night last night?'

'No, nothing to do with alcohol or getting to bed late. It's more about what's happened this morning.'

Nigel could spot a decent bit of gossip from a mile away,

and teased out every element of her interaction with Kate Summers.

'So you reckon there's more to this?' he asked after mulling things over a while. They were in Lancaster now, making their way through the one-way system all around the city towards the infirmary.

'You can say that again. You heard Tiffany Irwin; she thinks she's a prisoner in Briar Bank. And with the way DCI Summers warned me, I'm telling you: if it is Callie Irwin, everything's going to kick off. And what about the wind farm Jon Rogers told me about? I'm going to look up that company; it had some weird name. Just give me a moment, I'll check his voice mail message again.'

Charlotte found the name of the company and typed it into her smartphone twice until she found the correct spelling.

'I'll call the site manager to see if we can get a tour,' she said after finding a contact name and number. 'He's called Sam Halford. It's a mobile number, so hopefully I'll get straight through to him.'

Charlotte couldn't believe her luck when Sam Halford answered almost immediately. Using a trick she'd seen Nigel deploy from time to time, she played it completely innocently, flattered Sam into believing the newspaper was genuinely interested in running a feature about renewable energy and bagged herself an appointment to visit the same day.

'You're kidding. He agreed, just like that?' Nigel asked.

'Yes, he's on site this afternoon. Although he can't give us a formal tour, he's happy to meet us there. He's in Cumbria at the moment, but he's making his way back down from Walney. He offered to take me up in one of the turbines at a more convenient time. Regardless of whether it leads to anything, it'll still make a nice feature, won't it?'

They'd arrived at the infirmary. Charlotte felt her stomach churn, recalling how she and Will had been forced to flee from here in the dead of night to avoid the men who'd come to kill her. She felt a wave of panic gathering momentum, gripping her body. It had been some time since she'd felt this way.

'Are you OK coming in here with me?' Nigel asked. 'I'm so sorry; I should have thought to ask. You look like somebody's just drained all the blood from your face.'

'I'm OK, honestly. Just give me a moment, will you? Every now and then I get a rush of fear with flashbacks. It's less regular now; I'm getting better at working through it.'

'I'll buy a parking ticket. Take as long as you need,' Nigel reassured her.

By the time he'd returned, after spotting somebody he knew in the car park and spending five minutes chatting with them, Charlotte was ready to move on again. Her reaction to seeing the infirmary had taken her by surprise. She'd thought things had settled down, but the panic attack made her feel as if she'd taken several steps back.

They approached the reception desk, and Charlotte felt her cheeks burning up as the nurse on duty recognised her. She must have been on duty the night she came in after the rescue at sea. Two of the nurses had lost their lives that night; did these people hate her for it?

Nigel was careful enough not to give away the reason for their visit. Charlotte was gradually learning how to limit the level of information they should reveal, in order to avoid a block.

'Ward 38 is the ICU,' he said, 'It's in the main Centenary building. We'll have to play this one carefully.

There's usually only one cop on the door for a case like this.'

They moved through the hospital, its corridors filled with purposeful staff going about their business, patients wearing gowns and slippers, and the occasional visitors with demeanours matching the gravity of their visits. Charlotte was always surprised at how much free movement was allowed around places like this, but she knew the real challenge lay ahead: getting through the locked doors of the ICU.

'Have you got a plan for getting in?' Charlotte asked.

'No,' Nigel looked back, smiling at her. 'Just a flash of my press card and a hope that they read their local paper.'

They arrived at the ICU doors.

'Watch this and learn,' Nigel said.

He walked up to the intercom and beckoned Charlotte over. He waited a few seconds until two nurses approached in their blue uniforms.

'I'm sorry, I messed it up, please would you press the button again?'

Charlotte wondered who he was talking to, since he hadn't pressed the button on the intercom.

'Could you help me with this door, please?' he asked, smiling at the nurses. 'I'm Nigel Davies from The Bay View Weekly.'

He held up his press card and Charlotte fumbled in her pocket to find her student equivalent.

'This is my colleague Charlotte Grayson. They keep buzzing me in, but the door locks again before I can open it. You couldn't let us in, could you?'

'Of course,' one of the nurses replied. 'You have to get your timing right with these electronic locks; they can be a nuisance sometimes.'

They were in. The nurses walked ahead while Nigel hung back, making a big deal about replacing his identity card in his wallet.

'That's terrible!' Charlotte scolded him. 'We shouldn't be cheating the hospital's security.'

'We're not here to do any harm,' Nigel replied. 'They can see we're legit; they wouldn't have let us in otherwise.'

Charlotte wasn't so sure. It made her nervous whenever Nigel did something to take advantage of people's trust.

'The room's up ahead.'

He changed the subject. Some elements of journalism challenged Charlotte, but she knew she'd have to find a way to navigate them. She'd rather let the hospital staff know they were there, but Nigel didn't seem to care.

A bored looking police officer was sitting outside on a wooden chair.

'Hold on, I think I've met this guy before,' Nigel said, moving ahead.

Charlotte stood back, self-conscious about her presence, expecting to be asked to leave at any moment. She could hear Nigel striking up a conversation with the police officer, gently pumping him for information. She looked around at the equipment in the ICU. It looked more like a car repair centre than a place where human beings were kept alive, with screens, consoles and cables all over the place.

'Can I help you?' came a voice from behind.

It was a man in overalls, carrying a bucket filled with cleaning materials. He had a hospital lanyard around his neck.

'I'm just waiting for my colleague over there. He's the one chatting with the police officer.'

'Everybody's talking about that patient. Do you know the story? If it's the Irwin girl, a storm's going to blow up.'

'Has it been confirmed yet?' Charlotte asked.

She was pleased she hadn't mentioned the local paper. In her limited experience, often people were more unguarded if they didn't realise they were speaking to a reporter.

'It's not official yet, but let's put it this way, I was cleaning in there yesterday and they've written the name Callie on the board by her bed. They're talking about her as if she is one of the Irwins. And there's been a police presence around here constantly, waiting for her to wake up so they can speak to her.'

'Is she conscious yet?'

'No, not as far as I'm aware,' the man replied. 'If you ask me—'

The fire alarm cut him off.

'Oh no, that's not the weekly drill. I'd best see if it's for real.'

He rushed off as various medical staff emerged from the rooms, checking to see if it was a genuine alarm or a routine drill. The police officer stood up and made his excuses to Nigel, moving away from his post to consult with hospital staff about what happened next. Nigel walked up to her.

'Did he tell you anything?' Charlotte asked.

'Nothing new, no.'

They stood to the side as people came and went, trying to decide whether an evacuation was needed.

'Surely they don't have to move all the patients out of this place every time a visitor lights up a sly cigarette in the toilets?'

'I hope not.' Nigel laughed. 'I'm pleased I'm not in charge of this unit. I'd have a heart attack myself every time the alarm sounded.'

The shrill sound dominated the corridor for several

minutes before the confirmation came that it was a false alarm. The staff began to return to their stations, but Charlotte spotted the police officer walking up to them, an anxious look on his face.

'Were you standing here all the time the alarm was sounding?' he asked.

'Yes, why?' Nigel asked.

'Did you see anybody go into that room?' He nodded towards the wooden chair which marked his station.

'No. It was bedlam out here for a while. We picked the wrong time to pay a visit. Anyhow, what's up? You look like something just spooked you.'

The police officer held up a brown envelope in his hand.

'This envelope was left on the patient's bed. Someone broke into her room while the fire alarm was ringing.'

CHAPTER TEN

'Have you checked inside the envelope yet?' Nigel asked the police officer.

'No, not yet. I'm out of my depth, to be honest with you. I've a feeling I'll get a dressing-down for leaving my post when the fire alarm went off.'

'We'll vouch for you,' Charlotte chipped in. 'Nobody seemed to know what was going on, and whoever left the envelope walked straight past us in the confusion.'

'I'm not sure my sergeant will see it the same way, but thanks for the vote of confidence,' the officer replied.

'Did you look at what's inside?' Nigel prompted.

The blank face that met his question gave them their answer.

'It might hold some crucial information,' Charlotte suggested.

The officer seemed unsure.

'It's not even sealed.' Nigel pointed his finger at the envelope, in case the young officer had missed it. 'It might give you some crucial information to pass onto your superiors. It would certainly distract them from you abandoning your post.'

Charlotte stared at Nigel, realising exactly what he was up to. She was only a cub reporter herself, but she understood that as soon as anybody involved in the case caught wind of the envelope, the press wouldn't get a look in until the police were ready to share its contents with the rest of the world. She moved to the side of the corridor, having spotted an opened box of protective gloves on a trolley nearby. She took two out and handed them to the officer.

'Here, I know you've probably thought of this already, but if you use these medical gloves, you won't mess up any fingerprints or DNA evidence that might be retrievable from the package.'

Nigel smiled at her. The young cop relented and put on the gloves. It was a good job they'd reminded him about prints, she thought, as he almost handed the package over for them to hold while he put on the gloves. Thinking better of it, he placed it on top of the metal surface of the nearby trolley until he was ready to look inside. He put his gloved hand inside and pulled out a single item. It looked like a blank piece of A4 paper at first, but as he turned it round, it became clear that it was a photograph, albeit a bad one. The officer glanced at Nigel and Charlotte as if inviting them to comment.

The image was in colour, but grainy and out of focus. Charlotte thought it looked like the sort of photo she'd have extracted from her old Nokia phone years back. The shape wasn't right for a modern-day device.

Two people were in the image, a man and a woman. Charlotte identified the woman immediately, but the young officer clearly hadn't got a clue. Without asking permission, Nigel took a photo on his smartphone. The officer didn't even blink or challenge him, even though Charlotte flinched slightly when she saw what he was doing.

'Doesn't seem particularly useful,' Nigel said. 'We'd best be going. Thanks for your help. And if you need me to put in a good word for you to your sergeant, just say.'

He was in a hurry to be on his way. Charlotte wasn't sure why, but she followed his lead.

'Thanks for your help. Cheerio,' she said, as she rushed to catch Nigel before he left the ICU.

'You're in a hurry,' she said as she drew up behind him.

'I've had an idea, but we need to move fast before that copper rings it in to somebody who knows what they're doing. You saw who it was in the photo, right?'

'Yes, DCI Summers. A young DCI Summers. It must have been taken around the time the Irwins went missing. But who was the man?'

'I don't have a clue, Charlotte, but I'll bet a month's salary it's Callie Irwin in that ICU room, and I'll bet the following month's salary that she's come back from the dead for a very good reason. Call it a hunch.'

'So what happens now?' Charlotte asked.

'I want to view the security footage before the cops put in a request for it. Ready to tell another white lie?'

'Another one?' Charlotte replied. 'Couldn't we try to do it honestly for once?'

'Sometimes you have to do what's necessary to get the story, Charlotte. I'd never lie in a way that harmed someone. But this is a game of cat and mouse, and sometimes it's unavoidable.'

'I may be able to help,' she interrupted, spotting the cleaner who'd been chatting with her earlier.

'Hello again,' she said, walking up to him. 'I wonder if you could help me? One of your doctors dropped a twenty pound note during the fire alarm. I saw who he was, but I couldn't catch him in all the commotion. Could we check the security footage in the corridor to see if we can get it back to him?'

'Yes, you can; any excuse for a chat with Simone in security. She keeps snacks handy for friendly visitors, and I'm about ready for something to eat. I'll take you to her. Follow me.'

Charlotte gave Nigel a thumbs up sign, and they followed her new friend to an office marked Security. Inside was a woman eating a chocolate bar and studying an array of CCTV screens stacked up in front of her.

'Hi Mike,' she said, with a look that suggested she was grateful for some company. She leaned forward and opened a drawer packed with every kind of chocolate bar you could imagine. Stuck in the corner was a shrivelled orange which had seen better days.

'Don't mind if I do,' Mike said. 'Help yourselves; Simone is legendary for her chocolate drawer.'

Nigel and Charlotte took the opportunity for an impromptu snack and thanked Simone, who was immediately likeable and friendly. Before long, and with extraordinarily little persuasion, they were working through the CCTV footage along their corridor, with Simone inputting digital codes to move backwards and forwards to locate the specific time when the fire alarm sounded.

Nigel had his smartphone at the ready, quietly taking pictures of the screen behind Simone's back. Mike was working through his second chocolate bar, totally disinterested in what was happening. Then the moment came, but it was only a quick glimpse. The person passed directly behind Charlotte and Nigel and quickly darted into the room past the chair where the PC should have been sitting.

Whoever they were, there wasn't a chance of identifying them from the CCTV extract.

Charlotte ran through the details as the frames advanced. Possibly around six foot, indeterminable gender and hair colour, wearing surgical scrubs and a medical face mask, no doubt as a disguise. Nigel maintained their cover and pointed to some random doctor on the video footage, making a big deal of writing down his name and hospital department.

A knock at the door made Simone jump in her chair. She threw the half-eaten chocolate bar in the bin beside her desk.

'Management alert!' she warned them.

An authoritative woman wearing angular spectacles and with her hair drawn back into a severe bun strode into the office.

She stopped, obviously not expecting Simone's small room to be so busy. Mike moved towards his cleaning equipment and gulped as he swallowed the last of his chocolate.

'What's going on in here?' the woman asked.

CHAPTER ELEVEN

Charlotte had the situation summed up within seconds. This lady was a senior member of staff with all-access permissions, able to walk directly into the security office. Simone's confidence had withered the moment she saw who it was, transforming her from a friendly employee to a subservient staff member in an instant. Silence hung awkwardly in the air like a foul stench until a man wearing a firefighter's uniform stepped in behind her.

'We were just on our way.' Nigel was first to shatter the discomfort. 'Simone was just explaining your strict rules on data protection. She's good at her job; you run a tight outfit here.'

The woman looked at him dubiously as Nigel fumbled in his pocket.

'Nigel Davies, pleased to meet you,' he continued, holding out his identity card. 'And this is my colleague, Charlotte Grayson. We were just being sent packing by Simone as you walked through the door.'

The fire officer coughed.

The lady took her cue from him. 'Simone, the fire officers need to examine some footage to identify who set off the fire alarms. It was done maliciously.'

Charlotte glanced at Nigel and raised her eyebrows slightly.

'Where did it start?' Nigel asked the fire officer.

'In the female toilets along the corridor.'

'Thank you, Mr Davies. We can take it from here.' She dismissed them with a snooty look.

It wasn't a bad result, considering they'd been caught red-handed. Mike had already had the good sense to sneak out before he was challenged; at least he had some excuse to be in a sensitive area of the building.

'Thanks for your help, I'll do as you advised and submit a freedom of information request though the formal channels, as you advised. I appreciate your professionalism.'

Charlotte felt Nigel was laying it on thick, but it was the best they could do considering the interruption.

'Did you get what you need?' she asked, as they made their way down the corridor.

'Yes, I managed a couple of shots on my phone. We can't use them in the paper; I reckon we'd end up with a legal action of some sort. But we can use them for our own purposes, maybe to get a head of steam on what's going on.'

Mike was further along the corridor, keeping his head down, wiping a plastic cable retainer that ran along the length of the corridor.

'That was a close one!' he said, smiling as he saw them approaching. 'She's terrifying. I've just escaped with my life.'

'Where's this toilet the firefighter was talking about?' Nigel asked.

'Just along there; it's on my round. Look, another firefighter just came out.'

'I know it's a personal question, but you don't need to use the ladies, do you, Charlotte?'

Charlotte grinned at Nigel.

'I do now.'

She made her way up the corridor and pushed open the door into the female toilets.

'Oh, I'm sorry,' she said as she spotted two male fire-fighters investigating the smoke alarm which was attached to the ceiling.

'Don't mind us darling,' one of them replied. His mate gave him a sharp nudge, no doubt to remind him that they weren't living in a seventies sitcom.

'We'll be another five minutes. There's a disabled cubicle next door if you want to use it.'

'What's been going on here?' she asked. Below where the men were working were the burned fragments of a hospital leaflet.

'Somebody triggered the alarm on purpose,' the second man said. The first had evidently decided to keep his mouth shut. 'I have no idea why they do it; it's not like we don't have better things to do. It was probably some junkie.'

'Any idea who it was?'

'No, but she – or he – must have been tall. The flame from the paper has scorched the rim of this smoke alarm, so they must have held it right up close. We're just checking it for damage now.'

Charlotte left them to it and joined Nigel back in the corridor.

'Looks like there's some cleaning up to do, Mike,' she said, 'You might want to move quickly and get yourself in that manager's good books.'

Mike picked up some cleaning items, knocked, and entered cautiously.

'Did you learn anything interesting?' Nigel asked.

'How about we go to the cafeteria for a coffee?' she replied. 'We're meeting this Sam Halford guy shortly. We can compare notes then.'

When she put the tray on the table with soup, a roll and a coffee for both of them, Nigel had just finished filing the update to the other reporters back in the office.

'I put in a call while you were getting served,' he said. 'The police have called a press conference this evening; we'll be able to run the bare bones of the story online. It'll be tight, but at least we won't get caught out with the wrong headline. Do you want to come? Are you covered at the guest house?'

'I wouldn't miss it for anything. This story has got its claws into me now. I want to know if that person in the ICU really is Callie Irwin.'

Nigel changed the subject.

'So what did the fire guys have to say?'

'They think it's some junkie.'

'That's unlikely,' Nigel replied. 'We saw whoever it was who left the envelope in the ICU. How tall would you say they were? And what gender?'

'It looked like a male, but I can't be sure. I think it was a woman.'

Charlotte thought back to what they'd seen on the CCTV footage.

'Exactly, I agree,' Nigel continued. 'The firefighters said whoever set off the smoke alarm was tall. Over six foot, I'd say. But if you were trying to keep a low profile, you wouldn't go into the female toilets alone if you were a bloke. If someone walked in, it would immediately raise the alarm.'

'The alarm was just to the side of the cubicles,' Charlotte said, reflecting on the layout in the female rest rooms.

'You could lock yourself into the centre one and set the alarm going from there. If someone walked in, you'd just wait until they left. It's not like it's core visiting hours either, so the hospital is quieter.'

'Who would it be though? Why would somebody want to create all that fuss just to leave a grainy old photograph? It would have been safer to send it in the post. It doesn't make sense.'

Charlotte's soup was cool enough to sip, so she took a mouthful before replying to Nigel.

'What if dropping off the photograph wasn't the main reason for them coming to the hospital?'

'I don't understand; how would that work?' Nigel asked. He hadn't even started on his food yet.

'What if they were there for the same reason as we were? To find out who's inside that hospital room?'

CHAPTER TWELVE

Charlotte had driven past the wind turbine site at a distance many times, but she'd always accepted it as just a structure on the landscape. She'd never given a thought to who owned it, precisely where it was or even how long it had been there. She was predisposed to like wind farms, though she'd read enough readers' letters in the local newspapers to know their siting could be controversial.

As somebody who wasn't directly affected, she was agnostic. She'd rather have looked at the turbines than the nuclear power station which was situated not so far away from the former Sandy Beaches Holiday Camp. However, she also knew how many jobs the nuclear plant provided, and their household relied heavily on electrical devices around the house. If the power didn't keep flowing, it might create the Grayson family's biggest crisis yet.

She tried to count the turbines as they drew closer, but with the lanes winding left and right, she kept losing track of their vast, tubular bases and spinning clusters of blades.

'I count eleven, how about you?'

'Twelve, I reckon. Did you include the one right at the back? It's easy to miss.'

Charlotte counted again.

'Yes, twelve. It's a good job I can count better than that when I'm doing the books for the guest house.'

Nigel smiled and checked his sat nav.

'I'll have to navigate using traditional skills from this point. This is the post code, but I don't see the entrance yet, do you?'

Charlotte surveyed the area. She'd lost track of precisely where they were, but it was somewhere along the coastline between Middleton and Heysham.

'Are you OK being around here again, after what happened?'

Charlotte thought about it a moment. It was fine. The ghosts of the past at the holiday camp were laid to rest. She was doing her best to remember the good times she'd had there as a student. After all, it was where she'd met Will, and now they had their wonderful family.

'Yes; thanks for asking, but you don't need to worry about me. I'm inclined to stay away from the port for a while longer, but I don't even know where we are. We must be close, but I've lost my bearings.'

She'd barely finished the sentence when Nigel slammed on the brakes and reversed up the narrow road.

'Sorry!' he said as Charlotte tugged at her seatbelt which had locked with the suddenness of the sharp jolt.

'Here it is; if you blinked, you'd miss it.'

They drove up a narrow, gravel path, through a field and on towards the base of one of the turbines where a muddy SUV was parked. A man got out.

'I take it that's Sam Halford,' Charlotte said, as Nigel parked up.

Sam was friendly and welcoming. Charlotte had never been this close to a wind turbine. Looking up at the blades made her dizzy, but she found the steady swoosh to be oddly calming.

'So, this is Bay Mouth Wind Farm,' Sam said. 'It's not the biggest in the region, but it's capable of generating enough power for a small town.'

'How high are those things?' Charlotte asked. She found their constant movement hypnotising.

'The tower is 40 metres, only slightly lower than the Statue of Liberty, if that helps you to picture it better. The blades take it much higher, of course.'

'Impressive,' said Nigel. 'Can you tell us a little about the background to this place? How long has it been here?'

Sam leaned against his SUV, settling in to tell a story.

'It's been here almost two decades now. I've been on this site since the first foundations were sunk. It was just a field back then.'

'Who did the land belong to?' Charlotte asked, keen to steer him away from technical matters.

'It's Armstrong family farmland; it's been in their family for centuries. Just over the rise behind us is the old farm-house. It's privately owned now, but the outbuildings surrounding it are managed by Valdron Subramani. They're the company in charge of this wind farm and various others in Lancashire and South Cumbria. They've also got a couple out over Walney way too, across the bay.'

'Just to be clear, do the Irwins still own this land?' Nigel asked.

'Yes, and no,' Sam replied, studying something up ahead, slightly distracted. 'It all got rather complicated, but fortunately none of it impacts on me. I take it this is off the record?'

Nigel and Charlotte glanced at each other and nodded.

'Well, it was a family bloodbath. When old man Armstrong died, he gave his son Fabian control over the farm and land. He was traditional like that, an old-fashioned farmer, and when it came to the business, Tiffany was invisible.'

'Tiffany?' Charlotte asked. She wanted to hear it from Sam's mouth.

'Tiffany Armstrong was Fabian's sister. She married though, she's Tiffany Irwin these days. She's still alive, but has been off the scene for years.'

'Why the bloodbath?' Nigel probed.

'Fabian intended to sell the land for nuclear or chemical development. Tiffany wanted to preserve the farm for agricultural use. She was challenging the legality of the land ownership when her children disappeared.'

He hesitated a moment, as if wondering whether to continue.

'She claimed that there was historical paperwork which made the transfer to Fabian null and void. But Fabian had pulled a fast one and had stitched it all up while the father was still alive. She managed to get her own way in the end, because they leased the land for the wind turbines and the animal grazing continued around them. Fabian never did succeed in changing the land use. The lease is up on this land soon, I don't know if the turbines will stay here then.'

Sam looked at Charlotte, then Nigel, as if awaiting their comments. They said nothing, so he carried on speaking.

'Bay Mouth Wind Farm is the smallest part of Fabian Armstrong's portfolio. He was never really into renewables. I think this place is the respectable face of Valdron Subramani—'

'Wait, isn't Valdron Subramani a different company?'

Charlotte was having trouble keeping pace; it sounded like a family mess.

'Valdron Subramani is Fabian Armstrong's company. He's more into fracking these days, a much more controversial business. I just manage the wind farms side of things. I stay out of all the rest.'

Charlotte had a lot of questions, and she could tell by Nigel's fidgeting that he was struggling to contain his own curiosity.

'So, Fabian Armstrong controls all this land and the wind farm via an arm's length company, and Tiffany has nothing to do with it?'

Sam seemed to be tiring of the family questions. He sighed, enough to give them a hint.

'Yes. It was incredibly sad, what with her family disappearing and the decline in her health afterwards. She was cut out of the picture completely. It's sad; I always preferred speaking to her. I wish they could have worked it out between them. He's a nasty piece of work, Fabian Armstrong. Fortunately, I never see him these days. He has bigger fish to fry elsewhere. He probably keeps the turbines here in the hope that the nuclear plant will expand in the future, or that he might get a bite from the chemical processing or refining industries.'

'Final question, I promise,' Charlotte chanced her luck. 'The fracking is all happening further down in Lancashire. Where is Fabian based these days?'

'Blackpool. Valdron Subramani's headquarters is in Blackpool. The further away the better, as far as I'm concerned. I'm happy just managing this place along with the others in my brief.'

'You don't work for him then?' said Nigel.

Charlotte chuckled to herself. They were like a pair of inquisitors when they got started.

'No, I'm freelance, contracted in to do this. Fabian Armstrong isn't my boss, though I suppose he is indirectly. I haven't seen the man in years. Nor Tiffany, come to think about it.'

Sam stepped back and surveyed the site.

'I reckon that was an Iceland Gull flying over there,' he said. 'It's too far to be sure, though. They're rare; the local bird watchers will be getting excited if it is.'

Charlotte nodded. Birds weren't her thing, but at least she knew what had been distracting him now.

'I'll give you a tour if you want one,' Sam said without warning, as if he'd just remembered to offer a house guest a cup of tea. 'I don't mean now; we'll have to book it in. But if you want to go to the top of one of these turbines and do a feature for the newspaper, you'll be welcome.'

'Really?'

Charlotte scanned the structure from the metal steps at its base to the centre of the blades.

'How do you get to the top?'

'Via an exceedingly long ladder. You'll have to be kitted out with the proper safety gear over at the offices and get some health and safety paperwork done first. But you're welcome to climb up.'

Charlotte looked at Nigel, as a child would seek permission from a parent.

'It would make an excellent assignment for my course and the photographs would be amazing for the newspaper. What do you think?'

'I went up one of these things years ago, so I won't deny you the journalistic experience. But are you sure you'll be OK, after what happened at the port?'

'What happened at the port?' Sam queried.

'It's a long story,' Charlotte shrugged it off. 'I take it we'll have harnesses and hard hats?'

'Of course,' Sam answered.

'Then I'm in, let's get it organised. Besides, I'm doing an assisted skydive for charity on Sunday. How bad can this be?'

Charlotte made arrangements with Sam to meet him on site the following week, pending submission of the usual paperwork and health checks. He was interrupted by his pager and rushed away, making his excuses and leaving them alone at the base of the turbine. They watched him drive down the track, the crunch of gravel at last replaced by the calm swishing of the blades at their rear.

'This gets better and better,' Nigel said at last. 'This has all the makings of a bloodbath scene in a Godfather film. The moment it's officially confirmed that it's Callie Irwin in the ICU, I reckon we've got ourselves a story here.'

'I'm desperately sorry for Tiffany Irwin. Isn't there something we can do to help her?'

'Don't get too involved,' Nigel cautioned. 'Remember what happened last time.'

Charlotte gave a hollow laugh. It was too late; she was already caught up in Tiffany Irwin's story.

CHAPTER THIRTEEN

Charlotte was grateful when the bacon sandwich arrived.

They'd stopped off at a café after concluding their conversation with Sam Halford at the wind turbine site.

'Is this what journalists do all day? It doesn't say anything about this in my distance learning course. I've never eaten so much since I started working with you. It's a good job I've kept up with my Saturday runs, otherwise it would be playing havoc with my weight.'

Nigel finished the first mouthful of his sandwich.

'Before long you'll know every greasy spoon café in every corner of Lancaster and Morecambe.'

He wiped a spot of egg from his chin; he'd braved an egg and bacon sandwich, during a working day too.

'I've been researching this company of Fabian Armstrong's on my phone while you were driving. It seems he's worth a small fortune. I wonder if Tiffany gets to see any of the money? As far as I can tell, it all resulted from the original sale of the farmland; that was his business start-up money. We have to check this guy out, don't we?'

'I'm already on it,' Nigel replied. He looked like he hadn't eaten for days, the way he was making light work of the sandwich.

'I know a chap who works in radio down in Blackpool. He used to cover this patch in Lancaster, but got caught up in some trouble locally. I'll call him and see what he can tell us about Mr Armstrong.'

'A lot of terrible words have been written about him on the internet. He seems to swoop in on farmers, secure their land, then start aggressive fracking operations.'

Nigel finished his sandwich and placed his phone on the table. The café was quiet, with just two other customers, workers from somewhere on the industrial estate taking a break. He ran through his speed dial options and pressed the green telephone icon then placed the call on speaker-phone, loud enough for both of them to hear, not so loud that everybody else could listen in. After two rings, it was answered.

'Hi, it's Russ McGill.'

Nigel screwed up his face at Charlotte.

'Hi Russ, it's Nigel Davies from The Bay View Weekly. I was expecting Pete Bailey to pick up. Has he moved on again?'

'Yeah. Hi Nigel, I don't believe we've met? Pete had some personal issues; he's out in Spain these days, I think. He left the radio station, but I'm not sure what he's up to now. He was only down here for a temporary period. Can I help you?'

'I hope so. What do you know about Fabian Armstrong?'

Charlotte and Nigel exchanged glances across the table.

'Where do I start?' Russ began. 'On the one hand, he's

divided the entire county over his fracking plans. On the other, he's supporting local charities and communities by throwing money at them. They can't condemn him because they need his cash, yet few of them want the fracking on their doorstep. Is that the sort of thing you were after? I hope you weren't calling for a job reference, were you?'

Charlotte laughed more loudly than she should have. The two workers gave her a dirty look.

'Can we get to him?' Nigel asked, countering the guys across the café with his own dirty look.

'He won't talk about it, other than via bland press release announcements. His PR machine runs on overdrive, but they have a policy of not speaking to the press on fracking matters. He's always happy to talk about the charitable work, but the moment you draw breath to speak about fracking, he'll walk off. It doesn't make for very good journalism; all you can do is to puff up the good news stories without challenging him over the bad news. It's very frustrating.'

Charlotte's phone vibrated. She checked it briefly and saw it was a text from Will. She placed it on the table; she'd deal with it when Russ had finished his briefing. It would probably be something related to tonight's evening meal. A bag of frozen peas, a tin of beans or whatever it was could wait. Besides, there was no point living in a guest house if you couldn't raid the kitchen from time to time.

'If you want to hijack him in public, he's got a big charity event in Blackpool on Saturday. I'm covering it for radio. He's at the Winter Gardens, making an announcement about funding for a village hall refurbishment nearby. It's going to be packed with members of the public and representatives from some local charities. Is that any use to you?'

'What are you doing on Saturday?' Nigel looked up at Charlotte.

'What time?' Charlotte spoke at the phone.

'Mid-afternoon, two o'clock or thereabouts. It lasts an hour. You'll have to sit through a performance by a local kids' ballet group, but he'll be accessible at least.'

'Sounds good. You can pick me up after my parkrun,' Charlotte said.

'OK, the Winter Gardens you said?' Nigel checked.

'Yup, nice and open, the perfect place to get up close and personal. If you're planning to push him on the fracking issue, can you at least let me get my interview in first? You'll be as welcome as a bout of flatulence in a space suit, so don't expect a warm welcome when you raise it.'

'OK, thanks for the warning. So Pete Bailey is in Spain now, you say? Lucky thing, I wonder how he managed to wangle the move on a journalist's salary?'

'Last I heard, he was living out there with that Alex Kennedy woman from Crime Beaters on the TV. They go way back, my boss reckons. But no, he's not local any more. Did he ever get the house sold? Poor guy. What a liability that place was, after all those deaths.'

'Oh, I remember that media coverage,' Charlotte said. 'I read about it in Bristol.'

'Yes, the house was sold. I was sent over to Lancaster to report on one of the murders there,' Nigel added. 'If you see him again, please pass on my regards; he always seemed like a decent bloke to me. And we'll see you at the Winter Gardens tomorrow.'

Nigel ended the call and Charlotte returned to her sandwich. She'd have to master Nigel's skill at eating faster. The bacon was cold now, not half as tasty as it had been before the call.

'Remember the first time we knocked on Edward Callow's front door?' Nigel asked.

'Yes. What was it Russ said? A fart in a space suit. That's what it was like.'

'Are you sure you're up for this? I know people like Fabian Armstrong. They can be nasty pieces of work. If you're not up to it yet, there's no problem. I'll go to Blackpool on my own.'

Charlotte remembered the text message and picked up her phone to read it as she began speaking.

'I'm fine, seriously,' she said. 'I'm jumping back on the horse. If I let the past get to me, I'll become scared and cowed again. I won't let that happen—'

Her voice rose, full of determination.

'Keep the noise down, love,' one of the workers chided from across the room.

'Get lost!' Charlotte snapped back at him. 'This café is for everybody. You've been chatting and laughing away all the time. I'm sorry if you don't like women in your greasy spoon café, but hard luck, it's the 21st century. Get used to it.'

Nigel stared at her, stunned. The two workers appeared equally shocked.

'That was over the top,' Nigel whispered. 'Careful, these guys can be tough.'

'They've been looking down their noses at me since we came in. I'm not apologising for it; I wasn't doing anything wrong. Besides, I've just got a text from Will, and it's made me a bit tense.'

'Is everything all right?'

'Not really. He wanted to speak to me this evening about something important. But he's just sent me this text. Look.'

She held up her phone so Nigel could see. It was only brief, but it had rattled her.

Please DON'T worry, I'll tell you more tonight. But if a woman called Hollie Wickes tries to contact you, please don't engage with her. I'll tell you more later. Will x

CHAPTER FOURTEEN

Nigel's phone vibrated, but he ignored it and continued speaking to Charlotte.

'Who's this Hollie Wickes person? Do you know her?'

'I don't have a clue who she is. I'm getting tired of all these creeps and weirdos in my life.'

As if on cue, the two workers got up from their chairs, muttering something about *time of the month*. Charlotte bristled but decided to keep her mouth shut this time. They hadn't pushed in their chairs either. The lady who'd served them at the counter cleaned up the debris they'd left on the table and took care of the chairs.

As the owner of a guest house, Charlotte knew how rude some customers could be. The majority tidied their tables, stacked their crockery, and left the cutlery neatly organised in a convenient place, but slobs left their tables like they'd exploded their food rather than eaten it. These guys were the latter.

'I'm sorry for my outburst,' Charlotte addressed the woman who was clearing up. 'They just caught me at the wrong moment.'

'Don't you worry, love, those two act as if they own the place. They expect women to be doing what I'm doing, running after them all the time. You carry on just as you are. You weren't doing any harm. It'll do them some good to be called out. I can't do it; I'd lose my job.'

'There, you see. I wasn't rude, I was righting an injustice,' Charlotte said, buoyed up by what she'd said.

Nigel had been studying his phone while Charlotte had been chatting. He glanced up at her as he spoke.

'How pushed for time are you? Can you squeeze in one last appointment this afternoon ahead of the press briefing at five o'clock? The police update is at the town hall, so you can go still go along after this new appointment, which is just up the road. I can't make it; I've got to pick up my son from an after-school club. Best not miss my domestic commitment, not if I'm going to be in Blackpool on Saturday.'

Charlotte ran through the night's arrangements in her head. Will wouldn't be back until after 6 o'clock, but Piper and Isla were running the kitchen and check-ins between them, so they were covered for the early evening.

'I can manage one last job. Where is it?'

'It's in your part of town, if I drop you off, you can walk home afterwards. Are you sure it's OK? I don't want to get into trouble over apprentice exploitation.'

Charlotte smiled.

'You know I love this work. Anything that takes me away from boring essays and dull reading is a light relief. I learn better by doing, anyway. Where are you dropping me off?'

'Do you remember Rory Higson, the guy who used to be a reporter on the newspaper well before my time? He's retired now.'

Charlotte knew all about Rory Higson.

'He's the chap who photographed Edward Callow and his pals back in their younger days. I saw his name in the old newspaper cuttings. He's a great source of information. Why do you want me to talk to him?'

She saw her mistake the moment the words came out of her mouth. Rory's name was plastered all over the microfiche reports that she'd printed out. He was the main reporter on the case involving Tiffany Irwin. Of course Nigel had put in a call to him.

'Do former reporters ever get to retire?' she asked.

Nigel shook his head.

'Not really. They're such a great source of local information. Besides, men like Rory Higson love it. It takes them back to their reporting days. You know what it's like. Once you get hold of a story, it's difficult to let it go.'

Charlotte knew the feeling all right. She took two notes out of her pocket and left them on the table to pay for the food and drinks. She left a decent tip and waited for her receipt for the food. One aspect of journalism that the distance learning course didn't cover was the skill of saving receipts for expenses claims. Nigel was teaching her well. He'd told her the canny reporter could almost survive on food purchases through expenses, if they were careful to manage their diary properly.

Charlotte made sure everything was settled, then re-joined Nigel in the car. Twenty minutes later, she was standing outside Rory Higson's semi-detached house, waving goodbye to Nigel, having synchronised diaries for the town hall briefing and the next day's visit to Blackpool.

The small garden at the front was well groomed and carefully planted. Its owner was attentive to detail, with careful and precise planting, the mix of colours intentional. She knocked at the door, sneaking a peek inside the front room window. She was grateful to be visiting Rory. Will's text had unnerved her, and she wished he hadn't sent it in the first place.

Rory was quick to answer the door, obviously expecting her. As he shook her hand firmly, she wondered how many times that same hand had been in contact with the great and the good of Morecambe over the years. He led her to the lounge and gestured to her to sit on the settee. Charlotte heard the rattle of a dog's collar approaching and a friendly Labrador clambered up on the sofa, resting its head on her lap, as if she was a familiar visitor.

'You don't mind dogs, do you?' Rory asked, not settling in his seat in case he had to encourage the dog back into the kitchen.

'Of course not,' Charlotte said, stroking the creature as if they were best friends. 'What's his name?'

'Archie,' Rory replied. 'He's 12 years old now, an old man. You'll find him very friendly.'

Charlotte had fallen in love with Archie already. She had to re-focus on the reason for her visit.

'So, I take it Nigel explained why I'm here?'

'Yes, he did. Sometimes I wish I wasn't retired; I'd love to be working on this story again. It consumed me. It's what led to the break-up of my marriage, actually.'

'I'm sorry to hear that. I know some of these news stories can get a grip on you.'

'You can say that again. So, how can I help?'

Archie nestled his head deep into Charlotte's lap, looking like he might never move again. She'd seen Will adopt the same posture on many a Sunday morning.

'We're after anything you can tell us. What about DCI Kate Summers, for instance? What was her involvement?'

Rory gave her a blank look.

'Sorry, I've never heard of her. Is she connected with the case?'

'How about Kate Allan? You might know her as PC Kate Allan.'

If ever there was a moment when you could spot a penny dropping in a person's head, this was it. The immediate sign of recognition flashed across Rory's face.

'Is she still around locally? I always wondered what became of her. No wonder she seemed to disappear; she must have married and changed her surname. I can't blame her. You wouldn't want the name of Allan following you around in the circumstances.'

Charlotte was caught off guard. This didn't sound like the Kate Summers she knew; a serious, diligent, well-respected officer, totally dependable.

Rory continued, the glint in his eyes suggesting she'd just stoked a fire which still had plenty of life left in it yet.

'She was first on the scene; I guess you're aware of that already? But did you know about her brother?'

'I didn't even know she had one.'

There was no reason why Kate Summers would have mentioned him. Their relationship was professional, and she was vaguely aware of children and a husband in the background, but she didn't even know the age of her kids.

'He went missing at the same time as Tiffany Irwin's family. His name was Brett Allan.'

Charlotte felt her jaw drop. She thought it was a term used only in books. But it happened like it would in a cartoon; she felt her mouth open as he said it.

'Really? Was he involved with the Irwins in any way?'

'I don't think so, though some rumours were going around, none of which could be substantiated. I could never find any proof of it. But he vanished a week or so after the Irwins. The official investigation said it was pure coincidence. There were a few other disappearances around the same time, and the police insisted they were not related.'

Charlotte didn't know what to say. No wonder Kate Summers had been cagey. She felt a surge of guilt as she recalled how she'd pushed Kate for information. This news story was re-opening a wound for her.

'What happened to her brother?'

'Suspected suicide.'

'Oh no—'

'I'm afraid so. At Sunderland Point. His car was found abandoned and empty, with all the doors open. The tides come in fast over there; they've caught out many a person. There was no body, no note, no sign of him. Everyone assumed he'd died. It was the same with the other girl, Joanne something—'

'How did the police conclude that all these deaths were unrelated? It seems astonishing.'

'Not really,' Rory continued. 'It was a new millennium. You're old enough to have been around then. Everybody went crazy. People thought the world was ending. Joanne Taylor, that's the name of the other girl who also went missing.'

Charlotte leaned over to jot the name down in her small note pad. Archie looked up at her as if expecting to be disturbed. When he saw she wasn't moving, he settled on her lap again.

'What happened to Joanne Taylor? Was she another suicide?'

'That's a different story altogether. As far as the police

were concerned, she disappeared without a trace. She just vanished from Morecambe one day and was never seen again. I found out years afterwards that she'd worked as a live-in childminder for Tiffany and David Irwin.'

CHAPTER FIFTEEN

Charlotte couldn't grasp what Rory Higson was telling her. All the incidents seemed to have nothing in common, yet her intuition urged her to give it more thought. And there was DCI Kate Summers, who'd been at the scene, now avoiding her calls and personally involved too. The whole thing stank, yet as Rory had confirmed with her, it had all been thoroughly investigated and the cases were deemed to be coincidental.

As Rory explained how life was much less exciting in retirement, and why he missed the cut and thrust of a good local news story, Charlotte's mind began to drift. In the past year she'd had her own experience of a cop gone bad, although the events concerned had taken place years before she came to live in the resort. So what if Kate Summers was a cop gone bad, rather than being one of the good guys as she'd always thought? She dismissed the idea immediately; DCI Summers couldn't be anything but a straight-up police officer.

The ticking of Rory's old-fashioned clock drew her back

to the present, and she tuned back into his voice just in time to catch the tail end of something interesting.

'—I'm certain I could get the former DCI who dealt with the case to speak about it. He's still a pal of mine.'

'Just repeat that again, would you?' she asked, embarrassed at being caught out daydreaming.

'Evan Farrish; he lives locally. Like me, he's still alive to tell his stories. He walks his dogs on the beach at Half Moon Bay. We often stop there for a hot drink and something to eat. I'll see if he's up for it if you want? I'm certain he'll be happy to chat to you off the record. He might speak to you on the record, if you're lucky.'

'I'd appreciate it if he would,' Charlotte replied, glancing at the clock. Its persistent sound kept her focused on the passage of time. She'd need to make her way back to the town hall. They exchanged telephone numbers and Charlotte reluctantly evicted Archie from his newly declared territory on her lap.

'Sorry, Archie, I've got one last place to be before the day ends.'

She was pleased to have met Rory Higson. Just like Jon Rogers at the library, he was one of those locals who knew everything and everybody. It was a shame they had to retire.

It didn't take long to get to the town hall, and she was pleased for the fresh air and the exercise. They'd been driving around all day, and the salty breeze cleared her mind. She was grateful for some time on her own again too; sometimes it was easier to see things without somebody else's voice jabbering away in the background.

She felt a sharp and sudden sadness for Kate Summers; what must it be like to lose a brother at such a young age? And for a body never to have been found; it must have been painful and difficult for her. She wondered how a person could ever recover from such an event, yet DCI Summers had. It must be a heavy burden to bear.

The town hall grounds had just been replanted. The council always ensured the entrance to the resort's key municipal building looked colourful and well-tended. She walked up the steps and through the heavy wooden doors which had been left open for the briefing.

There was an atmosphere of professional anticipation as members of the press and police made small talk in the room reserved for the gathering. Both sides knew that in a matter of minutes it would be police versus reporters, the latter seeking as much information as possible, the former carefully controlling it. Refreshments beforehand were an attempt at peacemaking.

Charlotte helped herself to tea and biscuits. Boiling water was dispensed from an urn which could only ever be found in a British town hall. Any similar specimens would have been scrapped or placed in museums years ago. She took a chair and looked around for Nigel; unusually, he was late.

The police were gathering at the rickety table at the front, on which a tablecloth had been placed along with cabled microphones from the various media outlets. It had generated considerable interest, with TV and radio there, but most of it was local. She couldn't see any national reporters in the room.

Nigel darted in at her side just as one of the officers began calling order in the room.

'Sorry I cut it fine,' he whispered, 'I've lined us up a nice little interview to illustrate the news story. So long as they're not about to blow it out of the water,' he added.

'Welcome to this informal briefing of the press. It's good to see so many of you here,' the leading officer began.

'How was Rory?' Nigel whispered.

Charlotte wasn't keen on chatting during the briefing. As a former teacher, she knew how annoying it could be when she was competing with the drone of other voices during a lesson.

'I'll tell you afterwards,' she said, focusing on the activity at the front of the room. Nigel took the hint.

'My name is DI Comfort,' the officer continued. 'I'm leading this investigation into the appearance of a young woman on the slipway opposite the RNLI building in the early hours of yesterday morning.'

'At least we're in the right place,' Nigel whispered again. 'I thought we might have gate-crashed the adult education flower arranging class by accident.'

Charlotte stifled a giggle.

'To my right is Toni Lawson, the press officer who'll be fielding your queries on this news story, and DC Redmond, who was the first detective on the scene. I'll begin by reading out a prepared statement which Ms. Lawson will be happy to make available in full at the end of the briefing.'

Charlotte was a veteran of just two police press conferences, apart from those she had seen on the television. As far as she could tell, they took a long time to say not very much. She sat as patiently as she could, jotting down the gist of it. It was an excellent real-life opportunity to take her newly acquired shorthand skills out for a spin, if nothing else.

They dragged out the bit everybody was waiting for. The facts of the case were confirmed: a young woman in her mid-twenties had been found on the slipway in a bad state of health, and she remained in a coma. She had a distinctive birthmark and was wearing a wedding ring believed to be the one Tiffany Irwin had lost in 2000. They knew this because photographs had been placed in the police files during the original investigation. Charlotte realised this information would allow them to report what had gone on officially, rather than relying on hearsay and tip-offs which couldn't be verified. Eventually DI Comfort got to the point.

'After accelerated DNA tests, owing to the importance of this case, we can now confirm the young woman shares the same DNA as Tiffany Irwin and is believed to be Callie Irwin. I would sound a note of caution in your reporting; we are unable to confirm if this is Callie Irwin or Jane Irwin, but it is most likely to be Callie, based upon the presence of a birthmark—'

A spark of excitement flared through the room.

'Thank God for that; we just got our front-page story,' Nigel whispered. 'I was getting nervous; if all this turned out to be a storm in a teacup, we'd have been left high and dry.'

'Why can't they say it's Callie?' Charlotte asked.

'It's a technicality, but as the kids were so young, they can confirm the DNA link, but there won't be dental records, fingerprints or anything like that for individual identities. All three kids would have had no teeth, or just baby teeth. I don't envy the police, having to sort this one out.'

'The investigation into the disappearance of Callie, Jane, Rowan and David Irwin has been re-opened and I will be the officer leading it on a day-to-day basis. I would remind members of the press that family members are still alive and living within the county; sensitivity will be appreciated in your reporting. A local woman who believed her children to be dead for two decades has just found out that at least one of them is alive. This young woman remains in a critical condition in the ICU at Lancaster and it may be some time before she is able to help us directly with our enquiries. I'll now open the floor to members of the press—'

DI Comfort had barely finished his sentence when the questions started flying, tossed like grenades without a care as to where they landed.

'Does this mean the other children and the father are alive?'

'Where has Callie Irwin been for the past 20 years?'

'Was this an abduction rather than a tragic accident?'

'Did Morecambe Police bungle the original investigation back in 2000?'

The mood changed all of a sudden; détente formally ceased, as the police defended their position and the press started smelling blood.

Not much more of substance emerged, other than that the woman thought to be Callie was a Type 1 diabetic, hence her state of ill health. Medical staff had taken some time to work it out, but were now treating her properly.

DI Comfort appeared flustered and browbeaten by the time he concluded the briefing, looking like he'd just gone several rounds in a boxing ring with Tyson Fury. The TV and radio reporters had their evening deadlines to make, so the room cleared swiftly as they rushed to file their reports.

'This is the advantage of working in newspapers,' Nigel said. 'With only one weekly deadline, we can dig a little deeper than the other guys.'

Charlotte made her excuses, left Nigel to it and wandered around the town hall, searching for the rest rooms. A female voice echoed in the long, dark corridor.

'Are you trying to find the ladies' toilets too?' she asked.

Charlotte turned around. It was Toni Lawson.

'Hi, yes. Any ideas?'

'Down here, apparently,' Toni guided her with her hand. 'I haven't seen you about before; are you new?'

'Yes, I'm training to be a newspaper reporter, I'm with Nigel Davies from The Bay View Weekly.'

'What did you make of the press conference? I'm new too. Not to this line of work, but to this police force.'

'It's still a novelty for me,' Charlotte said. 'I find it all fascinating.'

They reached the toilets, and each took a cubicle. Charlotte was glad there was more than one; it might have ended in a fight to the death otherwise.

Toni continued the conversation from her cubicle. They had gaps at the top and bottom of the doors, offering little privacy, so it seemed as natural as anything to carry on talking, even though they'd just met.

'I notice DI Comfort didn't mention the incident at the hospital earlier today,' Charlotte ventured. 'We just happened to be there when it all kicked off.'

'No, he kept his powder dry. We were hoping the press hadn't got hold of that one yet. Well done, you're ahead of everybody else already. You don't have any paper in there do you?'

Charlotte did, and she passed some under the gap between the cubicles.

'Do you know who entered Callie's room yet? Was there more than just the one tall person?'

'Wow, you have done your homework.' Toni smiled at her as they emerged and headed for the sinks.

'I'll let you into a secret,' Toni began as she tested the temperature on the hot tap. 'It's not a secret as such; regard it as a scoop. We have no idea who it was who caused the incident at the infirmary earlier today or how many people were involved. But whoever it was, they took something from Callie's room. Tiffany Irwin's wedding ring has vanished from the side of her bed. We reckon they're linked to the family in some way.'

CHAPTER SIXTEEN

Charlotte and Nigel sat on a bench outside the town hall before going their separate ways for the evening. After her conversation with Toni Lawson, Charlotte had returned to the press briefing room to find the chairs and tables being packed away. Several metres ahead of them, DI Comfort was getting ready to be interviewed via a television satellite van, the urgent activity suggesting they'd be going on air soon.

'Have you met Toni Lawson yet?' Charlotte asked Nigel as she watched the TV engineers working methodically through their set-up routines.

'No, she's new. I mean, very new. Her predecessor was a chap called Brian Whittle, who's been at the helm for years. He was there when I started working on the paper. He retired due to ill health. What's she like?'

'I liked her. And she was kind enough to tell me someone has stolen the wedding ring from Callie's bedside at the hospital. That has to be significant, surely?'

Nigel was also watching the TV crew at work, so he paused a while before answering.

'If it wasn't for the photo they left behind, I'd say it was just a chancer stealing it while Callie Irwin was out cold. She didn't mention that, I'll bet?'

'No, no mention of the photo,' Charlotte confirmed. 'What about this diabetes thing too? Surely they'd know Callie had diabetes from old medical records?'

Nigel's attention snapped back into full focus.

'Ah, I know about this because my sister has Type 1 diabetes—'

'Oh, I'm sorry Nigel, I didn't realise.'

'It's fine, it's just one of those things. It was detected at a young age, so it's just something she manages on a daily basis. I wasn't aware of this until it happened to Amy, but Type 1 diabetes usually appears when children are around four to seven years old – which is when it happened in our family – or from about the age of ten into the early teenage years.'

'So if it is Callie Irwin, which seems pretty certain, she wouldn't have had diabetes before she disappeared. Which means wherever she's been all this time, she has to have been engaging with the health service for at least eight years, maybe even more.'

'Yes,' Nigel replied. 'And if this coma is related to her diabetes, it suggests she couldn't access her treatments for it. Maybe she ran away or escaped from somewhere. I've been wondering if she was kept against her will.'

Charlotte stopped following the progress of the TV team and gave Nigel her full attention now.

'Is that possible? The police didn't say anything—'

'The police only tell us what they want us to know. They had to share something with the press, and they've re-opened the case now, so they need us to help them find leads. But why else would she be found unconscious at the slipway? She hadn't been assaulted or anything like that; at least nobody has suggested she has. She's a grown woman, not a kid, which means she'll have been managing her diabetes for some years. It will have taken her some time before she went into a coma. We can't say anything in the newspaper yet, but I'd venture a small bet she was running away from something. Or someone.'

'Have you ever thought of becoming a detective?' Charlotte smiled at him. 'Inspector Davies of the Yard, I can see it now. The Rebus of Morecambe Bay.'

Nigel laughed.

'It's not quite my scene. There's too much danger for my liking. I enjoy playing armchair detective as a reporter. You get all the cerebral challenge with none of the physical risks. That's much more my style.'

They paused a moment as they watched the TV team working in synchronised, professional harmony. Charlotte consulted the clock on her phone; it was evening TV bulletin time. It was exciting to see how it worked live on air.

'Oh, I forgot to tell you, we have a busy day tomorrow.'

Nigel looked like he was getting ready to finish for the day, gathering up his notepad, phone and pen.

'Another one?' Charlotte asked. 'I'm not supposed to be working at the paper tomorrow, but I can probably manage it if Isla can cover the early evening shift. I'll check when I get back. What's going on tomorrow?'

'I've fixed up an interview with Yasmin Utworth, the lady whose daughter Morgan has been missing for twenty years. She's not officially connected with this news story, but I want you to write what's called a backgrounder—'

'You want me to write a full feature? With my name on it?'

'Yes, it's high time. This is a nice feature item, you're well ready for it. It'll impress your tutor on the distance course too.'

Charlotte was in danger of exploding with pride and excitement. That would have given the television viewing audience something interesting to watch.

'What's the job? I'm excited already.'

'I want you to speak to Yasmin Utworth about what it's like when a person you love goes missing. Get a feel for how it works with the police and the various agencies. It'll help us flesh out our coverage until Callie comes out of this coma and starts talking. Are you up for it?'

Nigel was fiddling with his phone.

'Of course I am. Just tell me where to go and I'll take care of it.'

'I've just texted you the details. I'd better be on my way now; we've done quite enough for today. Oh, and when you're finished with Yasmin Utworth, let me know when I can come and pick you up. We're heading out to Sunderland Point for a look around.'

'Where Brett Allan went missing?'

'Yes. I want a sense of what happened, and I'd like to explore the area. All my journalistic instincts are telling me we have a big story on our hands. I'll see you tomorrow. Thanks for your help today.'

After Nigel left, Charlotte remained on the bench watching the TV crew until the interview concluded. The satellite van rig was packed away as fast as they'd set it up. It was time for her to make her own way back home.

It was only a ten-minute walk, precious time alone to process the day's events before she had to slip back into guest house and family mode. But most of all, she couldn't believe she was getting her first-ever newspaper by-line, the holy grail for every new reporter in her position.

When she walked through the doors of the guest house, it was all hands on deck to feed some late walk-ins. Isla was grateful for the extra pair of hands, despite Will having rolled up his sleeves to help when he'd come in from the bus. His involvement was usually restricted to routine food purchases from the cash and carry store and light mainten-ance tasks; at his own request Charlotte tried to keep him away from the catering side of things.

It was eight o'clock before Charlotte set the final table for breakfast the next day. She'd just finished when George came through the front entrance with Una on her lead, ready to collect Isla. Having checked that Isla was happy to cover the next day, with a little help from George in his usual helpful way, Charlotte headed upstairs to the family accommodation, ready for something to eat.

Will was sitting at the kitchen table, his phone in his hand, his face tired and drawn. He hadn't looked that way for some time, not since the terrible events of the previous year.

'What is it you wanted to tell me, Will? From the expression on your face, it's not good news.'

He looked up at her, weary and struggling for words.

'I wanted to protect you from this as long as possible, but I have to tell you now, for your own safety. We've got a problem, Charlotte. And I'm afraid it might get out of hand.'

CHAPTER SEVENTEEN

'I can't take any more of this, Will. Please tell me it's not connected to what happened last year.'

Charlotte felt a wave of nausea wash over her, pulling her back to a dark place once again.

'It's nothing to do with what happened at the old holiday camp,' he answered, as if expecting the question to be raised. 'This is something different.'

Charlotte pulled up a chair at the kitchen table and picked up two chips from Will's plate. She could see the oven was on low and he'd left her food in there. She was famished, but this announcement – whatever it was – had made her knees feel like they were about to give way.

'It's connected with the university. I've got caught up in a bit of trouble.'

'Please tell me you're not suspended or anything, Will. Your job isn't under threat, is it?'

'No, it's nothing like that. Not yet, anyway. I've got a problem with a student—'

'Oh no.'

Charlotte's mind transported her back to her last day in

the classroom. She began to sweat, recalling the incident that finally marked the end of her own career. But Will was dealing with adults, not teenagers. They were paying to learn. What could go wrong?

'I'm getting unwanted attention from a female student.'

'What kind of attention?'

'The kind that made it uncomfortable enough to report it to my department head. Inappropriate attention. I thought I'd better raise it in case it escalates.'

Charlotte didn't know what to think. Had Will encouraged this? Was it an unsuitable relationship with a student? If so, this was a powder keg ready to explode in their faces.

'What's been going on, Will. Are you having a relationship with this woman?'

'Whoa, no, Charlotte, absolutely not. It's nothing like that. I'd been feeling uncomfortable around her. She was always lingering after lectures... she seems to be everywhere I am. I reported it to Suzy, my line manager, and she asked me to keep a diary of my interactions with this woman. She reckoned I'd done the right thing. I thought it was over until she called me in this morning for a chat.'

'Why didn't you tell me this was going on?'

Charlotte knew the answer to her question. Why on earth did he still treat her as if she was delicate? She'd put the past behind her; if only everybody else would.

'I didn't want to worry you. You've had enough on your plate.'

There it was, Will being over-protective.

'What did Suzy have to say? Why are you telling me this now?'

'Suzy has recommended I conduct any tutorials or feedback sessions somewhere public, where there are witnesses. She's told me not to get caught alone with her, or else the department would have to take any allegations seriously.'

Charlotte glanced up at Will. He looked like he'd already been found guilty and was awaiting his sentence.

'Your instincts were right in reporting it to Suzy. How old is this woman? Is she the one you warned me about in your text?'

'Yes, she is. Her name is Hollie Wickes. She's 21, a second-year student, probably had a year out as she's a little older than the others in her year group. I thought I'd better mention it in case it turns into a stalker kind of thing. She might start trying to find out more about the family, for instance. I'm scared you or the kids will get caught up in this.'

'We can't tell the kids, not after the year they've had.'

Will's face suggested he thought otherwise.

'We kept secrets from them in the past which we shouldn't have done. They're adults now, Charlotte. We can't treat them with kid gloves; they need to know.'

'OK, but let's be gentle about it. I don't want them terrified; they've already had more to deal with than most young people of their age. Do I need to worry?'

Will paused before answering.

'I don't think so. There's been nothing threatening or sinister. She's just too needy, overstaying her welcome, being over-friendly, asking too many personal questions. I almost didn't report it; I thought I was being over-sensitive.'

'That'll be the day, Dad!'

Lucia had walked into the kitchen, wearing a onesie and with garish, furry slippers on her feet.

'I take it you're staying in this evening?' Charlotte said, eager to change the topic and pick a better time to bring up Will's issue.

'Yup, I need my beauty sleep. We've got the parachute jump on Sunday. How's your sponsorship coming on?'

Charlotte hadn't even checked. Lucia had shown her how to set up her donations web page and she'd shared it a couple of times on Facebook, but she had been distracted by the Irwin news story. She pulled out her phone to check the donations page.

'I've raised over four hundred pounds,' Lucia added, in the absence of an answer from her mother.

'Wow, I'm over five hundred pounds,' Charlotte announced, refreshing her account to make sure it wasn't a mistake.

'You might have me to thank for that,' Will confessed. 'I've been complaining to everybody at work that it's too soon for you to be doing this parachute jump, and they've all been telling me to stop wrapping you in cotton wool and let you get on with it. Then they've all been asking how they can support you.'

'I can't believe the figure. Thanks Will, I appreciate that. Daisy and Abi will be delighted; we've raised just under a thousand pounds between us for the Down's Syndrome charity. I thought we'd barely scrape three hundred pounds between us if we were lucky.'

'I still don't think you're ready for it—'

This was a long-standing source of tension and Charlotte was sick of it.

'The doctor gave me the all-clear, Will. We've discussed this a million times already. It's a tandem jump, and I'm in the hands of an expert. People with disabilities do these jumps. I read about a woman who's over a hundred years old doing one the other day.'

'But this is you, Charlotte. I don't care about those people—'

Charlotte couldn't suppress her anger any longer.

'I'm doing this, Will! Don't you think I deserve the chance, after the year we've had? I'm not really doing it for Abi or the charity; this is all about me. This is about proving I'm over it, about showing everybody that those bastards didn't break me. When I jump out of the plane, I'll be terrified. But after what Lucia and I went through, I have to do it. I need to stare fear in the face on my own terms and prove it can't beat me. So I'd appreciate it if you'd keep your thoughts to yourself and just let me get on with it.'

A silence hung between them, then Lucia put her hand on Charlotte's shoulder and gave it a squeeze. She'd even chosen the shoulder that hadn't been dislocated. They were all handling her too gently in their own way.

Will didn't say another word, and Charlotte was grateful for it. She'd got more fired up than she'd wanted to, and she didn't want it to escalate into a row.

Lucia put a stop to that. Breaking the silence after it had become unbearable for everybody, she changed the subject.

'So who's this Hollie Wickes person I heard you talking about?'

CHAPTER EIGHTEEN

Charlotte thought it best to leave the house with Will the next morning, since the conversation had been so heated between them the previous night. She'd been busy helping in the kitchen from early on, so relations hadn't had a chance to thaw over breakfast. When Will had come down from the family accommodation to remind her that he was making a later start, she seized the opportunity.

'Mind if I walk up the road with you towards your bus stop? I'll just finish a few things and I'll be with you.'

She'd half expected to be given the brush off, but it didn't come, so she rushed into the dining room to finish setting the tables for the evening meals, then made certain Piper had everything under control.

'Any news of Jenna?' she asked. One of the few benefits of their previous problems was that Piper and Jenna were now reconciled. And it had given Piper the impetus to break away from her previous profession; Charlotte had been glad she'd finally taken her up on the opportunity to work at the guest house.

'One month to go and she'll be out. I can't wait. We're

talking about getting a place together; me, Mum and Agnieszka. I'm very grateful to you, Charlotte. Seriously, I'd still be entertaining weird men in my bedsit if it wasn't for you. God, I could even be dead.'

Charlotte sometimes forgot some of the details of their previous drama. It had all happened so fast that night. Piper was right; she'd done much more than just providing her with a job and a safe route out of her escorting work. She didn't ask Piper if she still entertained clients. The money here wasn't anywhere near as good, but Olli had helped her secure some grants and benefits. Hopefully that horrible life was behind her now.

Things were better with Will on their short walk; he was chatty and cheerful. They had been forced to form an alliance when Lucia asked them about Hollie Wickes.

'I can't believe she heard us talking last night. She's a little minx, that one; she's had ears like an elephant since she was tiny.'

It emerged that Lucia had been listening outside the door, taking in the tense voices and the hushed conversation.

'I think I managed to warn her about Hollie Wickes without frightening the life out of her. I'd rather have chosen my time to tell her, instead of her forcing it out of us.'

They chatted freely, but it irked Charlotte that they had to go their separate ways so soon.

'Who are you seeing today?' Will asked, after giving her a kiss on the cheek before they went their separate ways.

'A lady called Yasmin Utworth. Her daughter has been missing for two decades.'

Will scrunched up his face.

'Poor woman. That will require some sensitivity. I hope it goes well. See you later.'

He walked off in the direction of his bus stop and Charlotte wove her way through the streets towards Bare.

Yasmin Utworth's house was easy enough to find, even though Charlotte didn't know Bare particularly well. Yasmin soon appeared, an immaculately made-up woman with a neat, tidy, and restrained style. She was immediately friendly, but the moment they spoke, Charlotte saw the veil of sadness hanging behind her eyes.

'Come in, come in,' Yasmin encouraged her. 'I'm so pleased the newspaper is doing this feature. The more information we can get out about Morgan, the better. I sometimes think the police have given up entirely, though they assure me they haven't.'

She guided Charlotte to the lounge and motioned for her to sit in an armchair nestled in a bay window, opposite the television.

'That was Morgan's chair,' Yasmin said. 'She loved to sit in it and read; the light is excellent from the window. She was a bookworm before she could read. Remember those little rag books? She always loved those.'

As Charlotte sank down into the armchair, she got a sense that she was sharing the space with a ghost. How many times had Yasmin watched her daughter sitting in this chair? How many times must she have stared at it whilst empty, willing her daughter to let them know she was safe or even to come home? For the first time, she felt the weight of the job she'd been given to do.

'If I ask any questions which you'd prefer not to answer, or if you want a break, just tell me,' she offered. It was as much for her own benefit as Yasmin's. Until this point, she'd covered trivial local stories or been able to hide behind

Nigel's experience and expertise. She felt alone and exposed, uncertain whether she was up to this job.

'Ask whatever you want,' Yasmin reassured her. 'I've heard every question a hundred times already, and I've thought it more than a thousand times. Can you imagine how long a night can be when you don't know if your only daughter is alive or dead?'

Charlotte recalled how they once thought they'd lost Lucia. It had driven her to desperate measures, willing to risk her life and do extraordinary things to ensure the safety of her daughter. She had no doubt Yasmin Utworth was capable of reaching the same extremes for her own daughter, despite her orderliness and self-control.

'Is Morgan's father still around?'

Charlotte knew the moment she said it that she'd asked a clumsy question. She admonished herself. A simple glance around at the photos in the room would have given clues. She did it now, belatedly, and got her answer before Yasmin even responded. Every photograph in the house was of Morgan. On the wall behind Yasmin was a faded rectangle where a large, framed photograph had once hung. It had been replaced by a small graduation photo of Morgan, too small for the spot. She looked like any other young woman: educated and intelligent, at the start of an incredible life of opportunity. There were two pictures from Thailand too; Charlotte guessed it was in a gap year.

'My husband and I are separated. The marriage couldn't take the strain. It was nothing to do with him or me, we just found it unbearable spending every hour of every day in this house, asking the same questions about Morgan. We couldn't share the sadness. It's easier to carry it alone and not talk about it every day. We still love each other, there's no hatred. We just can't be together until we know what happened to our daughter.'

Charlotte tried to hold the tears back, wiping her eyes in an attempt to make out it was an allergic reaction rather than an emotional one.

'Do you want to see her room?'

Charlotte hadn't expected the question. She'd assumed it would be a lounge-based interview, hoping to borrow a few photographs to scan for the newspaper article.

'Yes, yes, that would be... helpful.'

The Utworths lived in a compact detached bungalow, one of many in Bare. Morgan's room was at the end of the central corridor which gave access to every room in the house. On the door was a name sign, in the shape of a rainbow. Yasmin opened the door, walked in a little way, then froze and began to cry. Charlotte placed her hand on Yasmin's arm.

'I'm sorry, I haven't been in here for a week; I try to force myself not to come in. It's not that I don't care... it's just that I know I have to accept Morgan is dead now. After all this time, she has to be dead.'

Charlotte placed her arms around Yasmin and gave her a hug. She didn't know this woman, but it was the only thing she could offer. As she held her, she scanned the room. It could just as easily have been Lucia's bedroom. There was a combination of pink, girlie memorabilia preserved from her youth and a new backdrop of angsty, more sophisticated tastes including a bare-chested poster of a pop star, signalling the awakening of sexual curiosity.

A bookshelf displayed primary school reading favourites alongside academic texts from Dickens, George Eliot, Shakespeare and other classics. On the bed, a large, framed photograph from her graduation was awaiting placement on the walls. A sturdy trunk, pushed into the corner, showed that Morgan's life was in transition, back home from university but ready to move at a moment's notice.

Yasmin thanked Charlotte, pulled away, then dabbed at her tears. The control this woman exerted over the small things in her life – her hair, her make-up, her clothes – represented her personal fight against the unbridled mayhem she was obviously dealing with inside.

'I haven't moved anything,' Yasmin said, after composing herself once again. 'How could I? For weeks, months even, we just expected her to bound through the door and pick up her life. If I change her room, I'll have given up hope. And I'd rather be dead than give up the last tatters of hope I'm clinging onto.

Charlotte forgot any notion of covering up how much this was affecting her. She let a tear trickle down her cheek and made no attempt to wipe it away.

'What happened to Morgan? Do you have any idea why she disappeared?'

'The police maintain she either took her own life or felt the need to disappear. They discounted foul play. I know my daughter, and I can tell you she had nothing to run away from. She had everything to live for: a lovely boyfriend from university, and a plan to get jobs in Manchester so they could live together. She couldn't wait. There's no way she would have run away. Did you know that the police held an investigation into whether I killed my own daughter? Can you imagine that? My husband too, the number one suspect. All sorts of terrible questions about physical and sexual abuse. Can you believe you have to endure such things when your child goes missing? It's like a hell on earth.'

Charlotte was familiar enough with police questioning

to know the score. It was usually the father or an ex-lover, or else the mother or another relative, seldom a stranger.

'What do you believe happened to Morgan? You're her mother; what does your intuition tell you?'

'I think she's still alive. I know in my heart she's still out there. Either somebody took her, or she was in some trouble which she couldn't tell us about. Morgan would never end her own life, nor would she run away without good reason. It's the same with that poor family on the news, the Irwins. I remember reading about it then, thanking God it wasn't my child. Then look what happened to me soon afterwards. One thing I can tell you with absolute certainty, Charlotte, is that people don't just disappear. There's always an untold story, a secret or a terrible event. It's what happened with Morgan and I'll bet it's the same with the Irwins too. Someone is keeping a terrible secret and we won't find our children until we know what it is.'

CHAPTER NINETEEN

Charlotte was so overcome after speaking to Yasmin Utworth that she was grateful for some time alone before she prepared for the next appointment. She couldn't comprehend what it must be like to carry so much fear, doubt and hope for so long without going completely mad. Yasmin managed all the tiny parts of her life because the single most important part of it was wildly out of control and could not be brought to heel. She made sure she'd got the key elements of her newspaper report in place, then made her excuses.

Grief and fear permeated every corner of the house, overwhelming her. She hugged Yasmin hard before she left, in the only insignificant, useless act of solidarity she could offer. There were no words, assurances or platitudes. All Yasmin could do was sit and wait until they found Morgan's body, or until she got in touch to say she was still alive.

In the short time she had spent with Yasmin Utworth, Charlotte learnt about Missing People UK who supported the families, and was astounded to learn that thousands of people of all ages simply vanished every year. She discovered there was a UK Missing Persons Unit and found out how the local police got involved. And there was the heartbreaking part of the process too: when to declare Morgan dead, if at all. It was a sad and desperate world which Charlotte had no experience or knowledge of at all, yet all around her, families were living with the anguish of loved ones who'd disappeared without a trace.

Charlotte walked towards Lancaster, following the path of the bus route as she did so. She needed the fresh air and physical activity. She was never quite sure where Bare ended and Torrisholme began, but she was struck by an overriding urge to see Tiffany Irwin again. If she was fast, she reckoned she would have time to make an impromptu visit to Tiffany before Nigel got in touch for the pickup. She began to jog slowly. She was joining Daisy Bowker for their weekly parkrun on the promenade the next morning, so this would be a good warm up. For months she'd had to build up her strength again, first walking the course using crutches, then managing without them, and finally covering the 5km at a very slow jog. At that point, she'd agreed to the tandem charity parachute jump, a little hastily perhaps, but as a celebration of her recovered health. She had no intentions of becoming an athlete, but after the physical trials of the previous year, she was determined never to be out of shape again.

It wasn't long before she reached the square in Torrisholme, close to Tiffany's care home. She'd driven past the square on many occasions, and the return bus stop was nearby, so she spent a few moments sitting on a bench and admiring the planting in the flower beds, which made the small, grassed area a stunning oasis along a busy road.

She was feeling guilty about the way they'd dealt with Tiffany Irwin, blundering in there, only focusing on their news story. This was a woman who'd lived with the disappearance of four family members for over two decades. Three of those people were her children. No wonder her mental health had deteriorated. Charlotte reckoned nothing short of sedation would have helped her to endure the agony of uncertainty. Even suicide wasn't an option, as it might have been if the children had been found dead. However much Yasmin insisted she was resigned to a terrible outcome, it was evidently the last flickers of hope that kept her going.

Charlotte checked the time on her phone. She'd be cutting it fine, but she reckoned she could squeeze in a visit to Tiffany. If she encountered Quinton Madeley again, it would be game over. But she'd seen the look on Zabrina's face when they'd been sent packing from the care home; she didn't appear to agree with her husband's point of view.

The care home was closer to the square than she remembered, and she'd cooled down from her jogging by the time she arrived. She was intending to head for the main entrance, but it was a nice day and she could see some residents out in the gardens. The lawn cutting team were at work, so the gate beside the main building was open; she chanced her luck.

The gardens were beautifully kept, a refuge of tranquillity for the residents on a pleasant day like this. Some of the bedrooms had double doors which opened onto a patio area. There were plenty of staff about, no doubt in case of incidents or runaways, but none of them had spotted her. In her mind Charlotte retraced the steps they'd taken in their previous visit to Tiffany. The gate had brought her out on the right side for Tiffany's room, but she would have to figure out how far along the building she was.

Scanning the area, keeping an eye out for Quinton, she made her way along the patio, trying to recall the details of Tiffany's room. There were some nursing staff talking to residents in the gardens, but they still didn't appear to have noticed her. Ahead of her, two doors opened outward and a Carole King song could be heard at a low volume from inside. She walked over cautiously, making sure she hadn't been spotted. She could see an armchair had been moved in front of the window. Somebody was sitting in it, motionless, with her head slumped forward. It was Tiffany.

Charlotte checked nobody else was in the room, then stepped inside. The main door was also wide open and she could hear voices in the corridor, but it looked like Tiffany was alone. She seized her chance.

'Tiffany... Tiffany. It's Charlotte Grayson from the paper; do you remember me?'

She raised her head slowly, as if she was drunk.

Looking down at the bin beside Tiffany's chair, Charlotte saw a collection of three discarded containers, the size of the milk cartons found on the trays in hotel rooms. Drugs. Tiffany had been sedated.

'Tiffany, are you able to talk to me?'

Tiffany slowly raised her head, struggling to focus.

'Fabian? Is that you?'

'No, it's Charlotte. From the newspaper. I just wanted to apologise to you. It must have been terrible for you, losing your family. I'm sorry for the way we questioned you. We were insensitive, and I should have known better, being a mother. I'm sorry.'

'Fabian. Stop Fabian. He... he's coming today. They...

just keep giving me these damn drugs. Can't get my head clear.'

Tiffany's head slumped again. Charlotte looked around the room, trying to get a sense of this woman. By her bed was a photograph of the children, obviously taken years ago. There was Tiffany too, young, happy, and fresh-faced, but with no sign of a man in the picture. The children were beautiful, grinning, happy young things, none of them older than three or four years old.

Charlotte pulled out her phone and took a picture of it. She spotted the birthmark on what must have been Callie; there was no missing it. Lucia had had bright red marks on her skin as a baby, but they'd faded as she became a toddler. Stork bites, other mothers had called them. If the woman in the ICU had similar marks, surely there could be no doubt it was Callie?

Men's voices echoed along the corridor. Tiffany raised her head. Charlotte recognised one of them as Quinton Madeley. At least he'd given them plenty of warning.

'Fabian… that bastard Fabian. He keeps me here… you need to help me get out.'

For a moment, Charlotte considered making a dash for it and leading Tiffany out beyond the double doors and through the gate to the gardens. But she stopped short of it. They were too close; she'd get caught red-handed and be in all sorts of trouble for attempted abduction.

'I'll be back, Tiffany, I promise. I won't leave you here. I'll help you find your children.'

Charlotte darted outside just as the two men entered the room through the other door. She hovered beside the double doors, out of sight, scanning the gardens in case she'd been spotted. She could hear Tiffany slurring her words inside: 'Charlotte… don't go. I'm all alone here… Charlotte.'

Then there was an unfamiliar voice, presumably her brother Fabian.

'Hello Tiffy, guess who it is? I thought it was high time you and me had a little chat. Mr Madeley here tells me we need to ramp up your drugs regimen. Apparently it's for your own good.'

CHAPTER TWENTY

Charlotte wasn't sure whether to run away or confront Fabian Armstrong. The decision was made for her; either Fabian or Quinton closed the double doors leading to the gardens. She'd also been spotted by a member of staff who was trying to catch her attention. She did what anyone else would have done, bearing in mind she'd just entered what was supposed to be a secure building by slipping through an open gate: she made a run for it.

Keeping her head down, she began to half-run, half-walk, pretending not to have seen the staff member making his way over to her. She darted around the corner at the edge of the building, expecting to make good her escape through the open gate. But the guys doing the lawns must have packed up the van while Charlotte was talking to Tiffany and the gate was now locked. She gave it a shake, as if that would make any difference.

Charlotte felt like a trapped animal in a corner. Excuses flashed through her mind. What could she say? She'd got lost trying to find the reception area; that seemed to be the best bet. Then she spotted an escape route which was far more preferable to a confrontation, though it would mean sacrificing her dignity. She bent down and started to squeeze through a small hole in the thick hedge bordering the gate. As she pulled herself through, she heard a shout; someone had spotted her. Her body jerked upwards with the surprise of it and she hooked her top on a branch.

'Excuse me, madam, may I just check your visitor's pass?'

If she hadn't been so desperate to make her escape, Charlotte would have burst out laughing. All her pursuer would be able to see was her backside pointing at him from the dense foliage of the hedge. He'd have a job identifying her in a line-up parade. It was ridiculous, a grown woman caught on a branch, trying to pull herself to safety on the other side of a hedge. As she wrestled with the obstruction, the staff member grasped her ankle and began trying to pull her out of the undergrowth. She could picture how funny it looked, and she'd have been in hysterics if she hadn't also been trying to make good her escape. She couldn't afford to be identified, because she had every intention of seeing Tiffany Irwin again.

At last, she managed to disentangle herself from the branch, snatching her ankle away from the grasping hand on the opposite side of the hedge. She was away. Back on her feet, she took off at speed, the fastest she'd run for many months. As she made her way along the road, then down a narrow alleyway which ran along some houses, she congratulated herself on how good her recovery had been. She'd rather not have had to test her fitness by running away from a care home, but given the situation, she'd fared well.

Charlotte was desperate to speak to Nigel and update him after her eventful morning, so she was glad when the bus back to Morecambe arrived on time and delivered her close to the clock tower on the sea front where Nigel had texted to arrange a pickup. She made it with ten minutes to spare.

'We're heading out towards Overton,' he said as she opened the door to the company vehicle. 'Is that OK? By the way...'

'By the way, what?' she asked, waiting for him to complete the sentence.

'It'll wait,' Nigel replied. 'You look like you've been dragged through a hedge backwards. I asked you to interview Yasmin Utworth, not have a fight with her.'

Charlotte pulled down the sun visor as Nigel drove away and re-joined the traffic. He was right; she'd give a scarecrow a run for his money. She tidied herself as best she could, pulling a bramble stalk from her hair.

'Has a bird been trying to build a nest in there?'

'Something like that. Where are we going first?'

'Sunderland Point. How well do you know it?'

'Not well, but I'm more than happy to have a look around, especially now we know what happened to Kate Summers' brother. Poor Kate, I wish I'd known. We've been rampaging around chasing this story, when it's a very sensitive matter. I found my chat with Yasmin Utworth very moving.'

Charlotte and Nigel exchanged notes as they drove along the promenade, past the boarded-up Battery pub, and towards Heysham.

'Now don't start panicking, but we've had a complaint about you,' Nigel said as they passed the Heysham Village sign.

Charlotte felt her stomach knot.

'Remember those chaps you hurled abuse at the other day? They put two and two together when they saw the newspaper's name on our car outside and made a complaint to the boss. I hope I've managed to smooth it over for you, but you might want to pop your head around the door and show how contrite you are. I told him it wasn't without provocation, but you know what management are like. With so few people buying newspapers these days, he wants to hang onto every single reader we've got. Telling them to get lost tends to make them cancel their subscriptions. I told him you've got a brilliant feature coming in about Yasmin Utworth, so I'd make it a good one if I were you.'

Charlotte felt wretched. This was a fresh start for her. The newspaper didn't have to take her on; it was an unpaid mentorship to support her distance learning. Now she'd put that in jeopardy and she'd let Nigel down.

'I'm so sorry, Nigel. Thanks for covering for me—'

'Those guys had it coming,' he interjected. 'You don't owe me an apology. I'd just recommend smoothing it over with the boss. I love working with you; you've got all the makings of a superb journalist. You just need to handle this, but don't worry, he won't want you to self-flagellate or anything. Just pop in, apologise, and it'll go away.'

Charlotte sat in silence for a few moments as they approached the turn to Middleton Sands.

'Are you OK?' Nigel asked.

'Of course,' Charlotte said. 'But I'm more worried about this complaint than I am about what happened at the old holiday camp.'

'Would you just check out the tide times before we lose a signal?' Nigel asked, pulling the car over into the drive of the former pub Charlotte and Will had drunk in when they were students. 'I should have found them before I left the office,' he scolded himself.

Charlotte looked up at what was once The Old Roof

Tree Inn; they'd spent some wonderful nights there, Will and her, their young love blossoming during a summer vacation job, in spite of what had happened at the camp.

She pulled out her mobile phone and opened up a web browser. It didn't take long to find the tide information, and she handed it over to Nigel.

'This is how people get into trouble in this neck of the woods,' he said after jotting down the high tide timing. 'Plenty of time,' he continued, 'but we'd better not get too distracted.'

Nigel pulled back onto the narrow road once again and Charlotte opened up a local history web page which outlined the basics of Sunderland Point. She was pleased she had the page up on her phone, because her phone signal died soon afterwards.

'You know, I haven't been out here before. I was getting confused with somewhere else. It looks fascinating though, and very remote. Who lives this far out when you can get cut off by the tides?'

'Well, some people prefer it. There are days when I'd like to get isolated by high waters, especially when there are bills to be paid.'

Charlotte carried on reading as they entered the coastal area, which was now flat and slightly marshy.

'This article is interesting. People seem to get caught along the causeway on a regular basis, despite the warnings all over the place. It's no wonder it was so easy for Brett Allan to disappear here. This place looks like it could be deadly.'

CHAPTER TWENTY-ONE

Charlotte had never seen a place like Sunderland Point before. It was a small village of around thirty houses at a rough count, at the end of a tidal causeway, almost at an equal distance from both Lancaster and Morecambe. The causeway itself seemed long and exposed, winding through mud flats, with frequent puddles giving the impression you'd had to part the waves to drive there.

Isolated wasn't an extreme enough word according to the article Charlotte was reading, which explained the causeway and car park where they'd stopped were both flooded at high tide. There were frequent signs warning that the area would be under several feet of high water when the tide came in. With the tide out, it was a splendid location to visit, part marshland and part beach, surrounded by flourishing farmland and views to die for.

'I love this place. How come Will and I never made it out here?'

Nigel pulled up the handbrake and switched off the engine.

'I've lived here much longer than you have, and even I

have to admit I don't get out here as often as I'd like. It's not on the way to anywhere, but it's one hell of a place. But you'd need to know your tide timetables if you lived in one of the houses.'

They got out of the car and Charlotte scrolled down the web page on her phone screen.

'The article says it used to be a big port at one time. That seems incredible. According to the official web page, only London, Bristol and Liverpool did more trade than this place and Lancaster. What a changed world we live in. Maybe the traders stopped coming here because the mobile phone signals are so bad.'

'It certainly has an incredible history. But it's the more recent events I'm interested in. I want to understand what happened to Brett Allan if I can. Now we know the person in Lancaster ICU—'

'It's Callie, isn't it?'

'Yes, but the police have to remain circumspect about these things. There's no way it can't be Callie, bearing in mind the birthmark. But until she's awake to confirm it, they have to allow for a margin of error. I don't envy the police. Cases are much easier when adults are involved.'

Charlotte and Nigel walked along the narrow road running alongside the houses. Several boats were sitting on the mud flats, mainly small fishing and leisure vessels, many of them so old that it was hard to believe anyone would risk going out to sea in them. There were signs the tide was moving in rather than out. Water was beginning to pool in the curving mud channels and the smell of salt water permeated the car through the ventilation system.

'We should be safe for an hour,' Charlotte suggested. 'I'm no expert at tide times, but the time on the chart is when the water reaches its peak, isn't it? So it starts to rise beforehand; you can't use the high tide as your departure time, can you?'

'Sounds about right,' Nigel answered, watching a man working on his boat. 'Let's keep moving and take as many photos as we can. I'd like to head over to Sambo's Grave too, before we go—'

'What did you just call it?' Charlotte asked, stopping in the street. 'You can't say stuff like that nowadays, can you?'

'It's fine, honestly, it's a place of historical significance, a short walk from here. You can't visit Sunderland Point without knowing about Sambo's Grave. Sambo was the servant of a ship's captain who died in one of the cottages here. It's very much a story of its time, and most of the details were handed down from person to person. He's supposed to have died from a broken heart because he thought his master had left him. I'm not so sure about that part of the story, but his grave is just over there.'

Nigel pointed vaguely to an area in the distance, but Charlotte was none the wiser.

'Presumably he couldn't have been buried on consecrated ground. People paint stones and leave them on the grave as a sign of respect. I'm sure modern history would have a different tale to tell about his life, but it doesn't stop us paying our respects to him.'

'What an incredible story. It's so hard to imagine any of it taking place here, it's so quiet.'

'Speaking of which, I'm going to have a word with that fisherman over there. He looks like he's packing up.'

Nigel rushed ahead, his feet crunching through the stones. Charlotte clicked the Sambo's Grave link on the website, but it just went to an error page now the signal was gone.

'You'd be in a panic if you got stuck out here and your phone didn't work,' she called over to Nigel.

'Don't get stuck out here, that's the trick!' Nigel shouted back.

He was deep in conversation with the fisherman when she caught up with him. Her canvas slip-ons were already caked in salty mud, and her jeans were wet at the bottom and pebble-dashed with mucky brown splashes. They were talking about Brett.

'My father was the one who found the car. He's dead now; I was just a teenager then. I remember all the police were here, combing the area, and divers, too. As a young boy, it was exciting, and the police officers were patient with me, telling me what they were doing. Now I fish here, I can tell you, I understand how serious it was. These waters are deadly. You respect them like they're your worst enemy; if you don't, they'll take your life.'

The fisherman spoke in a strong, local accent which added gravitas to the tale he was telling, as if passing along folklore that would survive over generations.

'Speaking of which, I'm packing up here now, and you shouldn't dawdle either. The tide's coming in.'

'You've lived here all your life, haven't you?' Nigel asked.

'Yes, in my house over there,' he replied, pointing at it.

'Could that young lad have been swept out to sea? Is it possible to commit suicide here if you were desperate to end your life? He can't have been much older than you at the time.'

The fisherman thought a moment, looking over to the causeway.

'I haven't spoken about this for a long while. But I'll tell it again, seeing as you seem to be the interested type. I never thought he killed himself, but nobody would listen to a boy like me. They all thought he'd driven out to the causeway in the dark, left his doors open and let the water take him. That's what they said in the newspapers. It's possible, but the body fights back when it's under water. The lungs want to breathe; it would take a force of will to let yourself be taken by the sea. It's more likely he got trapped and couldn't raise the alarm, so he drowned.'

Charlotte recalled the previous year's incident at the stone jetty when she'd rescued Olli. She knew what it was like to fight with an incoming tide. She agreed with this man: the body fought for air. A good job too, or she and Olli would be dead.

'So what do you think happened?' Charlotte asked, so engrossed that she took the lead from Nigel.

'I think he wanted everybody to believe he was dead, but I'm not convinced his body is out at sea.'

'Really? That's quite a stretch after what the police investigation concluded,' she replied.

'Well, as I said, they ignored me when I was a kid. It put me off the police. There's an old pillbox from World War Two around here. My friend and I used it as a den. The day after this young lad was supposed to have drowned, we found a bag with clothes and documents in there. I told the police the next day, but when they checked it out, there was nothing there. They told me I was lying. My father gave me the strap, the only time it ever happened. But I know what I saw, even if nobody believed me. I'm telling you, that boy didn't die out there; it's just what he wanted everybody to think.'

CHAPTER TWENTY-TWO

'You'd best be getting back to Morecambe,' the fisherman said, apparently unaware of the bombshell he'd just dropped.

Charlotte looked out at the water. She knew it was deceptive; she'd been living along the sea front long enough to know how fast the water can come in when you're not giving it your full attention.

'Can I take your contact information, just in case?' Nigel asked.

'I'm Jed. We don't have a phone at the house; can't say I've ever needed one. Just come and ask for me. Everybody knows me around here.'

'Seriously? You don't even have a mobile phone?' Charlotte asked, shaken from her distraction by the news that there was still someone alive in the 21st century without immediate connectivity.

Jed put his hand in his overalls and pulled out a battered, old-fashioned mobile phone.

'I have this, but nobody ever calls me on it. There's no signal at home or out here, but I can get one out on the boat.

I keep it with me in case I get in trouble out on the water, but it's no use to me anywhere else. As soon as I spot Morecambe on the shoreline, my signal appears.'

Nigel took the details of Jed's mobile phone and the name of his house before the fisherman said his goodbyes.

They watched as he walked up the narrow road in front of the row of houses which made up part of the village. His feet crunched in the pebbles, then there was silence as he stepped onto the road. They followed him up the street and he went into what seemed to be a cluster of properties.

'I can't imagine living in the same house all your life,' Charlotte said after a while. The lapping of the water beyond Jed's boat was almost hypnotising. She loved the way the smell of salt made her breathing so clear. Will had once told her it was the increased ozone in the air by the sea, but she preferred the less scientific explanation.

'It's a blessing for humanity that there are still people on this planet like Jed, but it wouldn't suit me.

I always want to know what's over the horizon; there's so much to explore.'

'How do you feel about checking out the pillbox and Sambo's Grave?' Nigel asked. 'The water still isn't coming up to the causeway, which I reckon is our trigger to get out of here.'

Charlotte stared at the narrow road winding across the mud flats. It was a wonder it didn't get washed away by the sea. It looked like they still had plenty of time.

'Let's do it, but I'd rather not cut things too close, not after what Olli and I experienced. I've had enough scares with the sea to last a lifetime.'

Nigel led the way, evidently sure about where he was going, judging by his sense of purpose. Charlotte followed, admiring the earthy character of the boats that were tied up along the shoreline and wondering what stories they could tell.

It wasn't a long walk to the bunker, but it made sense to take photographs while they were out there.

'You know I'm risking falling out with Kate Summers about this,' Charlotte said as they made their way over to the other side of the peninsula. 'Imagine if her brother was still alive? We have to tell her about Jed.'

'What if she already knew he could be alive?' Nigel replied.

'What? Do you think that's possible?'

'She was a young police officer then, so she must have had access to all the documentation. At the very least, the investigating officers would have been more honest with her than they would a regular family. It's possible she might know already.'

Charlotte carried on walking, trying to work it out.

'But you'd never stop searching if you thought that. If you were convinced someone was still alive, you'd be like Yasmin Utworth; you'd do whatever was in your power to find them. Wouldn't you?'

'What if you'd fallen out with the person?' Nigel suggested. 'What if they were trouble? Would you keep searching then?'

Charlotte mulled it over for a while. They'd reached the end of the lane and could see the sea again.

'Yes. I'd keep searching. However angry you are with somebody, you'd have to know. It's her brother, Nigel. She's a DCI with resources at her disposal and the clout to use them. Jed might be mistaken. The police wouldn't ignore a lead like that. If Kate's brother was still out there, she'd know.'

'This is the pillbox,' Nigel said, stopping at a slope

which bordered the edge of a field. In the distance, not too far away, was a farmhouse. They climbed up the banking and over the wire fencing.

The pillbox was constructed from red brick and concrete. If you didn't know what you were searching for, you'd assume it was some small construction used by the farmer, a shelter for sheep perhaps, or even a store for hay.

'Are we OK to take a look?'

Nigel was already on his way, not being one for seeking permission.

'How's the charge on your phone?' he asked. 'It's dark, and I'd like to take a proper look.'

Charlotte switched on the torch app and shone it through the large, letterbox-style opening at the front of the pillbox. She had to kneel to complete the manoeuvre, as so little of the construction was above ground.

'I'm surprised they even have one of these out here. Who would attack a place as remote as this? You'd be just as safe in your house with the lights switched off.'

'Who knows?' Nigel replied, peering inside. 'They can't even pick your bins up from inside your garden these days, but in World War Two they could provide guard posts like this for communities in the middle of nowhere.'

Charlotte had lost interest in the history lesson, because she was trying to fathom out whether Brett Allan might have abandoned his car on the causeway and hidden in this place overnight. Inside the pillbox, the dirt floor was covered with various items of rubbish. There was something at the far end; she strained to move the torch so she could see it properly.

'Let's go inside,' she said, but Nigel was already ahead of her.

There wasn't much to see. She wondered how much it

might have changed in the twenty years since Brett Allan might have sheltered there. The object she'd been trying to identify through the opening of the pillbox turned out to be an old coat.

'Somebody has been here,' she said, not wanting to pick it up. It was damp and musty, as if it had been on the floor for some time.

'I bet generations of kids have used this place as a den. You'll get teenagers in here, photographers, history buffs and maybe the odd tramp. It doesn't compare to your guest house though, does it?'

'But if you were on the run, or desperate to get away, it would do for the night.'

'We'd best get a move on,' Nigel suggested, checking his watch. 'We can make a quick dash over to Sambo's Grave, then we'd best be on our way. I'm not sure Jed would welcome two house guests overnight. He looks like a man who's more used to his own company.'

Once they'd taken plenty of photographs with their phones, Nigel led the way to the grave, a short walk in the opposite direction. Charlotte watched the water moving closer to the track, and began to get anxious about the timings.

'Do you mind if we pass on Sambo's Grave this time? We don't need it for the news story, do we? I'm just getting slightly nervous about the water. I'm sorry—'

Nigel stopped her.

'You should never apologise, not after what you went through. You're right. We should get back.'

Nigel would never know how thankful she was that he didn't make a big deal of it. She felt her heartbeat settling and within ten minutes, they were back in the car with the engine running.

'You were right to hurry us along. The water's lapping at the causeway,' Nigel said, pointing ahead. 'We should have taken Jed's hint, but I didn't want to miss out on the pillbox, not after what he told us.'

The causeway was still clear to drive across, but puddles were forming where the water had washed up high, then receded.

'Ready to go?' Nigel asked.

Charlotte nodded, and he pulled off. When they'd driven across the causeway earlier, it had been flanked by mudflats on either side. Now the water was rising, she realised just how dangerous it was along the narrow and vulnerable track. It was perfectly possible for Brett Allan to have been carried out to sea from there, surely?

'Oh shit—'

'What was that?'

A massive splash of water shot up at the side of the car on Charlotte's side, making her jump in the passenger seat. Nigel had hit a puddle, and it had sent a sudden rush of water across the front of the car and up the side of Charlotte's door. The car spluttered a little, and Nigel revved to keep it going, then it slowed and kangarooed to a bumpy stop.

'Damn it!' Nigel cursed. 'I've soaked the engine. We're stuck.'

CHAPTER TWENTY-THREE

Charlotte's heart started racing.

'What do you mean, we're stuck? What's happened?'

'That puddle must have splashed the engine. It probably soaked the spark plugs. I'll need to look inside.'

Nigel rolled up the sleeves on his shirt, then searched for the bonnet catch near his right leg.

'We've got to get out of here. We can't just wait. Look, the water is coming in.'

Charlotte could sense her anxiety raging, like waves crashing on the rocks.

'Whoa, steady Charlotte, we're OK for a little while. The tide doesn't come in that fast, and it's only a five-minute walk back to the village. Give me a moment to see if I can get the engine started. I won't risk anything, but see if you can sound the alarm via your mobile phone. Try mine if you can't get service out here.'

Charlotte opened the door a little and peered at the narrow road outside. The water had just sloshed up over the asphalt and was receding, ready for the next wave.

'We're almost surrounded by water, Nigel. The road

will disappear in a moment. If we don't move, we'll get cut off—'

As she said the words, her thoughts returned to when she rescued Olli at the stone jetty. The sea had been so powerful, waves coming at them in successive punches, never allowing time to recover, punishing them until they submitted to their force. She still carried the memory of her son gulping in the water and coughing it out. The alert had gone out to the RNLI, and they'd recovered them in the nick of time.

But today, nobody knew they were out here at the causeway. And look what had happened to Brett Allan. Charlotte's mind raced, imagining the water reaching the floor of the car, gradually spilling over into the foot well. She wondered when you would know your time was up. Was it when the causeway was covered, and you could no longer navigate your way to the village on foot?

She slammed the door shut and tried to control her breathing, sensing Nigel turning towards her.

'Charlotte, I need you to focus. I realise this is scary for you; I haven't forgotten what happened. But we're fine for time. I'll give it ten minutes at the most, then we'll return to the village and wait until the tide goes out again. It will give me several hours to figure out how to explain it to the boss.'

Charlotte watched as he stepped out onto the road and lifted the bonnet. He moved round and tapped on her window, and she wound it down a little. All around them was the gentle lapping of water, teasing them, hinting at what was coming.

'Move over into the driver's seat and turn over the engine when I give you a shout. Don't overdo it, or you'll exhaust the battery. The water sloshed up inside the engine, it's soaked under the bonnet. It's my fault, I should have driven steadier. We'll give it a couple of turns, then I promise we will head back to the village.'

Charlotte nodded, not daring to speak for fear of breaking down. She closed the window, then shuffled across into the driver's seat. She checked her phone. Of course there was no signal; why would there be when she needed it?

'OK, give it one turn,' Nigel shouted from outside.

Charlotte tried the engine. It didn't even budge, stubbornly giving an insolent electronic click.

'OK, wait please...'

Nigel disappeared behind the raised bonnet. The sound coming through the dashboard suggested he was fiddling with something. Years ago her dad had taught her how to check the oil, the tyre pressures and the bulbs in her first car. She couldn't remember the last time she'd lifted a car bonnet; she wasn't even certain how to top up the water for the wipers in their current vehicle. It was about time she found out, instead of expecting Will to do all the checking.

'One more time!' Nigel called.

Charlotte swallowed, then placed her hand on the key and turned it. The engine made some half-hearted attempt, then gave up. It reminded her of waking up Lucia at the weekends. The will was in there somewhere; it was just staying well hidden.

'Again?' Nigel suggested.

Charlotte was already on to it. Again, the engine turned a little, then gave up.

'OK, just as I promised, we're out of here,' Nigel said. 'Let's see how hospitable Jed is feeling.'

'Damn it!' Charlotte cursed, punching the steering wheel. She looked in the rear-view mirror at the path they'd have to cover to reach the settlement before they were cut

TRUST ME ONCE   143

off by the sea. The road was still clear when the waves receded, but it would be terrifying walking along it, even with the level still so low. She couldn't face it.

She decided to give it one more try. If the car was a write-off anyway, it made more sense to keep going until it was completely dead. She moved the key. The engine turned over, then nothing. Again. It turned, then made a protesting groan and stopped. One more time. She thought it might die, but as she was about to release the key, it fired. It wasn't much, but there were signs of life.

'Rev it up!' Nigel shouted.

Charlotte moved her foot to the accelerator and floored it. For a moment she thought she'd killed it. But just like a dying ember fanned into a flame, the engine suddenly found its strength and surged back into life. She revved it several times, refusing to let it die again. Nigel dropped the bonnet and got back into the car on the passenger side.

'Nice one, Charlotte. I thought we'd lost it. I know you're not insured to drive the company vehicle yet, but I figure the boss would rather you kept the engine running for the length of the causeway, in preference to writing off the vehicle.'

Charlotte kept the revs up and gently moved off as soon as Nigel's door was closed.

'Nice and steady, don't do what I did and we'll be fine.'

Charlotte took it cautiously, wanting to scream the entire length of the causeway. She was furious and frustrated that they'd cut it so fine. Jed had warned them, yet they hadn't believed how fast the tide could rise. It was a mistake as old as time; respect the tides.

At the end of the causeway, safely beyond the warning signs which punctuated the route, Charlotte brought the car to a stop, keeping the engine running. Her body was shaking uncontrollably.

'Thank you, Charlotte. I was having visions of having to explain why I'd wrecked the company car,' Nigel said.

His voice barely reached her, as she struggled to breathe, the images of Olli's head about to sink beneath the waves mingling with the realisation of what might have happened if she hadn't started the car. She was rooted to the seat, paralysed with fear at losing her mind to the power of the sea.

'I can't believe we just did that. Sometimes I wonder if I'll ever learn my lesson.'

CHAPTER TWENTY-FOUR

Walking along the promenade the following day, Charlotte's escapade already seemed like a distant memory. It had felt so real, but after a fish and chip supper at Will's suggestion and a deep sleep, Charlotte was ready to go again. Her weekly run always cleared her head, and she enjoyed meeting Daisy Bowker. She'd always liked Daisy, and despite the history between them, she looked forward to running with her.

'You're walking normally now,' Daisy observed as they reached the start line. 'What a change; you've done so well.'

'Thanks. I can genuinely say I feel strong now. It took some time, but I trust my leg again. Which is just as well, since it has to see me through our tandem parachute jump tomorrow.'

Daisy seemed relaxed and happy. She'd relocated to Morecambe now, and it seemed to be working out well for her. She leaned in towards Charlotte.

'Now that you've put last year behind you, I wanted your permission to erect a headstone for Bruce. I finally managed to bury his remains in Newcastle, in a council cemetery. I wanted to make sure you were OK with it first.'

Charlotte thought back to how Bruce Craven had almost derailed their lives, over a year ago now. Daisy was entitled to her peace, however much she still hated the man. Even Daisy was a victim of Bruce.

'Honestly, I'm fine with it; you should go ahead. It helps me to put the past behind me too. He was your half-brother, even if he did terrible things.'

Charlotte thought back to the causeway incident the day before. She hadn't felt such fear since Bruce Craven had come back into their lives. She'd been here before, long ago, when she had her breakdown in the classroom, and she'd promised to tell Will if she ever felt like things were spiralling out of control again.

If there was one good thing to have come out of those terrible events, it was that they had reset the terms of their marriage, agreeing never to hide things from each other again. Yet here she was, lying to Daisy, telling her every-thing was fine. She'd said the same to Will, to George and Isla and everybody else who cared about her. The incident at the causeway had revealed the truth. Day by day, things were fine, but any hint of crisis drew her back to that dark place again.

The run started sooner than she expected, pulling her out of her thoughts. One moment she was chatting with Daisy, and the next the horn had sounded, sending hundreds of runners along the promenade.

'I want to keep up with you this week, Daisy,' Charlotte said, setting off at a steady jog. Something still wasn't right with her leg, but it wasn't painful and she was gradually becoming accustomed to the sensation.

'OK, I promise I'll keep up my regular pace, but let me

know if you're getting any twinges. I want you in tip-top condition for tomorrow's jump. How are you feeling about it?'

'I'll be honest, I've barely had time to think about it. After we did our run-through last week and the doctor gave me the final sign-off, I've been so busy at the newspaper.'

The joggers around them were thinning out already. The athletes were away in the distance, the fun-runners and walkers were behind them, and they were part of the middle runners, committed enough to jog all the way, but not serious enough to be wearing full Lycra.

Daisy gave a nervous laugh. 'Probably just as well. I'm looking forward to it, although I know I'll be terrified when it comes to jumping out of the aircraft. It's a good job we're strapped to a professional; I could never do it solo.'

Charlotte felt the same. Their tandem jumpers would take the strain, and all they had to do was to turn up, not chicken out when they were up in the air, and bank the sponsorship money for Abi's good cause, Alzheimer's research in people born with Down's Syndrome. What better way to put the past behind them than to help an old friend?

'Hey, how's it going?'

Charlotte glanced to her side, not recognising the voice. She was used to other runners encouraging them along the way and shouting greetings. It was one of the reasons she'd stuck to the weekly parkrun after struggling through her first event when she met Daisy. This woman appeared to be coming for a chat. She was young, brunette, fresh-faced and with no notable features other than a pierced eyebrow with a spiked barbell. Charlotte only noticed because Lucia had been talking about getting one and, having done the mum thing warning her about infection risks and potential negative stereotyping at job interviews, she was trying to get her head around it and come to terms with the prospect.

'Hi,' Daisy and Charlotte replied, almost at the same time.

'How far along the promenade do we run? I'm a first timer, I need to pace myself or else I'm likely to flake out by the time I reach the Eric Morecambe statue.'

Between them, Charlotte and Daisy explained the course, continuing to run at a steady pace. Charlotte couldn't resist asking some questions while she had a captive audience.

'Do you ever get any infection problems with your piercing? Does it hurt when they do it? It must take out a large section of skin.'

She winced as the woman gave her a summary of the installation and maintenance of eyebrow piercings. It made Charlotte grimace just thinking about it; she had never even plucked up the courage to get her ears pierced. However, there was nothing in the woman's description to justify her discouraging Lucia any further. Besides, although her daughter was behaving much better of late, Charlotte knew that whatever she said, it would be unlikely to deter her from getting it done one day. Plenty of places in Morecambe would be willing to oblige.

The chatty woman bade them farewell and ran ahead. Daisy and Charlotte allowed their conversation to subside, concentrating on keeping their breathing steady and completing the full five kilometres at a reasonable pace.

They finished the run within half an hour, and having confirmed plans with Daisy for the following day, Charlotte excused herself from their customary weekly coffee at the Beach Café and headed back home. She was in time to catch the entire family at the breakfast table after she'd showered. Willow was there too, having stayed with Olli overnight.

'I feel like I ought to get an oil painting of this moment,' she smiled as she walked into the kitchen, her hair still wet. 'I don't often get to see my entire family in one place, at one time. How are you, Willow? It's nice to see you again.'

They exchanged pleasantries, caught up with their snippets of news and, as fast as they came, the youngsters left again. It was Saturday, and they had plans for the day.

'Don't forget we have an early start for the parachute jump tomorrow!' she called after Olli and Willow, who were first to head out.

'Wouldn't miss it, Mum. Willow and I have a wager. I bet five quid we'll hear you screaming the moment you leap from the aircraft.'

'Cheeky devil,' Charlotte laughed, 'I'll be screaming as soon as I step on board the aircraft, so you've lost that bet already.'

'Oh, good,' Will said, looking up from his phone. 'That's what I bet. I'll accept cash and cheques, everybody.'

Lucia got up and hugged her mum from behind as she took a bite of toast.

'I'm proud of you, Mum. I notice these cowards weren't lining up to help Abi. It's left to us girls to do the hard work.'

There was more gentle teasing, and before long Will and Charlotte were left alone at the table.

'It will be quiet when they're gone,' Charlotte said. 'I miss them already. It's as if they're halfway out the door.'

'Like the Lion King, the circle of life,' Will replied, looking up from his phone.

'It's not that woman again, is it?' Charlotte asked, suddenly concerned.

'No. Sorry; I got caught up reading about the person

they found on the promenade. The nationals have got it now. It's a big story. I bet you're having a great time.'

'I love it,' Charlotte replied. 'No other job has ever captured my attention like this.'

'Do you think we ought to consider selling this place?'

It was the last thing she expected him to say.

'Are you serious?'

'I'm not having a go at you, but when we moved to Morecambe, this place was just what we needed, a fresh start. But I have a decent job at the university now, and you've stumbled on journalism by accident; the guest house is like a third leg.'

Charlotte considered what he'd said as she finished her toast and tea.

'I know Rex Emery would be interested if we did sell. It's looking like he'll land a significant compensation package. He emailed me the other day to say the reconciliation with his family is showing signs of progress. I didn't clear out the basement because it still contains things dating back to his time here. I'd like to offer it to Rex first if we do sell. I'm not against selling it in principle, but it's paying my salary at the moment, albeit a small one. I'd need to land a job in journalism first, and with the way things are going for newspapers at the moment, that will be tricky.'

'There's no rush,' Will replied. 'It's just something I've been thinking about recently. This business with the student at uni has unsettled me. I thought a move might be good—'

'You mean, leave Morecambe?'

'Potentially,' Will ventured.

'No, not Morecambe. I love it here, Will. All the problems we had when we first moved here are all over now. I'll consider the guest house, but Morecambe is not on the table.'

They sat in silence for a while until they were interrupted by a phone vibrating.

'Is that you?' Charlotte asked.

'No, mine is on silent. It must be yours.'

Charlotte never took her phone on her weekly run for fear of damaging it. As she scanned the kitchen, she saw she'd left it on top of the fridge while pouring a glass of orange juice before she'd left the house earlier.

'What are you up to today?' she asked Will, getting up to check who was trying to contact her.

'I'm seeing Vern. He's finally sold the video repair shop and moved into sheltered accommodation. I said I'd pop round and help him settle in.'

So many of the people surrounding them had been involved in the events surrounding Bruce Craven. They seemed to be picking up waifs and strays, people washed up on the beach by the waves they'd created in their past. Vern was a good guy. He'd helped Will, and without him, that terrible night might have turned out a lot worse.

'Send him my love,' Charlotte said. 'Did I mention I'm in Blackpool today?'

Will looked up, a caution on the tip of his tongue.

'Jeez, Charlotte, go steady—'

The look she gave him had the desired effect, preventing him from finishing his sentence.

As far as Charlotte was concerned, he'd made his thoughts clear on the subject of her physical recovery, but it was her body. She felt strong enough, and it was important to her sanity that things seemed back to normal. She would keep quiet about the ticking-off she had coming from the newspaper owner. It might be wise to keep their powder dry for now and halt any potential sale of the guest house. She didn't spend much time there, and she could draw a small salary from it. Anyhow, the frequent flow of guests also kept the roof over their own heads.

Charlotte checked the time on her phone. She'd need to get a move on; Nigel was picking her up shortly. Activating her phone screen, she clicked on the text notification.

She immediately tuned out of whatever Will was saying to her and gave the text her full attention. It was from DCI Summers, brief and straight to the point.

We need to talk. 5pm at The King's Arms today. Please be there and keep it between you and me please, Kate.

CHAPTER TWENTY-FIVE

Charlotte kept the text to herself and replied to Kate Summers immediately.

I'll be there at 5pm.

She agonised over whether to tell Will or Nigel, then decided against it. She'd once relied on DCI Summers to keep her mouth shut and she'd been as good as her word. Because of her discretion, and in spite of every alarm bell that must have been sounding in her head at a professional level, Kate Summers' silence had saved her family. She owed her one, that much was certain.

Charlotte kissed Will, gathered a few things together and headed downstairs. George and Isla were managing the kitchens and George was checking out a guest as she reached the first floor.

'Everything all right George? We don't get as much time to talk as we used to.'

'Hello, Charlotte. Yes, everything is good, thanks. The doctor keeps giving me the all-clear, so fingers crossed we won't be running into any more health scares. You're looking fit and healthy now; it's good to see you leaping down those stairs again. I used to think you'd be reliant on a stick.'

Through the open entrance, Charlotte saw Nigel pull up outside.

'I thought the same thing,' she replied. 'We must get together for a meal some time – my treat.'

As she passed the kitchen, Charlotte popped her head around the door and brought Isla into the conversation.

'How about it, Isla? A staff night out – it's about time, isn't it?'

'Count me in.' Isla turned from her plate scraping and smiled. 'Just let me know when you have a date.'

Charlotte wished them both well and joined Nigel in the car.

'So, Blackpool today. How long is it, 50 minutes or so? Mind if I doze? I may have peaked too early going for a run.'

They chatted a little until they joined the M6, then Charlotte closed her eyes and Nigel left her to it. He reached over and put the radio on.

Charlotte didn't want to sleep; she was just grateful for some thinking time. Kate's text had come as a shock. From being cold and dismissive, here she was calling a meeting. An urgent one, too. What could she want now? It had come at an opportune time. Charlotte was dying to ask her about her brother. Her involvement in the Irwin case seemed to run deep, and she was keen to know why.

A news bulletin jingle sounded on the radio, attracting her attention. The authoritative voice of the young newsreader spoke over the distinctive jingle.

'The news headlines at 11 o'clock. I'm Naga Balakrishnan. In our top story this morning, doctors have revealed that the woman discovered on Morecambe's promenade this week is fully conscious and speaking to police—'

'At last!' Nigel said. 'We'll find out what the hell happened to her and how she got there.'

So that was why Kate Summers was ready to talk. It couldn't be a coincidence.

'Although she has been tentatively identified by police following DNA tests, they're still keen to question her, as she has been presumed dead for over two decades. The medical team treating her at Lancaster Infirmary say she is still in a serious condition following complications around Type 1 diabetes—'

'The police won't have anything new for us until Monday, but this is welcome news. We can trickle it out through the website, but we still need to make a big splash when the paper comes out on Wednesday. How's your backgrounder on Yasmin Utworth coming along?'

'Let's just say it's in the formative stages, shall we?'

The news feature was one of many things swirling inside Charlotte's head. She'd save it until after the thrill of the parachute jump. It would be a nice, restful activity.

Nigel left the radio on low in the background and allowed Charlotte to play dead until they reached the outskirts of Blackpool. She was always excited to see the brown signs for the Pleasure Beach and the zoo, even though she had no special connection with the resort. The sight of Blackpool Tower in the distance reminded her of fun days by the beach as a child, even though her local beach had been Cleethorpes. There was something universal about the British seaside, and she loved it.

Blackpool was so much busier than Morecambe, like her home resort on steroids: more noise, more visitors, more ice creams and the flashing lights of arcades and gaudy signage everywhere. The smell of burgers and fish and chips found its way through the car's ventilation system, giving her hunger pangs. The trams ran confidently up and down the sea front, their bells warning pedestrians of their presence. It was all an affront to the eyes and ears, but Charlotte loved it.

They parked in the centre and Nigel checked the time.

'We can grab a bite to eat before we head for the Winter Gardens, since we made good time on the journey down. What do you fancy? Whatever it is, it'll come with chips.'

Charlotte scanned the area. There was so much to take in, with activity all around them.

'Oh look, a fortune teller! Do you mind, Nigel? I've always wanted to give it a go. It won't take long. I'll go for the cheap and cheerful option.'

'Be my guest,' Nigel replied, 'I'll get an ice cream and sit over there to eat it.'

Charlotte was a little wary of entering the small kiosk. The name *Mystic Zelina* was emblazoned across the top, with photographs of the fortune teller alongside celebrities from days gone by: Ken Dodd, Bob Monkhouse, Bernie Winters and many other faces which brought back fond memories of Saturday evening TV in the UK.

'Come in, my darling,' came a voice from inside the kiosk.

Charlotte stepped inside. An elderly lady, perhaps 70 or thereabouts, was sitting on an ornate, velvet-covered throne-like chair, mobile phone in hand. She wore large, round glasses and a glittery shawl, every bit the fortune teller.

'What is it you want, my darling? A full reading?'

Charlotte was nervous about paying too much, so she felt in her jeans pocket and pulled out a ten-pound note. She'd have to pay for lunch with a bank card. Mystic Zelina took one look at the note and motioned Charlotte to the cushioned stool at her side. As Charlotte sat down, the fortune teller pulled the sparkling curtain across the doorway, presumably to give their conversation a modicum of privacy should any further customers take one of the three stools which made up the waiting area. Mystic Zelina had used the tiny space well.

The first bit of palm-related activity was to remove the ten-pound note from Charlotte's hand. Once it was safely tucked into the pouch strapped around the woman's waist, Charlotte was encouraged to stretch out her hand. Mystic Zelina made a big deal of studying the lines and gazing earnestly into her face.

Charlotte felt a sense of anticipation, on the one hand treating the reading as a bit of fun and nonsense, and on the other being primed for any nuggets which might be revealed.

'These are very troubled lines,' Mystic Zelina began.

'That's not the half of it,' Charlotte thought to herself, keeping her face serious and straight.

'You've experienced intense pain very recently. Your body was wounded but is healing well. Your family are particularly important to you. You have a family, yes?'

Charlotte nodded. She thought of her friend, the clairvoyant Steven Terry, and had a sudden urge to see him again. The man's abilities were uncanny. She wondered if he was due to play any of the theatres in the region. It would be good to catch up with him.

'Trouble follows you; did you know that? It's always on your shoulder, never far away. You've embraced it too. Have you changed a job or profession recently?'

'Yes, I'm training to be a newspaper reporter.'

Mystic Zelina barely reacted to the answer, as if she knew already.

'You have a happy relationship; you're married, yes? And your family are healthy, they love you but are worried about you—'

She furrowed her brow. Charlotte had seen that look before, from Steven Terry. She wondered if these people went to a training school to learn all the dramatic tricks and phrases to use.

'Take care, my darling. There's a senior person, somebody in a place of importance. They're in your life now, or they'll be entering shortly. This person is dark, I can only see them in the shadows...'

Charlotte was beginning to wish she'd spent her money on an ice cream, like Nigel. Yet something inside her wanted to hear this. With everything that was going on, she craved guidance, if only for reassurance that it would work out all right.

'My darling, take care. Please, take great care. You'll be making a leap of faith and it will test you. It will test you to your core. And in taking the risk, you will place everything and everybody you love in danger once again.'

CHAPTER TWENTY-SIX

Charlotte had saved a chip drenched in both salt and vinegar until last. She eyed it on the polystyrene tray, chased it around with a small plastic fork until she succeeded in spearing it, then downed it in one delicious mouthful.

'You can't beat seaside fish and chips eaten within a stone's throw of the sea,' she said. 'There's something about the tang of salt in the air, the electronic beeping of the arcades in the distance and watching out for aggressive attacks by seagulls that makes it taste ten times as good as usual.'

Nigel had finished his lunch, having opted for a chicken pie, chips and gravy. They wanted to attend Fabian Armstrong's public event on a full stomach.

'That was delicious. If only it wasn't destroying what's left of my heart. I wish they'd hurry up and invent something that will allow us to stuff ourselves with food like this without adversely affecting our health. You can't beat traditional British grub.'

They'd eaten mostly in silence, content to watch the

seaside activity all around them. Charlotte had made light of her reading from Mystic Zelina, certain the fortune teller to the stars of Blackpool had simply got lucky. Charlotte wished she'd been watching more closely. The woman must have thrashed around until she'd caught a look on her subject's face, then embellished her words. She knew in her head it was complete and utter nonsense, even if her heart was telling her it seemed uncannily close to the truth.

If only she could speak to Steven Terry. There was a man she trusted. Since they'd first met in Morecambe, she'd been aware of him popping up all over the region with his stage show. She'd spotted adverts in The Bay View Weekly for local appearances at Lancaster's Grand Theatre and Kendal's Brewery Arts Centre. She'd heard him mentioned in the local radio events guides too: Preston, Blackpool, Fleetwood, Liverpool, Chester, Wigan... they were all his venues, and he appeared to be constantly on the road in the North West of England. It wasn't quite the Rolling Stones in terms of tour dates, but she assumed it allowed him to make his living.

She wished she'd paid more attention, then she might stand a chance of chatting with him. She was also worried about getting in too deep with the Irwin story; it wouldn't be the first time it had happened.

'We'd best head towards the Winter Gardens; we didn't drive all this way just for a lovely day at the seaside.'

Nigel stood up from his perch on a low wall and stretched out his hand to take Charlotte's litter. He placed it in a nearby bin and they made their way through the back streets, weaving towards the Winter Gardens.

'So what's this all about today?' Charlotte asked. 'Is it a show?'

'It's more like a positive press opportunity,' said Nigel,

'There's a cheque being handed over, a short performance by a local dance school, a gathering of some local officials – you know the sort of thing. If kids are around, we should manage a question or two without Fabian Armstrong swearing at us. It'll be good to see him and get the measure of what he's like.'

'I heard him when I was at Briar Bank the other day, during my undignified escape—'

She broke off, realising Nigel had stopped dead.

'What?' Charlotte asked.

'I'm sorry, I forgot to tell you. To be honest, I wanted to pick my moment, after the fright you had out at Sunderland Point. But I must tell you now you've reminded me, or you'll be livid with me when you go back into the office on Monday.'

Charlotte braced herself. Mystic Zelina might have given her a heads up.

'Quinton Madeley put in a complaint to the newspaper about you being on the premises without permission—'

'Oh.'

Charlotte saw her journalistic career fluttering away like a bird chased away from newly laid grass seed.

'I'm sorry, Charlotte. Two complaints in one week takes some doing. You have my full support and I told the boss as much. But Quinton Madeley knows how to rattle an editor. He used terms like press intrusion, client confidentiality and safeguarding. To be honest, you don't stand a chance against a barrage like that. Madeley has the moral high ground, and he knows it.'

'I didn't think anybody had got close enough to identify me. Will they ask me to leave?'

Charlotte didn't want to hear the answer.

'They must have identified you from the soles of your

trainers while the nurse was trying to pull you out of that bush.'

Charlotte gave a rueful smile at the thought of her close escape. Journalism was certainly providing more potential for funny situations than teaching ever had.

'Seriously though, it's fine; it's a hazard of the job. If we end up landing a great news story out of this, you'll be the hero of the hour. Good journalism takes persistent investigation. Ruffling feathers goes with the territory. Just apologise to the boss on Monday morning and promise it'll never happen again. And make your interview with Yasmin Utworth a good one; show him what you're capable of. You'll be fine.'

The white woodwork and glass roof of the Winter Gardens appeared ahead as they turned a corner, the sun glinting off it and dazzling them both. The stunning building dated back to the late 1800s and had all of the architectural magnificence and splendour of the period. It had been pulling in the seaside crowds for well over a century, and looked like it was as popular now as it had ever been.

'It's better concealed than I expected it to be. I always imagine it as a building surrounded by lots of space, and it always takes me by surprise, hidden away like this.'

Charlotte couldn't focus on the complaints now; they'd have to wait until after the parachute jump. The weekend was becoming too packed; a Sunday morning lying in bed would be nice, after the past couple of days.

They walked through the Horseshoe and Pavilion, both which resembled a bustling street market, until they found the main entertainments area.

'Take your pick, Empress Ballroom or Spanish Hall?' Nigel said, scanning the area for clues.

'Empress Ballroom,' Charlotte answered, without hesitation.

'How do you know that?'

'You're standing in front of the sign, look.'

In front of them a notice outlined the event they were searching for.

Community Celebration Event. Cheque presentation and performance by pupils from Rose Wallace School of Dance. Sponsored by Valdron Subramani. In aid of Fylde Together Community Initiative.

'They need to sort out their branding, Valdron Subramani sounds like the person who ought to be running the dance school—'

Nigel had barely had time to laugh at his own joke before a man carrying a notepad, pen, microphone and recording device walked up to them, as if he was expecting them.

'Hi, you must be Nigel and... Charlotte, is it?'

'I recognise that voice,'

Nigel said, turning to check whether he was right.

'Charlotte, this is Russ McGill, the radio reporter who replaced the chap I was telling you about, Pete Bailey. I'll bet he's missing the sunshine of Blackpool on a day like this. Is it Spain he's based in now?'

'Yes. I heard he and Alex Kennedy are getting a name for themselves as consultants in high profile crimes. Sounds like he fell on his feet, but knowing a TV personality like Alex won't hurt, will it?'

Russ motioned them towards the entrance.

'Better get a move on,' he suggested. 'They're starting with the cheque presentation and press questions before the tedious bit with the dance school. I can't imagine Fabian Armstrong will want to hang around. That's cruelty beyond measure; I wouldn't wish it on my worst enemy.'

Their timing was perfect. The event was only using the lower tier of the Empress Ballroom. The audience was made up of doting parents, coerced siblings and elected officials whose penance for their public spiritedness was to spend their weekends attending events like this, the equivalent of Strictly Come Dancing on a primary school budget.

'Here's Fabian now,' Russ prompted.

It was an informal affair, with a suited Fabian Armstrong flanked by a man wearing an ornate chain that would put the Bee Gees of the 1980s to shame, and a woman who looked as scared as if somebody had told her this was a Pagan festival and she was the sacrifice.

A couple of newspaper reporters were taking photographs from every conceivable angle and three radio reporters hung around with microphones at the ready, awaiting the time when they could ask questions.

'We're all here about the new land purchase Valdron Subramani just completed. Nobody gives a toss about the cheque,' Russ whispered.

As Fabian began to speak, a man stepped out from a side door and stood just behind him, his hands clasped lightly across his front as if he were a doorman of some sort. His hair was razored as short as it could be to still make it worthwhile calling it hair, and his ears were misshapen, like they'd been kicked a hundred times in the past. Although he wasn't tall and didn't seem muscular, he exuded power and confidence.

'Who the hell is that guy?' Charlotte said as quietly as she could. 'I take it he won't be dancing for us this afternoon?'

Russ turned to reply to her.

'That, Charlotte, is Vinnie Mace, Fabian Armstrong's hard man, a former paratrooper who saw some serious action in Helmand Province in Afghanistan. He's the one who'll throw you out of here if you ask a question which Fabian Armstrong doesn't like. Whatever you do, don't get on the wrong side of him. Journalists are a piece of cake to deal with compared with Afghan rebels.'

CHAPTER TWENTY-SEVEN

It began badly and only got worse. Fabian Armstrong and his small group of officials were intent on keeping to the subject; Vinnie Mace said as much before the press questions began. His voice was deep and authoritative. How much testosterone did it take to fuel a body that compact with wall-to-wall, 24/7 machismo? She was no biology expert, but she wouldn't have been surprised if a pipe had been creeping out of his trouser leg into a vat of the stuff concealed nearby.

Charlotte had little experience of men like this, other than her youthful and misplaced dalliance as a young student, a lesson quickly learnt. She preferred men who knew one end of a child from another and who would need to be rushed to Accident & Emergency if they banged their thumb with a hammer, if they ever used a hammer in the first place. Will was just that kind of man. Nigel was the same too, the more cerebral type. She found it easier to relate to them.

So when Russ McGill told her about Helmand Province, Afghan rebels and military action, it sounded like an alien world. She didn't know anybody who'd been in the military, except for the occasional guest, most of whom had retired long ago. This man looked sharp, alert and menacing. She'd been on the receiving end of menace before, but it had been from thugs and louts. Vinnie Mace was clearly intelligent, more than just hired muscle.

'I'd like to remind members of the press that today's event is to celebrate Mr Armstrong's substantial contribution to the Fylde Together Community Initiative, and we will restrict questions to that topic. I would also politely ask you to respect the many families and young children here today, and to temper your questions accordingly.'

Vinnie stepped back and Fabian extended his arms, encouraging the assembled interviewees into a huddle to make it easier for the microphones to pick up what was being said. It was an unusual arrangement; even in her short time working with The Bay View Weekly, Charlotte already knew enough about these events to understand that they were usually held at arm's length, with the press sitting in rows on uncomfortable chairs and the assembled dignitaries or experts safely tucked away behind a table. This was more informal than she was used to, and she soon realised why.

Fabian Armstrong read out a bland statement, which might as well have contained the words *blah, blah, blah.* She paraphrased it in her head: *Massive company with financial muscle buys off small, desperately under-funded community with paltry donation after securing land for fracking which will lead to significant monetary gain for said company.* Talk about the emperor's new clothes; the emperor himself was within arm's reach, completely naked and still swearing blind that he was fully clothed.

A young woman reporter, from an independent radio

station she'd never heard of before, barely waited for Fabian
to finish before calling out a question.

'How true is it that this is just another example of
Valdron Subramani bribing a local community with blood
money?'

Charlotte could sense the collective tension that
descended upon the group.

'Rookie error,' Nigel whispered. 'She's gone in too hard,
too soon. If she's not careful, they'll cancel the entire press
briefing and we'll all walk away empty-handed.'

Fabian Armstrong seemed unruffled and carried on
speaking.

'Thank you, Melissa from Fylde Coast Community
FM. As Mr Mace said, we won't be taking questions on that
topic today. Next question, please.'

As Fabian turned away from Melissa, leading everyone's attention to the opposite side of the gathered group,
Vinnie Mace moved in swiftly and grasped the reporter's
arm.

'We made the terms of the interview very clear. I'd like
you to leave now,' he said to her, loud enough for Charlotte
to make out his words, but not detracting from Fabian
Armstrong.

Melissa looked ready to make a scene, evidently
unhappy about Vince's grip on her arm.

'Mr Armstrong is a sponsor of your radio station. I'm
sure you wouldn't want to put that at risk.'

It was almost inaudible, but Charlotte had moved in
close enough to catch it. Melissa's mouth formed in the
shape of an expletive and Vinnie led her towards an exit. It
was superbly executed, an efficient and stealthy eviction
delivered without a scene.

The question-and-answer session was in full flow now,

the more seasoned journalists understanding the tactic of softening up your opponent first before catching them out with a body blow.

'What impact will this make in the community?'

'How will the money help villagers?'

'How proud is Valdron Subramani to be supporting communities on the Fylde Coast?'

This was journalistic lift music, worthy of a column inch at most. Charlotte could almost sense the smell of blood in the air. These journalists had to lock and load the trivial story first, then they'd chance their luck with the controversial topic. After the assembled reporters had re-phrased the same question for what seemed like the hundredth time, the switch came.

'Valdron Subramani bought the land at a fraction of its market value. Is this just another case of buying silence in Fylde communities?'

'It's been shown that fracking causes earth tremors. What reassurances can you offer residents whose properties are in spitting distance of the drilling?'

'Valdron Subramani has a track record of making initial payments to local communities, then not following through on subsequent payments and project delivery. Is this corporate fraud, Mr Armstrong?'

'Why is your sister Tiffany languishing in a care home for people with psychiatric problems, after experiencing a traumatic event over twenty years ago? Don't you owe her the same consideration as you claim to be giving these communities?'

The last question came from Charlotte; she could barely believe she'd dared to say it. This time, there was an audible intake of breath. Fabian Armstrong had already given Vinnie Mace the nod the moment the first off-topic question had been asked. But the entire group was silent now and the seasoned hacks and reporters turned to see who'd dared to ask such an audacious personal question.

'Talk about killing a conversation,' Nigel muttered to her. 'Great question. But look at Vinnie Mace's face. You just booted Fabian Armstrong's guard dog in the balls. Excuse my language.'

The gathering swiftly descended into chaos, but Fabian Armstrong called it to order. The audience were gathered in the seats in front of them as he signalled to the lady who Charlotte assumed was Rose Wallace that the main show should start. She stepped up onto the stage to warm up the audience.

'I'd make yourselves scarce if I were you,' Russ McGill advised. 'Vinnie Mace looks as if he wants to make a house call.'

He nodded towards Vinnie, who was getting instructions from Fabian, both of them staring at Charlotte.

'You're right. Come on Charlotte, best not cause a scene and make it three complaints to the newspaper. They don't know us in this part of the world. You definitely hit a nerve with your question. Let's save this fight for another day.'

As Nigel led the way towards a side door, Charlotte glanced behind her. Vinnie Mace had spotted them, finished his conversation with Fabian and was in pursuit. She was grateful to Russ McGill, who stepped in front of Vinnie to ask some inane question and create a brief delay.

'What colour are they painting the new community hall?' she heard him asking. It was searching journalism at its worst, but it gave them a temporary head start. Nigel was right, she couldn't risk an altercation and a third complaint, or she'd have the most short-lived career in the history of journalism.

'This isn't the exit,' Charlotte said. 'We should have gone the other way.'

'Too late now. Let's go this way, along this corridor.'

Charlotte could hear applause and the start of music from The Nutcracker. The door slammed behind her and assured footsteps swept across the vinyl floor covering. An intense sense of panic welled up inside her, as if she were a child caught trespassing in somebody's garden, fearful of the consequences. She quickened her step, catching up with Nigel.

'He's just behind us,' she said, scanning the room for a side entrance. 'If we can make it to the arcade area, we can blend in with the crowd.'

'Why are there no doors in this bloody place?' Nigel cussed, checking they still had a lead on their pursuer.

At last they came to some steps, at the top of which were two doors.

'Which one?' Charlotte asked.

'Any one,' Nigel answered, as Vinnie's steps drew closer. He pulled open the door, and they stepped backstage. They could hear the sound of children's soft ballet shoes working their way across the stage ahead of them and Vinnie's terminator-like clunking behind them.

'I never got into scrapes like this before I met you,' Nigel said. Charlotte couldn't decide whether he was annoyed or not. He'd only come to report on the opening of the guest house when they first met; now here they were, fleeing from trouble once again.

'There's no way out; we'll have to cross the stage,' Charlotte said.

'Uh-oh, you're right. Can't we go behind the back curtain?'

The handle on the door they'd just walked through moved downward.

'Let's hope Mr Mace doesn't follow us,' Nigel began. 'Are you ready? What's your ballet like?'

The door opened and for a second, Vinnie could easily have grabbed Charlotte to stop her getting away. Instead, she ran across the stage like a whippet out of a trap. The lighting dazzled her at first, but across the front of the performance area, a line of ballerinas aged from toddler to teenager were in the midst of a carefully orchestrated ballet routine. For a split second, Charlotte considered jumping with a flourish behind the young dancers to disguise her presence. She thought better of it and opted to apologise instead.

'Do you mind?' came Rose Wallace's affronted voice from stage left.

'Sorry... sorry, everybody. Really sorry, kids...'

The stage seemed endless as Charlotte and Nigel crossed in the full beam of the stage lights, the clumping of Nigel's footwear contrasting with the gentle sounds of the ballet shoes, drowning them out over the accompaniment of Tchaikovsky. Charlotte wanted the ground to swallow her up, but as they finally reached the far side of the stage, she glanced behind them to see if they were still being pursued. They weren't. All she could see was Rose Wallace encouraging the children to continue their routine and Vinnie Mace on the far side of the stage, out of sight, looking like he'd just located a military target in Afghanistan.

CHAPTER TWENTY-EIGHT

Charlotte was shaken by their narrow escape. As Nigel drove them back up the M6, her trembling continued until they passed Preston. She didn't know whether to laugh or cry. Their getaway couldn't have been more farcical, but as a law-abiding citizen, Charlotte didn't do these things without guilt. She always worried about being in trouble with some authority as yet unknown, but Nigel was taking it in his stride, just another day for a man focused on getting his news story.

'Their reaction to your question tells us everything we need to know. I wish I'd had a camera on Fabian Armstrong's face. Even the other reporters were shocked. I'm sensing a wider news story here. For a man who claims to be bringing so much affluence to the area, there doesn't seem to be much love for him. Are you all right?'

Nigel was concentrating on the road, only occasionally glancing at her.

'You look like you're about to throw up all over the car.'

'I'm fine,' she answered, 'a little shaken, that's all. It's just that I could have done without this the day before my parachute jump; I should be getting into the zone right now. Did you see Vinnie Mace's expression? He obviously wants to shut down the news story.'

Nigel was silent for a while as he switched lanes to avoid the road to Preston.

'I always feel like we're as good as home when we pass the A6 turn-off,' she continued. 'It's where industrial Lancashire ends and rural Lancashire begins for me. I love this area.'

Nigel nodded, still focusing on the traffic until they were clear of the junction.

'I agree,' he said at last, 'this is where the driving gets easy too. You seldom hit a jam after this part of the journey. You're right, Vinnie Mace didn't look like he wanted to have a quiet word; he was about to lean on us.'

'Will they complain to the paper?'

'Probably not; dealing with protesters and annoying people from the press goes with the territory. Both Fabian Armstrong and Vinnie Mace know the game. The question about Tiffany rattled them; my guess is nobody has asked about her for a long time. Reporters in Fylde will care more about the fracking, whereas you and I want the full story on Callie. I'm beginning to believe it's all linked.'

Charlotte would have preferred Nigel to drop her off at home, but she had to go to her five o'clock meeting with Kate Summers before she could put on her pyjamas and sit in front of the TV for the evening. She was worn out, having expended so much nervous energy worrying about Vinnie Mace. Nigel hadn't helped either. His comment before he dropped her off at the pub worried her.

'A man with Fabian Armstrong's resources will soon figure out who we are and which newspaper we represent. If Fabian knew somebody had been in his sister's room last time he visited – and I'd be surprised if Quinton Madeley didn't tell him – he'll soon put two and two together. Just stay sharp, Charlotte. These guys might play dirty.'

Nigel wished her well for the next day's parachute jump and drove off along the promenade. The King's Arms was within walking distance, which pleased Charlotte. They served food too, so since she was a quarter of an hour early, she ordered a meal. The pub wasn't yet packed, so she could find a seat with a view out of the window. From there she could see the Eric Morecambe statue. It always made her smile, bringing back happy memories of Christmas Day watching the TV specials with her mum and dad. There was never a time of day without somebody taking a photograph of a family member or friend posing alongside the statue in the distinctive stance. She was humming *Bring Me Sunshine* in her head when the food arrived. She fell on it like she hadn't eaten for days, despite the fish and chips she'd enjoyed earlier.

'Charlotte, thanks for meeting here.'

It was DCI Summers. Charlotte was enjoying her food so much that she'd forgotten about her. She'd never seen Kate look so drawn and weary.

'Hi Kate, can I get you a drink? Hot or cold?'

'I ordered a coffee at the bar when I came in, but thanks anyway.'

'You don't mind me and my glass of cider, do you? I was parched.'

'No, carry on. I won't keep you long.'

Charlotte cleaned her plate and DCI Summers' coffee arrived.

'So what's this all about?' Charlotte asked, not ready to part with the lingering taste of a well-cooked steak in her mouth.

'Some time ago, you asked me to trust you, Charlotte—'

'Yes, you did, and I'll forever be grateful.'

'It went against all my instincts. You made me break every protocol in the police handbook.'

Charlotte frowned at her, wondering what she was driving at.

'Yes, I understood. You put your neck on the line for me. If I hadn't made it out alive, you'd have got egg all over your face. Sorry about the reference, but that food was delicious.'

DCI Summers face barely moved. She had something to say and was intent on saying it.

'I need you to trust me, Charlotte, as I trusted you. You'll hear things about me that will make you wonder who I am and what I did. It won't happen yet, but it will soon; the storm clouds are gathering. I'm asking you for blind trust, Charlotte. This won't be easy, but I'm going to need a friend.'

Charlotte searched Kate's face and saw she was deadly serious.

'Of course. Can you tell me what it's about?'

'No, not really. But I'll bet you know all about Brett already?'

Charlotte felt her face colouring. Why did it feel like she'd just intruded on Kate Summers' private life? She nodded.

'It's why I'm trusting you, Charlotte. The reason you escaped that horrible man, Edward Callow, is because you're built of stern stuff. You don't realise it, but you have incredible strength, Charlotte. And you won't let things lie. I need your strength and your trust right now.'

Charlotte didn't agree with the DCI's assessment of her personal qualities, but saying no to her friend's request never occurred to her.

'I'll help, of course I will, Kate. What do you want me to do?'

'I've sent my husband and kids over to France for a month, to see his mum and dad. I want them out of the way. If they're difficult to track, I can concentrate on taking care of myself. I don't want the press hounding them either.'

DCI Summers seemed to be reassuring herself, as if running through the elements of a plan.

'I'm sorry I brushed you off the other day,' she continued. 'I just couldn't deal with it until I'd had time to pull my thoughts together—'

'Kate, it's fine, I've got your back with this, just tell me what you need me to do.'

Kate Summers took a long drink of her coffee and held her gaze, as if sizing her up, still not sure Charlotte was the woman for the job.

'I can't tell you the details, Charlotte; it would put you in danger. But you'll know when the time has come. When the shit hits the fan, I may need to do something that will feel out of character to you. They'll be saying all sorts of things about me. It will test you, but I need you to trust me and follow your instincts. Can you do that?'

Charlotte was becoming frustrated by the cryptic nature of her words, but Kate Summers was as serious as she'd ever seen her.

'Yes, I can. But can't you just get your colleagues to watch your back?'

'I can't trust the police. There's a rogue copper somewhere, but I can't figure out who it is. It's why I've come to you. When you figure it out, you'll work out who to go to. But in the meantime, we can't trust my colleagues. Oh... and one other warning: you must not put yourself or your family in danger.

'What?' Charlotte asked, her concern growing for Kate's safety.

'If you meet a man called Fabian Armstrong, do not get involved. Just walk away. If you cross his path, you're in too deep. If it comes to it, you'll just have to leave me to it and hope I can dig myself out of my own hole. Whatever you do, promise me you won't get involved with that man.'

CHAPTER TWENTY-NINE

Charlotte felt all the better for an early night and a good sleep. It was only after coming round in bed that she realised she'd forgotten to ask Kate about Brett and the pill-box. She cursed her forgetfulness and resolved to raise it the next time they spoke.

Breakfasts started later on Sundays and the guest house wasn't full, so Will volunteered to help in the kitchen, seeing as it was Agnieszka's shift that day. Charlotte could see the two of them had hit it off, after getting to know each other better on the bus to and from the university. She was thankful, because it detracted from the amount of time she spent running around with Nigel. She'd asked herself several times whether there was anything remotely romantic between them. There wasn't, on either side. They rubbed along well, but for both of them, it was a professional friendship; she'd never have taken up the training offer otherwise.

Similarly, Will had been at pains to reassure her that his relationship with Agnieszka was entirely platonic. After all, Charlotte had been the one to offer her a job and help her get her paperwork straight; the rest had just followed as a natural consequence. Will was still confiding in her, recently expressing amazement that he should end up such good friends with a former escort.

'I'm not in the slightest bit surprised,' Charlotte had said, proud of her husband. 'I always loved the way you didn't judge. It's why you helped Abi all those years ago. You haven't changed; you're still the nice guy I married.'

It was a busy breakfast table, with Olli and Willow staying over, Lucia excited for the parachute jump and Charlotte contemplating what DCI Summers had said to her, while still looking forward to the day. They'd been building up to this for some time. For Charlotte it was much more than a fund-raising jump; it finally drew a line under her physical recovery and all their troubles since moving to Morecambe.

This was the point from which she could move forward and embrace whatever the future held. With the business turning a reasonable profit, the kids settled and happy in their new home, Will content in his work and an exciting career ahead of her, she took a moment to appreciate the scene. She loved it when the kids were chatting and laughing and they all had to squeeze around the table.

Will joined them, the breakfast shift finished for another day.

'How's Agnieszka?' Charlotte asked. 'She seems to be gaining in confidence all the time. What a great find.'

'She won't be another Isla,' Will reminded her. 'Agnieszka has ambitions; she'll only be around as long as it takes her to complete her degree.'

Charlotte took a sip of tea.

'I've been mulling over what you were saying about the guest house,' she said to Will, as the kids shared some video that Lucia had spotted on Tik-Tok. 'I think you're right. But I'm not ready to move on straight away. How about I finish my course first and see where I am with work then? I'll sound out Rex Emery; I'm certain he'd be interested if he gets his legal settlement. We could avoid estate agents and save on fees.'

'Hey, Mum, you've raised over one thousand pounds now! That's amazing.'

Lucia passed her phone across so she could see the latest total on her web page. Charlotte had completely forgotten to check.

'I gave you a last-minute boost yesterday afternoon,' Will confessed. 'I promised my seminar group we'd pack up for an early Friday finish if they sponsored you, so it pushed you over the 1k mark.'

Charlotte squeezed Will's hand.

'Thank you,' she said, leaning over to kiss him on the cheek. Then she checked the time.

'OK, young people, you all take far too long in the shower, so let's get moving. We have to be at the airfield for 11 o'clock. I got an email from Abi this morning saying it's still on; the weather and jump conditions are perfect.'

Lucia, Olli and Willow made themselves scarce, leaving Charlotte and Will finishing what was left of the toast.

'Do you think Olli and Willow will stick it out?' Charlotte asked.

'Well, we were the same age when we met. There's no reason why it shouldn't work. She's a good kid, I like her. She fits in well. Lucia likes her too; she's a good influence.'

Will was right. She was grateful for Willow's positive attitude around Lucia. The time when they'd been scared they were losing their daughter seemed a lifetime away.

'You didn't run into anybody on your travels yesterday, did you?'

Charlotte was caught out by the about turn in Will's tone.

'No, why?'

She had no intention yet of telling him about her meeting with Kate Summers. He knew they'd met for a drink, but she'd implied it was just a chat about a newspaper-related matter. She'd convinced herself it wasn't really a lie. As for what had happened with Vinnie Mace and Fabian Armstrong, it was best if Will didn't know about that yet. She'd tell him after the parachute jump.

'Yes, on your morning run. Did anything happen?'

'No, it was a good run. I had a nice chat with Daisy; we discussed today's jump. I didn't hang around at the café; I came straight back home. Why?'

'Nothing in the pub when you met DCI Summers?'

'Will, what are you getting at? Stop beating around the bush.'

'When I went to see Vern yesterday, guess who I bumped into? Or rather, guess who bumped into me?'

'I don't know. Just tell me.'

Charlotte was already on edge; she could do without the cliff-hanger.

'Did anybody speak to you yesterday in town?'

Charlotte's tea splashed on the table as she slammed the cup down.

'Just spit it out, will you? I spoke to Daisy, Kate Summers, the barman and some lady who chatted to us for about two minutes on the run. That was it, Will. Everything else was in Blackpool. Now, what's your point?'

'Can you describe the woman who chatted to you on the run?'

Charlotte and her family had spent a lot of time in police questioning since they'd moved to the resort, and Will was giving her a sense of déjà vu.

'She was just a woman. People chat all the time on parkruns. They say hello as they're passing by, then move along. She was young and friendly. I couldn't pick her out in a line-up parade; that's how much impact she made on me.'

Will seemed ready to drop the topic.

'Oh no, wait, she had one distinguishing feature, now I think about it. Actually, you've just reminded me: I need to talk to Lucia about her piercing. This woman had a distinctive barbell piercing above her eye, the type you look at and wonder how much it hurt. But there's nothing else to report.'

Will's face changed the moment she mentioned the piercing. He paused for a moment before he spoke.

'I thought so. That was Hollie Wickes, the student from the university who's stalking me.'

CHAPTER THIRTY

Charlotte couldn't spare any head space on Hollie Wickes that morning. Once the youngsters were showered and showing signs of being ready at roughly the time she'd told them, Will and she prepared themselves and the group of five was assembled in the hall ten minutes early. She'd deployed a trick she used when the kids were at primary school, when time to them was an elastic thing which stretched to their personal agenda. The target time was always fifteen minutes before the real deadline.

With so much nervous excitement in the air, she couldn't spend her mental preparation time chivvying the younger members of their small group or worrying about Holly Wickes. Besides, Will had painted a picture of her as a Glenn Close figure, with a saucepan in one hand and a pet rabbit in the other. She'd seemed perfectly pleasant in the few minutes they were chatting, and there was no reason on earth why Hollie Wickes shouldn't have travelled to Morecambe to take part in a public running event.

She was glad to be in the jump preparation area by 11 o'clock, alongside Daisy and Lucia, putting on the required

red and yellow overalls. Abi was with them, recording the preparations with her smartphone. Her doctor had advised her not to make the tandem leap. That had been disappointing, since the entire venture had been her idea. She was the reason for Charlotte's determination to go ahead with it, terrified or not.

It was only a small airfield, dedicated to light aircraft, made up of a small cluster of buildings in a remote location, like a relic of a former Second World War RAF airfield. The buildings were functional and solid, mostly made of aged concrete. Charlotte was even convinced she'd spotted another pillbox at the far side of the landing strip. It set her thinking about Brett Allan, but she forced herself to stop. This day was about the jump, and she was with family and good friends.

They'd received a basic briefing before the event, though Charlotte had watched a couple of videos and the airfield's website told her everything she needed to know. They'd had to complete the inevitable declaration forms and doctor's certificates and she'd been amused to spot that a dislocatable shoulder and limb weaknesses were permissible on tandem jumps. She'd spotted the aircraft sitting on the runway as they'd parked up and got out of the car. It had a propeller, a novelty as far as she was concerned. From a distance it looked a snug affair, definitely not suitable for a transatlantic flight.

Three men were helping them to get ready, each one middle-aged, generally with over-long greying hair, beard growth and the kind of confident and plucky attitude you want from the person you'll be strapped to when you leap out of a plane. Charlotte imagined surfer-dudes became like this when they got older, adrenaline junkies with more cash to spend on expensive, terrifying pursuits. They all wore shaded visors, whereas the novices were given simple transparent goggles.

The harnesses were strapped on and the final safety briefing was delivered. Then the three women grimaced and nervously smiled at each other as the tandem jumping process was explained to them. Charlotte caught the rough idea of it. This was a skydive apparently, not a parachute jump, because there was an element of freefall. The parachutes were incredibly safe and the backup was an automatic activation device and a spare chute. All they had to do was go with the flow.

That was it; they were ready to go. They left the preparation area and headed out to the runway. The gathered supporters were waiting for them outside, along with Louise, Abi's daughter with Down's Syndrome, who they were all there to support. Photos were taken, good wishes passed on and two of the jump supervisors called time on the jollity and invited them to go over to the plane. Before long, the engine was fired, the propeller started spinning and everybody was in their seats except for the last instructor. One of his colleagues sent a radio message telling him to *move his butt*. A couple of minutes later, he came running out to the plane, shades down, helmet on, appearing calm and collected, as if he had all the time in the world.

The plane had a large, rectangular door at its side, where they would leap out. They clipped themselves to their jump partners, then took one of the seats, which were wide enough to accommodate two people harnessed together. The man who'd just got on the plane made straight for Charlotte and they secured themselves together.

Charlotte had never flown in such a small aircraft, but as they set off along the runway – which wasn't much more than a straight stretch of road with no traffic – she felt perfectly secure, happy to gaze at the Cumbrian country-side below them. She was surprised how quickly they rose above the clouds. Before long, one of the instructors had prompted Daisy to stand up. There was some activity at the front of the plane as her jump partner checked the harnesses and before she knew it, Daisy was giving the thumbs up sign and they were heading for the open door.

Suddenly the reality hit her. Everything up to this point had been familiar, as if it was just a regular flight in a smaller plane. But the sight of Daisy and her jumping partner heading towards an open door so high above the ground gave her an instant and sudden panic attack. She pictured the incident at Heysham Port, with Lucia precari-ously balanced on a cross-strut of the container lift, while she pleaded with Edward Callow for her daughter's life.

Lucia was standing up, looking as if she couldn't wait to get started.

'See you on the ground, Mum!' she shouted, over the humming of the engine and the roar of the wind outside. Charlotte felt paralysed as she watched Lucia perching on her jump partner's lap, forward facing and suspended thou-sands of metres about the ground, waiting to be thrust out at any minute. The count ended and Lucia was gone. She flinched as she watched her daughter disappear over the edge, plummeting towards the ground.

She was last. Her jump partner checked the buckles, and they moved forward to the open door. She could see the airfield below them, looking like a cluster of miniature buildings on a model railway layout. At that moment, she was completely in the hands of her instructor. Her legs felt weak and her head started to spin, as if she might pass out. She would have liked some encouraging words from him, but he appeared to be the silent type. He guided her to the door, and they manoeuvred themselves into position.

Charlotte's eyes were closed as they sat on the edge; she knew she was perched over open skies, but she couldn't bring herself to look down. She could sense her jump partner's head directly behind hers. They were harnessed closely together, so it was too late to opt out. They just sat there, Charlotte with her eyes closed, feeling the wind across her face and wondering how she'd breathe on the way down when they started to fall. She felt a small jolt and thought that was it, but it was her jump partner moving his hand to his shaded goggles.

Then she heard a voice that chilled her so much she felt like the grim reaper had just walked straight through her.

'Hey Charlotte, turn around, see who's here.'

She recognised the voice before she saw his face, but she had to turn and open her eyes to prove it to herself. He gave her a moment to register his identity, then pulled down his goggles and leapt out of the plane, taking her with him. She was at the mercy of Vinnie Mace. How the hell had he got up here with her?

Charlotte couldn't believe how fast the plane disappeared behind her. The wind took her breath away momentarily, but she quickly figured out how to control the flow. Vinnie turned them so they were aiming head first for the ground. They were still falling through small clouds; what was he planning to do to her?

'Hey, Charlotte!' he shouted. His gloved hand moved to the harness, and he was flicking it so she could feel the tension tightening then loosening.

'What do you want?' she gasped. She couldn't tell if he could even hear her. On the ground below, she could see Daisy and Lucia had landed safely, but Vinnie seemed to be steering them away from the drop zone they'd been told about at the briefing.

'I've got a message from Mr Armstrong. You need to forget all about him and go back to writing stories about lost cats and village galas. Got it?'

She only snatched parts of what he said as she moved her head to the side, trying to negotiate the force of the wind and hear him at the same time. He sounded so calm, despite the speed at which the ground was rushing towards them.

'Open the parachute!' she shouted. It was all she could come up with. They seemed to be getting too close to the ground; surely it was time to open the chute now?

'I need you to promise, Charlotte, while I have your full attention. I don't like people who think they can get the better of me. You can't out-run me Charlotte; I can find you wherever you are.'

She could barely comprehend his words and prayed that she would pass out, not wanting to live through what was happening, regardless of what Vinnie had planned. His fingers teased the harness straps as the ground came closer, closer, closer. The trees, the car, some sheep nearby... she could see them all. Surely it was too late? Surely he should have opened the parachute by now?

CHAPTER THIRTY-ONE

Vinnie held out his arms as they plunged towards the ground.

'Look, no hands! Are you gonna back off, or do we finish this now?'

'I'll stop... whatever you want... just open the bloody parachute, please!'

She could hear the cows and sheep in the fields below, and the ground was approaching faster as they continued to fall.

'OK then,' Vinnie said.

There was a flapping sound to her rear, then a sharp tug, jolting them upwards. Charlotte's heart was pounding against her chest like a football being kicked incessantly against a wall. She thought she was about to faint, but kept her focus on touching the ground.

Vinnie had steered them away from the airfield. Will and the kids would be wondering what was happening. As the long grass of the field below them came into sharp focus, Charlotte pulled in her legs to let Vinnie take the impact of the landing. It was smooth and efficient. She'd been told he was a former paratrooper, and his confidence and capability confirmed that must be true. He was in complete control while they were in the sky.

As Vinnie unclipped the harness and released her, she felt her legs crumple. Without wasting a moment, he peeled off his overalls and equipment, keeping his gloves on.

'Leave Tiffany Irwin alone and back off from Fabian Armstrong. This is a polite warning. I can find out everything about you, Charlotte. I will come for you again if you don't behave.'

All Charlotte could do was to nod, as if pacifying some bully in the school playground. She just wanted it to end, for Vinnie Mace to leave her. He stood and looked at her for a few seconds, then jogged over to the five-bar fence at the side of the field, leapt over it and headed for the white car she'd spotted parked at the roadside during their descent.

He'd planned it meticulously. Somehow, he'd found out about the tandem jump and arranged this in no time at all. Anyone could read about the jump on her charity page, but how the hell had he managed to get on board the plane?

The questions could wait for later. She sat in the long grass, still fully dressed in her jump gear, with Vinnie's clothing abandoned at her side and the discarded parachute catching the breeze and floating across the field. If her legs could have taken her weight, she might have tried to get some details of Vinnie's car, but it wouldn't have made any difference.

She knew how men like Vinnie Mace worked. Somehow, they circumvented all the normal problems such as police officers and gaining access to private information. They could even reach you from prison. Until you could absolutely corner them, they were dangerous and powerful. Edward Callow had had to lose his life to be stopped. This was a similar situation, but Fabian Armstrong didn't have to worry about being re-elected as the local MP. That probably made him more dangerous.

When Will and Olli finally drew up ten minutes later, she was still hyper-ventilating, keeping her hands on the ground, wanting as much of her body in contact with the field as possible. The rush towards the ground had been startling. She'd never felt velocity like it; it had been the most frightening sensation of her life.

Soon Will was running across the field towards her while Olli fastened the gate behind them. A second, then a third car drew up on the road.

'Jesus, Charlotte, what the hell happened? Where's your jump partner?'

He sat down at her side, hugging her tightly and glancing around, as if her jump partner might be hiding somewhere in the grass.

'Oh God, Will, I thought I was going to die. I honestly did.'

'Mum, are you OK? What happened?'

Olli was with them now, and she could sense others getting out of cars and making their way toward the gate. In spite of her body being seized by panic, her mind worked quickly. She'd have to confide in Will now. And in DCI Summers, too; she'd warned her about Fabian Armstrong. But she needed time to decide what to tell everybody else.

'They found your real jump partner unconscious and taped up, lying behind one of the outbuildings on the airfield. Who was that you jumped with?'

So that was how Vinnie had done it. It was why they'd had to wait for him on the aircraft. He'd been wearing gloves all the time too, so there'd be no fingerprint evidence either. She had to admit it was a well-executed scare tactic.

'I don't know what happened,' she lied. 'Somebody was trying to scare me, but I have no idea why. How is the guy at the airfield? Is he hurt?'

'He's fine, Mum, just shaken and bruised. He didn't see who hit him. They've got an ambulance there now; they're taking him for a check-up.'

'Are you hurt at all?' Will asked. 'You look like all the blood's drained from your face.'

'I'm not hurt, just shaken,' she replied.

Daisy, Willow, Lucia and Abi were making their way across the field together with one of the instructors, who was wearing the distinctively coloured overalls. He asked Charlotte the same questions as Will had, while Lucia hugged her. The guy from the airfield went to retrieve the parachute and after fifteen minutes or so, Charlotte was ready to stand up again.

'We'll probably have to report this to the police,' the man from the airfield said, the chute and discarded clothing bundled up in his arms. 'This has never happened before. Who the heck would do something like that? At least they knew how to handle the gear.'

All Charlotte could think was *more police*. She was fast getting on first name terms with the local constabulary, but she didn't dare tell them about Vinnie, not after the warning he'd given her. She'd need to work on her story.

'Let's give your mum some space and I'll help her back to the car,' Will said, shooing away the small, fussing crowd surrounding Charlotte. They moved away, leaving Will to help her to her feet.

'You're keeping something from me again,' he said, once he'd checked they were out of earshot. 'What's going on, Charlotte? Is this something to do with that bloody Irwin story you're chasing?'

'I will tell you what's going on,' she replied, 'but just give me a little time. And don't say anything to the kids or police, not until you and I have had time to talk—'

'Damn it, Charlotte! We couldn't help what happened to us last time. But this? This is of your own making. Is this intimidation? Have you been poking your nose into hornets' nests again? This puts everybody in danger, Charlotte. Why can't you just leave it alone?'

Charlotte could see Olli and Lucia looking back, as if they'd clocked something was going on. Will rarely raised his voice; he was not the angry type, so his current level of agitation had not gone unnoticed. She spoke as quietly as she could.

'I didn't plan it like this, Will. It just crept up on me. Do you think I wanted this to happen, that for one minute I would put myself through it all? It doesn't work like that. It creeps up on you, as it did with Bruce Craven. I'm not the bad guy; I'm just trying to help a mother who lost her three babies and is now incarcerated in some mental health facility. And I'm trying to support a friend who once helped me to save our daughter. Our daughter, Will! I didn't know I was going to piss somebody off again.'

Will stopped and released his supportive grip on her hand.

'I sometimes think you attract this, Charlotte. You can't help yourself. You need to learn to walk away and leave somebody else to sort out all the crap in the world.'

CHAPTER THIRTY-TWO

The best decision Charlotte had ever made regarding the
guest house was not to offer midday meals. It had been on
the cards when they were planning how they would run the
business, but Charlotte didn't want to be bound to
customers all day. Breakfasts and evening meals were
enough when she had a family life to squeeze in. As she
watched the long lines of customers at the carvery, she
allowed herself a moment of self-congratulation as she saw
how busy and constant it was, a feeding frenzy of beef,
gravy, roast potatoes and Yorkshire puddings, with
customers behaving as if it would be the last meal they ate
for a month.

She wasn't in the mood for the post-jump get-together,
but she felt obliged to go through the motions. They'd had
to bump their booking by an hour too, thanks to the police
wanting to gather details of witnesses and go through the
rigmarole of trying to figure out what had happened. All
Charlotte knew was that she'd been scared out of her wits,
and she thanked her lucky stars that Vinnie Mace hadn't
intended to harm her. He'd just wanted to terrify her, and

he'd done an excellent job. She wondered if Fabian Armstrong had an employee of the month award, because when it came to giving Vinnie a review for intimidation, it was definitely five stars from her.

So far, she'd been able to keep her mouth shut about Vinnie being the man responsible for the assault. The police had taken the basic details from her and agreed she could give a more formal statement at Morecambe Police Station after the weekend, when she was less shaken. Dare she mention Vinnie's name? While Lucia was regaling the assembled celebratory crowd with an enthusiastic recounting of the tandem jump in second-by-second detail, Charlotte was tussling with her sense of morality.

The jump instructor who'd been tied up wasn't seriously injured. He was shocked, scared, and bruised, but this was no attempted murder. Vinnie had simply needed him out of the way so he could put the frighteners on Charlotte. There was no more danger to the staff at the airfield either; it had all been focused on Charlotte.

In her amateur opinion, the chances of pinning down Vinnie as the man responsible were low to slim. He'd been wearing gloves, so wouldn't have left any fingerprints. She hadn't seen any CCTV on the airfield, but in any case he'd worn the cool jump instructor shades to conceal his face. She'd only recognised him from his voice. He'd parked his car in a country lane a couple of fields away from the airfield. Plane spotters parked along those lanes all the time; she'd seen them as they drove in. Vinnie's car wouldn't have been out of place.

She had nothing to gain by revealing Vinnie as the perpetrator of the assault, and a lot to lose. As Will leaned over to ask if she wanted her second Yorkshire pudding, she made her decision; it was safer to keep quiet about Vinnie.

'I'm not hungry,' Charlotte said to Will, who eagerly took the Yorkshire pudding. At least it might distract him from what she was about to do. She looked round the table at all her family and friends, who were high on the after-glow of the jump experience. They'd raised a lot of money and nobody was hurt. It was a good time to sneak out and make a call.

'Help yourself to my roast beef and potatoes,' she said. 'I'm just popping outside for a breather.'

The distraction of offering Will her food did indeed allow her to sneak off. They'd chosen a family carvery because it was easier for Abi and Louise. Sometimes Louise's Alzheimer's could make her difficult, so Abi preferred a venue which was packed with sugar-crazed chil-dren. It meant Louise could be as noisy as she wanted to be, because there was always a child who was louder.

Charlotte walked past the Manic Machine area, a complex soft-play facility which granted the feasting parents some respite from their energetic youngsters. It allowed them to reclaim some semblance of their adult lives for an hour or two while they ate a Sunday roast. Every wheel, opening and slide was occupied by a child, with no surface untouched by small, sticky hands. As she watched plastic balls flying, padded wheels spinning and excited children leaping, she figured her mind was probably acting in a similar way.

She walked through the double doors and found a bench to sit on, giving a sympathetic smile to a mother who was calming down a distressed child. By the child's lack of eye contact with the mother, she reckoned they were prob-ably somewhere on the autistic spectrum. In her teaching days, she'd done some special training on it. While the rest of the world rushed to make those kids fit in with them, she often wondered if the world could learn a thing or two from the kids on the spectrum. She'd always found them interesting, intelligent and stimulating in their unique view of the world.

For the briefest of moments, she felt a pang of loss at not being able to work with those children any more. Then she shuddered at the memory of the brutes in her regular classes. She was pleased to be out of there. Some of the kids she'd known might have given Vinnie Mace a run for his money.

The woman on the bench had done a fine job of calming her child and they were working their way along the flower beds, examining the shape of the petals. She took out her phone and dialled Kate Summers. The call was picked up immediately, almost as if she'd been waiting for it to come in.

'Kate, it's me. Can you talk?'

'Yes, I'm on my own. It's deathly quiet without the family here.'

Charlotte considered the young families inside the carvery, most of them craving a moment's peace from their family. Yet here was DCI Summers, having achieved just that, wishing the noise and bustle was back. Humans never seemed to be happy with their situation.

'What's up?' Kate asked.

'You know you warned me off Fabian Armstrong last night?'

Kate didn't answer. She probably knew what was coming.

'I couldn't bring myself to tell you last night. But we've already had a run in with him—'

'Charlotte!'

She couldn't remember hearing DCI Summers sound so exasperated before.

'I know. He's pissed with us, I'm afraid, really pissed.'

As Charlotte explained the events at the airfield, it reminded her of the time she'd rung her mother as a teenager to tell her she'd drunk a little too much at a friend's party and would need her father to come and pick her up after he'd already gone to bed for the night. Judgement and annoyance oozed from the other end, even though Kate Summers said nothing throughout.

'So what do I do, Kate? Do I tell them it was Vinnie Mace, or do I say I didn't get a good look at him?'

She could almost hear Kate thinking on the other end of the phone line.

'Charlotte, I want you to ignore what I said to you last night. I'll have to find somebody else to help me. You're already in too deep, and you need to back right off. Fabian Armstrong is a dangerous man; you've seen that for yourself already. I can't expose you to any more danger. Promise me you'll stop.'

'Should I say it was Vinnie?'

'You know that in my professional role, I have to tell you to report him. But as your friend, Charlotte... no, don't say it was Vinnie. If he and Fabian take some heat over the assault, you're right, nothing will stick; there's no evidence, and my colleagues won't be foolish enough to take legal action. When we come for Fabian Armstrong, the evidence has to be watertight and we have to sink the entire operation at once, otherwise it will be a hydra that keeps growing a new head. Back right away from this and let it play out. Just promise me that when they're calling me all the names under the sun, you'll remember I was only ever trying to do my best.'

CHAPTER THIRTY-THREE

After the meal, Charlotte decided she would walk home via the promenade. Will dropped her off at the Happy Mount Park car park, and after fending off everybody's concerns about her wellbeing, she finally had some time on her own.

'Are you sure you're OK?' Will asked. 'That was some fright you just had. Don't you need a check-up at the hospital?'

She couldn't help but be irritated by the constant fretting, but she cut Will some slack; it wasn't as if the past year had been a normal one.

'I'm fine,' she said. 'I just need a little time on my own to come down from the shock. A bracing walk along the sea front will do me the world of good.'

Physically, she felt in great shape. In spite of what had happened during the jump, there no damage done. That was a win. Mentally, however, things were different. She'd been here before, with violent men making threats and leaving her in no doubt they would carry them through. The question was always whether to back down and cower, or fight. If it wasn't for the kids, her answer would always be to fight, especially if a wrong had to be put right. In this case, it was Tiffany Irwin. Charlotte couldn't get over the fact that she was being kept in that care home against her will. Somehow, she didn't know how, Fabian had done something terrible to her. She couldn't let it lie; she had to do something about it.

The catering kiosk was open in the car park, so she bought herself an ice cream. Having barely touched her roast dinner, she was peckish and needed a quick fix of something sweet. Why not go crazy and opt for a double flake and chocolate sauce? She'd just have to run faster at next week's parkrun to make up for the calories.

She would have been ashamed to admit it to anyone local, but it had been some considerable time since she'd been to Happy Mount Park. Had the kids been toddlers, she'd be there all the time. She walked through the main gate and was immediately struck by how well-kept the gardens were.

The main path was packed with middle-aged couples, elderly people and families out for a free afternoon in the park. She smiled to herself as two children screeched with joy as their dad took a swing boat higher and higher. There was hope for the world while kids still loved the swing boats. As she ambled by the bowling green and the tennis courts, she heard a familiar voice.

'Charlotte?'

It was Nigel.

'You're the last person I expected to see here,' he continued. 'Isn't today the day of the parachute jump? Or have you done it already?'

Charlotte brought him up to speed with the events of the day, without mentioning Vinnie. She also told him what had happened after he dropped her off for her meeting with

DCI Summers. Nigel had been dispatched to get ice lollies from the café; his wife and children had gone ahead to scout for benches in the picnic area.

'I'd best not be long,' he said. 'No child waits forever for a promised ice lolly. It's one of the occupational hazards of working on the local paper; I can't walk a hundred yards without seeing somebody I know. So here's my probing journalistic question for you: why are you walking here alone after something as amazing as completing a parachute jump? Why aren't you with your family?'

Charlotte had a lot to learn from Nigel. He had the knack of getting to the heart of an issue.

She gave in and told him about Vinnie and the shock of the parachute jump, pausing for a moment towards the end to hold back the tears. She mustn't be that woman; if she let them make her cry, they were no better than school yard bullies.

'I can't believe they did that to you. You've made me nervous now; I'm concerned for my own family. It's very intimidating. Do you want to back off?'

She didn't want to stop pushing for information, but the memory of plunging towards the ground before the parachute opened made her go hot and cold. It had been the most terrifying experience of her life, even though she'd known Vinnie had to open the parachute; he wouldn't have killed himself. Besides, at the briefing, they'd said the chutes were fitted with emergency devices. He must have opened it at the last possible moment.

'I want to keep going, but we'll have to be more subtle about it. We can dig a little without getting in Fabian Armstrong's way – can't we?'

'I'm so pleased you said that,' Nigel replied, looking behind him to assess how busy the café was. 'I'd better get a move on, or I'll be in trouble. My wife is patient enough with my erratic hours as it is. I've got an appointment booked for us first thing Monday morning. Actually, it's not so much an appointment as a chance encounter.'

This was why Charlotte couldn't back off. News stories like this were like a loose thread which she just couldn't stop fiddling with until she'd come to its end.

'I have to be in early to get my ticking-off out of the way. I'll get my report written about Yasmin Utworth tonight and make sure it's a good one. Will I be OK?'

'You'll be fine, honestly. Just go into his office with a cup of black coffee, tell him how good your report will be and promise you won't get into trouble again. Honestly, you'll be fine. Besides, this meeting is at ten o'clock or thereabouts, so you'll be OK for time.'

'So, where are we going first thing?'

'Half Moon Bay. Do you know it?'

'I'm not sure. Is it Heysham way?'

'Yes, within spitting distance of where you and Edward Callow had your little fallout. It's a short walk along from the port.'

'Well, it'll improve my local knowledge. Why are we going there?'

'Remember our pal Rory Higson? He phoned the office after you met with him. It turns out that when he worked as a reporter on the paper, he was on particularly good terms with a chap called Evan Farrish, a former police officer. Farrish was the DCI in charge of the Irwins' case back then—'

'Yes, he mentioned it,' she replied, eager to hear where this was leading.

'I know. He wanted to sound out his friend before he confirmed it with us. DCI Evan Farrish is the man who headed the original investigation into the disappearance of the Irwin family. He still lives locally, but he retired years ago. Guess where he walks his dogs at around ten o'clock every morning?'

'OK, let me guess... Half Moon Bay? He mentioned that when we spoke.'

'You'll make an excellent detective someday, Charlotte. Yes; if we just happen to be walking there tomorrow morning, Rory says we're bound to see him. Rory walks out that way with his dog sometimes and they go for a coffee in the café opposite the car park. Are you up for it?'

'Of course. At least we might get some answers about Kate Summers' involvement in all this. And it can't do any harm as far as Fabian Armstrong is concerned, can it? Let's do it—'

Charlotte had suddenly noticed a woman approaching them at some speed. She was holding hands with a young girl who looked like she was being pulled rather than led. She didn't recognise her, but she was definitely making a beeline for Nigel.

'Do you know that woman?' she asked.

'Nigel, for Christ's sake, I've been looking all over for you—'

'Charlotte, this is my wife, Kerry. And my daughter, Michelle. Where's Freddie?'

'I thought he was with you,' Kerry said. 'The kids had run ahead, and I assumed he'd looped back through the trees and gone to get the ice lollies with you.'

She seemed panic-stricken, like her one hope had been of finding Freddie with his dad. Charlotte knew this scenario of old. Lucia had had a bad habit of wandering off as a child. She and Will had carried out many a frantic search when the kids were young.

'Why don't I wait at the gates, Nigel? I can make sure he doesn't leave the park. Do either of you have a photograph of Freddie to help me find him?'

'Thank you,' said Kerry, evidently grateful for an extra pair of hands. She took a purse out of her bag and handed over a small school photograph of the two children. He looked like any boy of that age.

Charlotte was about to go to take up her station when Nigel turned to his daughter, who had remained quiet and sullen throughout the panic.

Nigel gently pulled her over to him and spoke calmly.

'You were with Freddie when I went to get the ice lollies. Did you see which direction he went in?'

'I've been trying to tell Mum, but she wouldn't listen to me,' Michelle began. 'Freddie ran ahead; he was too fast for me. I saw him walking away with a man.'

'Did you know this man?' Nigel asked, panic beginning to rise in his voice.

'No, Dad, he's not a teacher or anything. I didn't know who it was. I don't think Freddie did either.'

CHAPTER THIRTY-FOUR

Charlotte had hoped the walk in Happy Mount Park would help to clear her head, but it did the opposite. The moment Michelle revealed Freddie had gone with a man, Nigel gave her a look which conveyed so much. It was along the lines of *Oh my God, my son is missing, we have to find him, we both know who took him, please don't tell my wife.* If there was a facial expression able to convey all that emotion in a single glance, Nigel just owned it.

'I'll stay at the gate until you come for me, I promise. I won't let him leave if he's still in here.'

Charlotte was turning to head off, but Kerry touched her arm to stop her.

'No, I'll take the gate with Michelle; we need to make sure he doesn't leave. Besides, you and Nigel can move faster and cover more ground; Michelle will slow me down. Go... go now, please find him. Please make sure he's safe—'

Nigel and Charlotte were on their way before she'd finished the sentence, the air charged with the spark of panic.

'Are there any other exits?' Charlotte asked.

'I'm not sure. You'll be able to get out other ways, but most of the flow is through the main entrance. Surely Vinnie wouldn't be crazy enough to snatch a child in broad daylight? There will be loads of witnesses.'

'What he did to me this morning was audacious, so I wouldn't put it past him.'

'By the way, Kerry wouldn't have told you, but Freddie is mostly deaf. He wears two hearing aids, but you can barely see them. We sign to him a lot of the time. Just so you know, if you find him.'

'Oh Nigel, I didn't know. I'm sorry—'

'He's deaf, not dead, Charlotte. Set that aside, and he's just like any normal kid of his age, but take care if you see him. He's not so good at lip-reading, but he's getting there. Stand in front of him so he can see you properly and he'll be fine, he'll figure it out.'

'OK, I'll go round the play area and the bowling green, you do the tennis courts and splash park, and let's meet up at the miniature railway. Then we can sweep the areas at the back of the park.'

Nigel nodded and left. Charlotte set off at a slow jog, mindful that there were dogs, toddlers and youngsters everywhere. She scanned the faces of everybody she passed, forcing herself to look for Freddie rather than just Vinnie. This was serious; it was bad enough scaring the life out of her, but a child? They were off limits.

Fabian Armstrong and Vinnie Mace had stepped over a line, but the stakes of pursuing the Irwin news story had just been raised. This might scare Nigel. He'd be well within his rights to insist they should only report on police press conference updates and refrain from the freelance investigations that had landed them in trouble in the first place.

In the packed play area, the kids were all running so fast that it was difficult to spot anyone. She convinced herself Freddie wasn't there and moved on to the bowling green area, which was a good deal quieter. Before long, she was beside the miniature railway. She'd heard the hissing of the steam engine as she'd moved away from the play area, so she knew it was running. Nigel joined her a few minutes later.

'Anything?' he asked.

'No,' Charlotte replied with a grimace. 'Not a sign of him.'

Nigel checked his smartphone.

'Nothing from Kerry either. Dammit, where is he? Where have you got to, Freddie—'

He cut his words short as the miniature steam train came around the corner, emitting a whistling sound as the passengers shrieked with joy.

Both of them idly watched as the train went by, packed with parents sitting with drawn-up knees and youngsters enjoying every minute.

'There he is, he's on the train!'

Nigel pointed, and Charlotte followed his finger. There was a solitary child sitting at the back, looking around as the train rushed by, happy and safe. They ran, following the train, until it came to a stop, then waited impatiently for Freddie to leave his seat and walk onto the small platform. He seemed to be searching for somebody, as if he'd been put on the train but had only just realised there was nobody to meet him. Nigel rushed up to him and gave him a hug. The two of them signed a brief conversation, then Nigel took his hand.

'Thank God, he's fine. He says he lost Michelle in the

park and a man asked him if he wanted a ride on the train. That's all. He's safe. I'll text Kerry and say we'll meet her at the gates. What a relief. I can imagine how you felt when your feet were back on the ground.'

Nigel texted Kerry and Charlotte smiled at Freddie. She wasn't sure how to communicate with him, so she made certain she had eye contact and began speaking, making her lip movements as clear as she could.

'Hi Freddie, I'm Charlotte, I'm a friend of your dad.'

'Dad, Dad, your friend is called Carrot. That's a funny name to have.'

Nigel laughed and ruffled Freddie's hair. He signed as he spoke.

'I told you it was early days with the lip-reading. I've told him your proper name. Kerry's relieved; she's taken Michelle to the kiosk for that ice lolly I was supposed to be buying. I'll meet her in the car park. My heart is thumping; I got such a fright.'

'Me too. I thought Vinnie was up to his tricks again. Let's ask the ticket collector if he saw anything.'

The train was loaded with the next lot of passengers, and the ticket collector waved his flag and blew his whistle. They waited until the train had set off, then caught his attention.

'Did you see who put my son on the train?' Nigel asked.

The ticket collector looked like he'd been retired for many years. He wore a cap on his head and had a small leather bag over his shoulder to hold the tickets. It reminded Charlotte of train trips as a child, before the days of apps and smartphones.

The man smiled at Freddie and pointed to the small devices in his ears.

'Yes, I did, because I realised your son had hearing aids

in. I'm the same,' he said, moving his head around and showing Freddie one of the more traditional ear pieces in his left ear.

'He was just a guy, wearing a plain black cap and sunglasses. Dressed in normal clothes like any dad. I thought nothing of it. Everybody pays in cash here; we don't take cards, so I can't help you, I'm afraid.'

'OK, thanks.'

Nigel couldn't conceal his disappointment.

'Oh, there was one thing,' the ticket collector continued. 'He seemed very strong. It was the way he moved, like he was sure of himself. A fit guy, that's the best way to describe it. Most of the dads who come here are regular guys like you and me. You know, we need to eat a bit less dinner and get out for more walks.'

Nigel nodded, smiled, and thanked the man.

'Sounds like it was Vinnie Mace then,' Charlotte said. 'Is it OK to speak in front of Freddie?'

'Yes, yes, go ahead. He picks up some of it, but not everything. I call it selective lip-reading. If you're asking him to tidy his bedroom, you need to sign it several times. If you're offering him an ice cream, the power of hearing is miraculously restored. You know what kids are like.'

'Will you tell Kerry?' Charlotte asked. 'Or are you going to be drawn into the dark world of secrets and subterfuge I seem to inhabit?'

'It's a tricky one, Charlotte. Scaring me with Freddie like that, it's not on. After Olli and Lucia were threatened last year, you of all people understand what it's like. I need to think it through. If it puts my kids in danger, it might have to be somebody else's battle. We can run features about Yasmin Utworth and report what the police tell us.

But we might have to draw a line under all this digging and interfering.'

Charlotte had hoped he'd be more infuriated by it, as she was, and adamant they wouldn't scare her off. She was petrified by what had happened, but she'd gone on protests for the CND back in the eighties and had campaigned against student grant cuts and funding cuts to the women's refuge in Lancaster. Lately that sense of indignation and justice had re-visited her.

'Do you want a lift? You can squeeze between Freddie and Michelle.'

'No, I'll walk thanks, Nigel. I'll just pop over to the car to check in with Kerry. She must have been going spare.'

They walked up to the car, and Kerry got out and ran up to Freddie, hugging him so hard it seemed like she might squeeze all the breath from him.

She signed frantically to him, speaking at the same time, telling him how much she loved him and how worried they'd been.

'Thanks so much for helping,' she said as she stood up. 'I'm so grateful you were around. It's lovely to meet you at last. I've heard a lot about you, and I've read all about your past adventures in the newspaper, of course. We should catch up for a coffee some time.'

'Dad?'

Freddie was trying to get Nigel's attention.

'I'd love that,' Charlotte replied.

'Dad?'

'One moment,' Nigel replied, signing it at the same time. 'I'll see you first thing tomorrow in the office. Make that article about Yasmin Utworth a good one, and the boss will be putty in your hand.'

'Dad?'

Nigel turned to face Freddie, following Kerry's lead by speaking and signing for Charlotte's benefit.

'What is it, Freddie?'

'Who's Vinnie Mace, Dad?'

CHAPTER THIRTY-FIVE

Charlotte hadn't experienced a Monday feeling like it since things had begun to deteriorate for her in the classroom while living in Bristol. A sense of foreboding and gloom settled in the pit of her stomach. She'd only ever exchanged pleasantries with the boss before, but now Teddy Solomon had asked to see her personally.

She'd been up until past midnight writing up her feature on Yasmin Utworth, honing it to within an inch of its life, and now she was standing in the office kitchen at 8.45 am. Thank goodness George had walked Isla to work that morning. Lucia had let his dog Una come into her bedroom and sleep on her bed, while George chipped in with the serving and table clearing, releasing Charlotte to her fate.

As it was, Teddy Solomon was a pushover. Charlotte had not expected it. She'd been terrified of him, aware that the Solomon family had owned the local press for many years. Teddy was presiding over its decline and probable demise, like many newspapers in the 21st century. She'd expected him to be overbearing, but it turned out he used to eat in the restaurant at the Lakes View Guest House in the days when Rex Emery ran a restaurant from the lounge, and he was more than happy to share fond memories of celebrations held there over the years. The complaints he'd received were almost an afterthought, after a conversation which was best summed up as warm and genial.

'These little complaints we've had about you—' he began.

The sinking feeling returned to Charlotte's stomach.

'When I started learning this business from my father, we were selling thousands of newspapers each week and the money was rolling in. We used to let the reporters do their own thing for much of the week, relying on their journalistic skills and local contacts to bring in the exclusive news stories. These days we're barely profitable, and we only have a handful of reporters who are forced to re-write press releases and report on village fetes. You have to ruffle feathers to find great news stories, Charlotte. That pisses people off. Excuse my language; I know we're supposed to be more PC these days. I can bat these complaints away; it's my job. There won't be a problem if you land the big story. If you can bring this home before anyone else, I mean the national news outlets, it's worth a couple of months of increased circulation and maybe even an award. We need both. From what Nigel tells me, you two have a great working relationship. I'll make these complaints go away; just make sure you and Nigel bring me something that makes my eyes pop out when I read it.'

Charlotte recounted the conversation as she and Nigel made the trip over to Half Moon Bay. Teddy had been so chatty that morning, she'd feared Nigel might have left without her. She made it in the nick of time.

'Well, we'd better do as he says and deliver a great story,'

Charlotte said to Nigel. 'Evan Farrish is an excellent person to start with, so let's see what he can tell us this morning.'

They parked up in the car park opposite the Half Moon Bay Café and made their way over to the beach. The wind caught Charlotte's hair; she instantly regretted not tying it up. She rummaged through her trousers and coat for a hair band, eventually finding one tucked away in her back pocket. It was a good thing, otherwise she'd have looked a wild mess by the time they ran into Evan.

'So what's the plan? We have to make this seem like a coincidence, right?'

'More or less,' Nigel replied. 'Evan walks from St Patrick's Chapel every morning, stopping at the café for a drink, before heading home. Rory Higson joins him for a catch-up occasionally. If we idly wander up and down the beach, we should meet them at some point. Rory has half sounded him out, but this is a bit of a set-up today.'

Charlotte and Nigel walked along slowly, looking out across the cold, grey sea and checking the walkers to make sure none of them was Rory and Evan. At one stage Charlotte looked behind them over to the port. She shuddered, remembering what had happened there. She and Will had promised themselves they'd try the Isle of Man Steam Packet some time in the future, but not yet. It was all still too raw.

'I don't know anything about St Patrick's Chapel,' Charlotte said as they walked on. 'Where is it?'

'Only a fifteen-minute walk from here, if that. It's worth visiting some time. The stone graves are up there too, just beside the church.'

'Stone graves? Honestly?'

'Yes, they're amazing. They're hewn out of the stone from the beach over there. Somebody told me they're used on a Black Sabbath album cover, though I can't say I've ever checked—'

He suddenly stopped, stared across the sand, then continued speaking.

'That's Rory over there; and I'd recognise his dog, Archie, anywhere. It must be Evan he's walking with. Let's see if Archie recognises me.'

Thanks to Archie's excellent canine memory, it wasn't long before Rory and Evan were making their way over to join them.

'Hello again, Rory,' Charlotte called over.

'Fancy meeting you out here,' Rory said, giving Nigel a wink. 'This is Evan Farrish, a former DCI, now enjoying a well-deserved retirement. I was telling him earlier that you're working on the Irwin story from way back.'

'What a coincidence, running into you out here,' Evan said, giving a wry smile. 'Anybody would think Rory here had been passing on some of his old reporter's tricks to the next generation.'

Charlotte and Nigel didn't bother protesting. They'd got what they wanted, and Evan Farrish was happy to play along.

'Can we treat you to cake and a coffee in the café?' Nigel asked. 'We'd love to hear your memories of what happened. You were leading the case, weren't you?'

Evan Farrish was happy to relive his memories back on the force and in no time at all they were sitting around the wood-burning stove in the Half Moon Bay Café, the two dogs content to take the lion's share of the warmth while Evan Farrish told them all about the case.

'I'll be honest with you, it was the only case that was still bothering me when I retired. I took retirement at 55; that's when I decided it was time to hang up my truncheon.

But I'd have carried on if they'd let me, if somebody had told me I'd solve it. It troubles me to this day. Three bairns don't just disappear. But no other explanation was offered at the time.'

'How was Kate Summers involved?' Charlotte asked. She was desperate to know, not just because of what happened to the Irwins, but also to imagine her friend as a young officer.

Evan paused a moment and took a long sip of his hot chocolate.

'Ooh, that's good hot chocolate. You can't beat it on a blowy day like today.'

Charlotte bent down to stroke Archie, who was happily resting at her feet, delighted to be fussed.

'When I see Kate's name in the newspapers, it's funny to imagine that wet-behind-the-ears PC reaching the same rank as I was when I left. She was always impressive, even back then, when she was barely out of university. She had an intensity about her; I reckon if you're a crook with Kate Summers after you, you might as well just hand yourself in.'

As he took another sip of his hot chocolate, they stayed silent, encouraging him to say more. Rory gave a faint smile; as a former reporter himself, he'd used the trick many a time.

'I had a lot of time for Kate Summers, but there were always some things that didn't seem to fit in that case. Why was she the first one to arrive at the scene? She was the one who called it in. I wouldn't have got excited about it if her brother hadn't gone missing so soon afterwards. There's something I can probably tell you, now I don't have to worry about breaking confidences any longer. She went AWOL from her job for three days before her brother's supposed suicide. They disciplined her for it. I still remember her face when she'd got her dressing-down, as if it was the end of the world for her. After that, I dug around a bit, some of it off the record. I never uncovered anything more about PC Kate Allan, or DCI Summers as I should refer to her now. But there was something that never sat right with me, even though I couldn't prove anything.'

CHAPTER THIRTY-SIX

Charlotte found the conversation with Evan Farrish fascinating. It was a remarkable experience to travel back two decades and hear exactly what happened. Evan might have been retired for some years, but he'd lost none of his sharpness.

Rory had lost none of his mental agility either. Listening to the two of them reminiscing about the cases they'd covered made her think that in another twenty years that might be Kate Summers and Nigel Davies. If she passed her distance learning course, it might even be her and Kate Summers chatting away.

'The funny thing is,' Evan continued, 'I considered Rory to be a pest back then. There were certain elements of the case which we didn't want the public to find out about, because it might have hindered our investigation. You may see a grey-haired man in front of you, but Rory Higson could be very persistent back in the day.'

Laughter came from near the log fire and Archie looked up from his slumbering, as if alerted to the possibility that they might be on the move. Charlotte's phone vibrated in her pocket. She used the lull in the conversation to check the message. It was Lucia.

There's a lady at reception wants to speak to you in person. She's a nurse at Briar Bank Care Home. She wondered if she could catch you today.

That was the last thing Charlotte had expected. This could move things on; perhaps she could offer a little more information about Tiffany.

Any idea where she wants to meet? I'm seeing your dad at the university for a late lunch today. I want to find out if they've got a book in their library I can borrow.

Charlotte tapped at her screen, keeping one ear tuned to the conversation.

She's not on shift today, she said she's flexible.

Charlotte thought through her plans for the rest of the day. After Vinnie's warnings on Sunday, she'd felt discouraged about what to do next. This offered some hope of progress without having to get into any more trouble.

Ask her if we can meet at the guest house at midday. I'll make sure I get back in time.

The response came immediately.

Will do x

She knew it was ridiculous, but Charlotte cherished every kiss in a text message from her daughter.

'Who were your prime suspects?' Nigel asked. 'Were any names in the frame?'

'We were at a total loss,' Evan answered. He looked like a man who missed being at the centre of the action, handling the questions as if it were a press briefing. 'The father was the chief suspect. There were rumours of extra-marital affairs and conflict in the Irwin household, but nothing we could ever substantiate. It didn't help that Tiffany Irwin had a breakdown soon afterwards. The poor woman was sedated for much of the investigation; can you blame her, losing three children?'

'But there were never any bodies found at sea,' Charlotte chipped in, putting her phone on the table. 'That seems odd, doesn't it?'

'I agree,' Evan continued, 'but do you remember the terrible case of the cockle pickers who were caught by the tide in 2004? They couldn't find all the bodies initially, and one wasn't recovered until six years afterwards. The bay is a unique area; the way the tides work can be treacherous.'

'I remember a chilling fact about that case,' Rory said. 'I know it was four years after the Irwins disappeared, but it has some bearing on their case. The chap in charge of the lifeboat operation that night described how his team came across a *sea of bodies*. It's a horrible image, but surely the same would have applied to the children if they'd been washed out to sea?'

Evan paused, then looked at Rory like the wily old fox he was.

'You're judging the Irwin case with the benefit of hindsight. The cockle pickers' tragedy was unprecedented. I'm sure my colleagues learnt a lot from the recovery operation; it might have helped us if we'd known about it back in 2000.'

'So what's your theory, now that they've found Callie Irwin? Have the police spoken to you yet?'

Nigel had been taking notes throughout. Between them, they were doing a surprisingly good job of raking over the past.

Charlotte checked her phone quickly. Lucia had updated her, but she'd been so engrossed, she hadn't heard the vibration alert.

12.15 is fine. She'll wait for you on the bench across the road from the guest house. See you later. x

Evan finished the last of his bacon and egg sandwich before answering. He took his time chewing then swallowing the mouthful.

'If this is Callie Irwin, and it sounds like it is, because the DNA can't be wrong, then everything we thought to be true two decades ago was clearly false. With the information we had at the time, we could only conclude the family had been lost at sea. We reached that conclusion after a considerable length of time; you don't just declare people dead. Tiffany Irwin's brother was the one who pushed for it. It's a legal procedure, you know, and it wasn't even introduced until 2014. But I heard from people on the force that Fabian Armstrong was straight in there when the new rules were introduced. And do you remember Lord Lucan, the man who went missing in the seventies? He got a presumption of death certificate 42 years afterwards. That allows the families to sort out their affairs. It's all very tricky from a legal point of view.'

Nigel was taking copious notes in shorthand. In a moment of frustration, Charlotte wondered if she'd ever reach his speed.

Evan got to his feet and his dog's ears pricked up. Both of them looked as if the last thing they wanted to do was to get moving again.

'Well, I know I'm retired, but I do have other things on today. I'll need to make my way back to the village now. You're welcome to walk with me, but I must be on my way.'

Charlotte checked the time on her phone.

'Mind if we walk over to the graves?' she asked Nigel. 'I'd like to see them while we're here. Is it far, Evan?'

'Fifteen minutes or thereabouts,' he replied.

'Sure, why not?' Nigel replied. 'We can have a chat about things on the way back.'

Nigel paid the bill, and they all left the warmth and comfort of the café. Charlotte resolved to visit the area with the family; there were so many lovely, secluded places like it tucked away along the coastline.

The walk back was as spectacular as Charlotte had expected it to be. Evan and Rory led them along a path they referred to as The Barrows, which criss-crossed the top of the cliffs. They stopped to let the dogs have a short run at a cove they came across en route, and Evan gave them the directions they needed to reach the ruins of the old chapel before they went their separate ways.

'If you ever need to talk more about the story, let me know. Just buy me a pint in The Royal and I'll happily chat to you all day.'

Charlotte and Nigel thanked the men as they headed back to their cars, and Rory gave them a conspiratorial wink before turning to call Archie.

'What Evan said about Fabian getting a presumption of death certificate was interesting,' Charlotte began.

'You can say that again. It needs some research. I'm not sure what happens about death certificates and other things when people go missing.'

'Sorry; I didn't question Yasmin Utworth about that. But if you ask me, I'd say she wouldn't want a death certificate for her daughter. It would mean she'd have lost all hope.'

'I agree. It sounds like Fabian was keen to get the legals all sewn up. But from what we know so far, he had it all stitched up nicely before Tiffany's family disappeared.'

'I wouldn't like him looking after my interests,' Charlotte said, walking faster. They'd reached the graves, human shapes carved into solid rock to create body-shaped hollows overlooking the sea. Charlotte found them fascinating; she'd never seen an ancient burial ground like it.

They walked up to the ruins of the chapel, which was remarkably well preserved in its position atop a cliff looking out over the grey sea and wet sands.

'What an incredible place,' Charlotte said. 'There's so much I don't know about this area. It's full of hidden secrets like this.'

They took the cliff top route to the Half Moon Bay Café. As the nuclear power station came into view ahead of them, Charlotte considered how much of her life had centred on this place. Beyond the power station was the holiday camp where the events of their youth had come back to haunt she and Will. Not so far beyond the café was Heysham Port, the place where she and Lucia had fought for their lives in a desperate race against time. And now, here she was, with a sense that the clouds were gathering once again, heralding a storm. She looked ahead, recalling everything that had happened to them in the short time since they'd returned to the bay area.

'I've been thinking, Nigel,' she said, watching the grey clouds forming over the sea. 'I know what Vinnie Mace did was terrifying. But we're still alive, and he was only trying to frighten us off. That tells me they're hiding something. And I'm desperately concerned about Tiffany Irwin. I say we press on. Whatever happens, we should keep going.'

CHAPTER THIRTY-SEVEN

Nigel and Charlotte had not parted on the best of terms. For the first time in their working relationship, she'd caught a flash of anger.

'You saw what they did to Freddie. I can't risk it, Charlotte, not with the kids. We're fine to report anything we get directly from the police, but I'm not goading Fabian Armstrong any more. The police will have to figure out that part of the puzzle; it's not the key element of the story we're reporting on.'

Charlotte didn't argue, having faced similar resistance from Will. She would keep her mouth shut and continue to investigate what was going on with Tiffany on the quiet. There was no way she was going to tell Nigel who she'd be speaking to at lunchtime.

'I say we stick to newspaper business only,' he continued. 'That means items about Yasmin Utworth are fine, and so is anything relating to police press briefings about Callie Irwin. If it comes through official channels and all the other media outlets get the same information, it's OK to use. But we can't do any more freelance investigations of Fabian

Armstrong. We stick to the story. I'm not prepared to put my family in danger.'

It was fair enough. Charlotte could hardly argue with what he'd said. He was being perfectly reasonable. And as her mentor on the newspaper, she understood he had a duty of care to her. But it wouldn't calm the indignation she felt at Tiffany Irwin's plight. She refused to just walk away. She'd play it safe, knowing better than to confront Fabian Armstrong directly. But she'd continue to dig into the matter quietly and then tip off DCI Kate Summers, if she wanted to hear what she'd discovered. Failing that, she couldn't imagine her new press office contact, Toni Lawson, wouldn't know who to pass some choice information on to.

Nigel dropped Charlotte outside the guest house. As the car was idling and they agreed their plans, he checked his phone for messages.

'So, I'm planning to catch up with course work and shorthand practice for the rest of today, if it's OK—'

'I've got an email from Teddy about your Yasmin Utworth article. It's effusive. He says it's the most powerful reporting he's read in a long time. Listen to this. *It resonates at a profoundly emotional level and brought me to tears, discovering what an impact Morgan's disappearance has had on her mother. This is excellent journalism Nigel, you did well bringing her on board.* Well, what can I say? You don't get praise like this from Teddy very often. Especially not after he's just had to field complaints about your behaviour. Congratulations, Charlotte, that's impressive.'

Charlotte felt like she was about to burst with pride. She'd worked hard on the feature, trying to place the shock of the parachute jump and the search for Nigel's child at the back of her mind. Until now, she'd written short inserts and informational content, nothing as sustained or personal like the article on Yasmin. It made her feel like she was making the right choice about her future career direction.

'Well, it's a good time to say goodbye and get my lunch; I should quit while I'm ahead.'

'It's great work; you should be proud of yourself. Teddy has sent you a personal email too, so make sure you let your distance learning tutor see it.'

They said their farewells and Charlotte walked up the path. It was quiet downstairs when she walked in; there were no guests due until after four o'clock, so it was a rare moment of stillness.

She ran up the stairs to the family quarters.

'Lucia? Are you in?'

She tapped on her bedroom door.

'Lucia?'

There was silence. She knew better than to enter the room without gaining specific permission, so she walked through to the kitchen. It was rare for her to have the place to herself, she thought, as she made up a small cheese and tomato sandwich and poured a glass of milk. Even though she was meeting Will for lunch, a pit stop was perfectly reasonable, after all the fresh air from the morning's activities. It was a source of constant wonder to Will how she kept on top of food and supplies for the guest house, but the family fridge rarely had much in it. He'd threatened once to book in as a guest because the service was better, and he had been forced to eat a takeaway that night.

She sat at the table and checked her phone. A new email had arrived. She was still fine for time, so she opened it up while devouring her sandwich. It was the promised email from Teddy.

Hi Charlotte, your article about Yasmin Utworth was superb. Excellent, tight writing and a strong sense of emotion without becoming sentimental. I don't mind admitting it made a grown man cry. It's an excellent start and we'll give you your first by-line. We'll also add your photograph too, make you look like part of the regular team. Keep it up; it was an excellent piece of writing. If you carry on like this, I reckon one day you'll be receiving an award for your work. Best, Teddy.

Charlotte wished Will was sitting opposite her, so she could show him the message straight away. After her breakdown in the classroom and the difficult times that followed, she'd wondered if she would ever feel successful in her working life again. This was like a second wind; the thought of a new career was exhilarating, after teaching had gone so disastrously wrong. She paused for a moment to celebrate. There was nothing like a cheese and tomato sandwich made with fresh bread to mark a career highlight.

It was time for her meeting. She finished her glass of milk then ran down the stairs, taking several steps at a time. Her contact was visible through the glass panels in the front door as she approached it. Once outside, she made sure the door was locked, checked the emergency phone contact message was visible in case of early arrivals, and walked to the kerb. The traffic was annoyingly busy; it took her several minutes to find a suitable break to cross over. The woman had already spotted her, and gave a small wave.

'Hi, I'm Charlotte Grayson. Thanks for getting in touch,' she said, shaking the woman's hand and taking a place on the bench at her side.

'Do you mind if we walk and talk, love?' the woman said. 'I'd prefer to go along the prom where it's busier. Morecambe is such a small place, and somebody is bound to spot us together if we sit here for too long.'

'Sure,' Charlotte replied, standing up.

'I'd rather not tell you my name,' the woman began, as they made their way along the promenade. 'I'm risking my job speaking to you like this, but you seem to be the only person who's interested.'

Charlotte was learning the tricks of the trade fast. She used Nigel's technique and said nothing. It worked every time.

'I saw what you did last week. Coming in to speak to Tiff like that was brave of you. I was also on shift the day Mr Madeley shouted at you and that man, when he asked you to leave. It takes a lot of nerve to stand up to Mr Madeley, and even more guts to come back and sneak in without permission. So I'm trusting you with this information in the hope you can help poor old Tiff.'

'What do you do at the home?'

'I'm support staff, my love—' the woman began.

'Oh, my daughter thought you were a nurse,' Charlotte replied. She'd hoped she might glean some medical information too.

'No, I just help with the patients, helping them with getting dressed and things like that. You get to know the residents well. They tell me more than the doctors and nurses do.'

Charlotte waited a moment. It seemed they were due some rough weather; the clouds over the bay looked ominous.

'I've been worried about Tiff for a long time. She's a lovely woman, always talks to me. But that brother of hers, he's a big bully. I've heard him speak to her. I wouldn't talk to my dog like that.'

'Do they—'

Charlotte almost didn't dare ask the question.

'Do they hurt her or abuse her in any way?'

'No, not physically, not that I've ever seen. They're too clever. Mr Armstrong and Mr Madeley are in cahoots, and her doctor. The three of them are pure evil, I reckon.'

'Tiffany has a doctor?'

'Yes, that's what I wanted to tell you about. Poor old Tiff, she spends most of her life spaced out or away with the fairies. They keep her on drugs, I reckon, to make her docile. I know, because I experienced it myself once, with my own daughter. She had a still birth, poor mite, and was depressed for a long time afterwards. She tried to take her life once, and they put her on strong drugs to help her manage her situation. I recognise the same look in Tiff, like there's no life left in her. It's so sad; it's criminal to do that to a person.'

'What about her doctor? Tiffany must have a profes-sional diagnosis so she can receive the drugs in the first place.'

'You're probably right, love. But that doctor isn't like a regular doctor. He doesn't have a surgery or anything; he's one of those private fellows who cost a fortune. They're not for the likes of you and me. He drives a big flash car, so somebody's paying him some good money, and he's friendly with Mr Armstrong and Mr Madeley. And if you ask me, I'd say Tiff is his only patient.'

CHAPTER THIRTY-EIGHT

'Where does he work?' Charlotte asked.

She checked the time on her phone. She had the afternoon free, so she could look him up, to see what he did and where he was based.

'I've no idea, but I know where he lives.'

'Really?'

'Yes, he's in a posh house near Heysham Road, where the great and the good live.'

Charlotte wondered if the woman saw her jaw drop. She'd seen it caricatured in kid's cartoons, but it was her own reaction when she realised where this man lived. He must have been near Edward Callow, if not on the same road. She'd always wondered how Edward's young henchman had got his hand patched up after his altercation with Will last year. Tyler with the purple hair was how she remembered him. He'd made it out alive, though it would be many years until he regained his freedom. Had this same doctor patched up Tyler that night? Was he an off-the-books professional who freelanced for whoever would pay the highest price?

She went cold as she thought of the second connection. She'd found Edward Callow unconscious outside the Midland Hotel. He'd been rushed to a private hospital in Lancaster and made a miraculous recovery the same night. Nigel had warned her of foul play and a private doctor then. This had to be the same man; how many doctors would be serving the higher end criminal fraternity in a small town like Morecambe? This made perfect sense to her, and she was determined to check him out. If she could link the doctor to Edward Callow, she might be able to help Tiffany without coming into direct conflict with Fabian Armstrong.

'Do you know which one? Can you give me a house number?'

'Sorry, love, I can't, but he drives one of those Tesco things. You know, the battery-powered cars. My son came to meet me at the care home from school one night and he saw it. He told me it costs more than our house. Imagine that.'

'You mean Tesla? Is it a Tesla car?'

'That's the one. Tesco is where I do my shopping. Mr Madeley put a charger thing in at Briar Bank especially. I wouldn't pay all that money if the battery keeps running down. I have to charge up my lawn mower every time I use it; it's always dying on me.'

'Just in case, what colour is it? I'll bet he's not the only resident with a Tesla in the area. In my day people used to buy a Rolex watch if they wanted to show off, but these days it seems to be a Tesla. I'll bet Rolex watches keep going longer too; most of them don't even have batteries.'

'It's blue, love. It looks nice when it's parked out there. I don't have a car myself. I use the buses.'

'Just to be certain, how did you find out that's where he lives? I don't want to be knocking on the wrong door.'

'I was in the work car once with Mrs Madeley when she called in to drop an envelope off. We'd been to some fancy event telling us about modern caring techniques.'

Charlotte thanked the woman and made an attempt at getting her to share at least her first name or her phone number.

She shook her head. 'This has to be private. When I'm in Tiff's room, I talk to her a lot, and she's always struck me as a decent person. I'm no expert, but I don't think she should be in there; I'm worried about her. If you can help, I'd be grateful. Tiff needs a friend. I daren't do what you did when you sneaked in. Nobody would listen to me, anyway. I will take your phone number though, so I can call you if I remember anything else.'

Charlotte passed on her number, thanked the woman, and headed back along the promenade towards home. It was frustrating that she didn't have a name or contact details, but it had given her a new lead, at least. This man had to be the same person who'd been involved with Edward Callow.

Were all these people linked in a fraternity of wealthy, white-collar crooks in the resort? It was a world that was unfamiliar to her, yet it seemed to make sense. While the shoplifters and burglars of Morecambe helped themselves to unambitious targets, why shouldn't there be a VIP tier for rich people, carrying out altogether classier and more lucrative crimes? Was that what this was all about?

As she neared the guest house, the flash of a blue light caught her attention ahead. As she got closer, she saw it was outside her guest house. A wave of panic gripped her. Had someone been hurt? Was it Lucia?

Charlotte darted across the road, making an angry motorist sound his horn as she dodged the cars to get to the other side. She jogged up to the property to see two officers inspecting the huge bay window at the front. It had been smashed.

She rushed up the path towards the police officers.

'Hi, I'm Charlotte Grayson, the owner. What the hell happened here? I've only been gone half an hour.'

'We got an anonymous call from a mobile phone saying some guy in a hoodie was seen running away about 15 minutes ago. He's made quite a mess. Aren't you the lady who—?'

'Yes,' Charlotte answered, used to being recognised by the local constabulary. 'Did this person get a look at the man in the hoodie?'

The officers smirked, like they'd rehearsed their lines beforehand.

'I'm sorry, it's why they wear these damn hoodies. He had sunglasses on too; it could have been anybody.'

'You don't have CCTV, do you?' the other officer asked.

It was Charlotte's turn to smirk this time. Of course she didn't have CCTV. It was a sleepy Morecambe guest house, not Fort Knox. She shook her head.

'Well, I suggest you get it seen to as soon as possible,' the first officer offered. 'I can recommend a chap who'll come round to make it safe, while you wait to get it re-glazed.'

'Thanks, that would be great,' Charlotte replied. They exchanged contact numbers, and she gave the two officers access to the inside, so they could further inspect the scene. Shards of glass had landed all over the two prime-slot dining room tables, which gave residents the best views across the bay. The window was single-glazed, which surprised her. She'd never given it much thought; maybe it was a big job to fit a window like that with better glass.

She dialled the glazier, a service offered by a man called

Rich who went under the name 24/7 *Lightning Glaziers*. He'd board it up, clean up the mess and remove the dangerous glass shards, then sort out the new glass once the insurance company had approved the work.

'You'll need a crime number for your insurance,' the first officer said, obviously happy that there was nothing further they could do. 'To be honest with you, it's probably just some bored kid causing trouble. We're unlikely to catch anyone. There are no fingerprints here; he's used a stone from your flower beds, by the look of it.'

He paused, then leaned forward and looked her in the eye. 'Still, it's a funny thing to happen out of the blue. You don't know of anyone who would want to do something like this, do you? Someone who wants to send you a warning, or who might be angry with you?'

Charlotte glanced at the faces of the officers; they looked like they had zero inclination to investigate any further.

'No,' she answered with a straight face. 'I have no idea who'd want to do a thing like this.'

CHAPTER THIRTY-NINE

As Charlotte gave Rich a wave from the path in front of the guest house, she turned around to face the sight of their bay window boarded over with chipboard and a large sticker declaring that 24/7 *Lightning Glaziers* had paid a visit. It was suddenly overwhelming. She walked through the front entrance, took a turn into the kitchen, and burst into tears, despising herself for it. Somehow the lethal concoction of fear, threat, adrenaline and terror had exploded inside her and found its outlet in the only way it could. She wiped away her tears, thankful nobody was around to see her like this.

Reflecting on what had set her off, she decided an explosion was the best way to describe it; she wasn't crying because she was sorry for herself. If anything, it was anger and the recognition that yet again, powerful people, much stronger than her, were threatening her in her own home. They were trying to intimidate her, to make her back down.

It scared the wits out of her, sure, and it made her whole body shake when she thought about standing up to them.

But it was indignation and rage that drove her. She wouldn't be cowed, even though fighting back would take her into dangerous territory, putting her family at risk. What if Lucia had been at home when the stone had come through the window? These people knew where to strike to put the fear of God into you. Nigel had made it clear he was backing down. She would not, though she knew direct conflict with Fabian Armstrong was probably not a clever idea.

'Mum? What the hell happened?'

It was Lucia, carrying a bag full of text books.

'Are you OK? Why are you so upset?'

She rushed over to Charlotte and put her arm around her.

'I'm fine, Lucia, honestly. I'm sorry, I didn't want anybody to see me like this. Things just overwhelmed me for a moment, but I'm fine now.'

'Sit down, Mum, I'll make you a hot drink. You've every right to have a little cry after yesterday. It must have been terrifying.'

Charlotte nodded, grabbed some kitchen roll from the worktop and dabbed her eyes.

'The window was just the final straw. To see our lovely guest house like that – looking like we've gone bust and been boarded up by debt collectors – it just caught me off guard. I'm sorry, I hate you kids seeing me crying.'

Lucia prepared the cups for their drinks and put her arms around Charlotte again. Not so long ago she'd wondered if she'd ever be this close to her daughter again. It felt magical.

'I'm surprised you don't cry more, after what happened last year. You always say you're not strong, but you're the strongest woman I know, Mum. What you did to rescue me... I can't ever thank you enough. The risks you took to save me from Edward Callow... I can't even find the words to describe how proud and in awe of you I am.'

Charlotte burst out crying once again. This time it wasn't anger. Lucia was right, she'd focused on recovery after the incident with Edward Callow, and hadn't taken the time to work through the issues. She'd been offered counselling, but she'd rejected it. A man in Lancaster had come highly recommended, somebody called Martin Travis who was exceedingly popular with many of the women she met, most of whom had been through couples' counselling with him. The majority of them had been ready to ditch their husbands and run away with Martin, only to find out he was gay and they were barking up the wrong tree. She had a phone number tucked away somewhere. Maybe it was time to look him up. He did all types of counselling, apparently.

Charlotte held Lucia tight, making the most of the moment. Times like this had been rare since the kids left primary school; she'd learned it was important to savour them when they came.

'What happened with the window?'

For a moment, she was tempted to lie to her daughter, instinctively wanting to protect her. But Lucia was a young woman now and had matured beyond measure since leaving school. She felt more like a friend than a daughter.

'I'm in trouble again—' she began.

'Oh Mum, I don't know how you manage it. What's happened? Is it this family that went missing? Have you got caught up in something again?'

Charlotte began to explain the entire thing. As she told

Lucia about the events at Briar Bank, the parachute jump, Nigel's son, and the various altercations of the past week, she felt like she was in confession, unburdening herself. Lucia pulled up a stool and listened as she sipped her drink.

'So that's it. The stone through the window is just the latest threat. Maybe I should follow Nigel's lead and throw in the towel. I can't risk putting you in danger again.'

Lucia scrutinised her mother's face with a look of understanding well beyond her years.

'When I was abducted last year, what went through your head, Mum?'

'That I would do whatever it took to help you,' Charlotte replied, without missing a beat.

'Why was that your instinct? Why didn't you just go to the police?'

Charlotte thought about it for a moment.

'Because there was no way on earth I was going to leave your welfare in the hands of somebody else. I couldn't have sat on my hands while the police were searching for you. I had to do something.'

'You have to accept that's who you are, Mum. Dad's a different kind of person; he'd rather bury his head in the sand until he's forced to do something. I saw a fierce rage in your eyes when you were coming to rescue me at Heysham Port. I took one look at you and I knew we'd get out, because you wouldn't let me die. And you're doing exactly the same thing for Tiffany Irwin now, because she has nobody else looking out for her.'

Charlotte considered what Lucia had just said. She was right about not looking away when someone was being bullied. If it took her to the eye of the storm, so be it. She simply could not walk away.

'Whatever you're reading in those books of yours is doing you the world of good,' she said, standing up.

'Where are you going, Mum?'

'You're right, Lucia, I can't turn away. I would hate myself if I abandoned Tiffany Irwin to her fate. And I think Kate Summers needs my help too. She's not telling me everything; she was caught up in something terrible in the past, but she can't talk about it for some reason. They both need my help.'

'I'm here for you if you need me,' Lucia said, squeezing Charlotte's arm.

'I know, but I'd rather keep you out of it—'

'Mum! I'm an adult now. I mean it. Whatever it is, just shout.'

'Thanks, I appreciate it. Don't mention this to your dad, will you? As you said, he has a different approach to these things. He still thinks I'm an invalid; he's indulging my work on the newspaper. Besides, he has his own worries at the moment.'

'It's fine, Mum, I'll keep it quiet. But my phone is on, so call me whenever you need me. I can't promise to come quickly, as I haven't got my driving licence yet. But I will come, eventually!'

Charlotte smiled and kissed Lucia on the forehead.

'The funny thing is, I think what we went through at Heysham Port was the best thing that could have happened to us. I know it was terrifying. But it brought us together again when we were moving apart. That's one thing I'll always be grateful for.'

'Me too,' Lucia said. Her eyes were welling up now.

Charlotte checked for her phone.

'Are you going back to the newspaper office?' Lucia asked.

Charlotte smiled at her, her resilience back again with a vengeance.

'No. There are two women who need my help. And thanks to my daughter's pep talk, they're getting it.'

CHAPTER FORTY

Charlotte was late for her lunch with Will; it would be more of an afternoon tea at the rate things were going. She wanted to speak to him first, to smooth things over, but she also wanted him to understand why she was doing this. If there was time on the way back, she would explore where this mystery doctor lived, the one who the support worker from Briar Bank had mentioned. She started hatching a crazy plan to turn up unannounced, pretending she'd mixed up his address with another, to see what kind of man she was dealing with. She was also keen to check him out online. He was bound to have a digital trail in his line of work.

She ran up the stairs three at a time to find the car keys. That wasted another five minutes; they weren't where they were supposed to be. She checked in on Lucia who was making herself a bite to eat in the kitchen, reminded her where she was going, and headed down to the car. It took a couple of turns for the engine to fire. She'd noticed that sluggishness of late and had hoped the longer run out to the airfield would charge the battery, but it didn't appear to have worked. A big repair bill was the last thing she needed right now.

Charlotte was distracted on her drive to Lancaster, but glad that the long snake of traffic through the city centre was running well. A dark car seemed to be following her out of the resort, but she dismissed it as paranoia once she reached Lancaster and the traffic mingled in the two lanes running through the centre. She took a shortcut along some back streets, and by the time she'd found The Lounge on campus, she was only twenty minutes late. Not bad, considering the day she'd had. The more immediate task was finding a parking place on the campus where she wouldn't be clamped.

She still remembered the core layout of the university campus, which was set around Alexandra Square. It had grown like crazy since she and Will had been students, but once she oriented herself, it was as familiar as when they were eighteen years old and newly in love.

'This wasn't here when you were a student, was it?' she asked as she kissed Will and sat at the table he'd secured for them.

'No, it wasn't as posh as this back in our day. They do a nice lunch here; it's all very civilised.'

They checked the menus and placed their orders while Charlotte brought Will up to speed on the developments of the day. He'd been there for some time and had bought himself a drink while he was waiting. She couldn't decide whether to tell him about the broken window first or not. She opted for mentioning it later.

'So, I wanted to clear the air with you. I chatted to Lucia earlier, and she helped me to clarify my thinking.'

'This sounds serious,' Will said, in an obvious attempt to keep things cordial and light.

'Not really. But I want to ask you a question. I already know what your answer will be, by the way.'

'That sounds worrying. Go on, ask away.'

The food arrived, served by a fresh-faced student with a glowing smile on her face.

'It's much better these days,' Will commented. 'Students have lots of opportunities to earn extra cash when they're not studying. I don't remember all these jobs being available when I was here. Go on, what were you saying?'

'OK, here goes. If you'd been working late on campus, you were walking along the south spine in the dark and you heard a scream, what would you do?'

Will finished his first bite of pizza before answering.

'I'd investigate and do what I could to help, of course.'

'Exactly. And that's how I feel about Tiffany Irwin and Kate Summers. Only they can't scream out loud. Theirs are silent screams. But they need my help, I'm sure of it. And I want to give it.'

Will shuffled in his seat and put his knife and fork down on his plate.

'The difference is, Charlotte, if I go to investigate a scream on campus, the worst it would be is a student who I could trace through university records. It won't be some psycho who threatens to crash me to the ground during a tandem parachute jump.'

Charlotte tried to keep her face straight, though inside she was cursing her opening gambit. Trust Will to fight with logic. He had a point, but that didn't matter; the principle still applied.

'I understand your concerns. Nigel has said the same thing. I get why you're worried about me, and I know how important it is to keep this a secret from the family. You have my word that I won't provoke Fabian Armstrong any more, but I intend to keep on digging. And if I do find something, I'll speak to DCI Summers and tell the police. Deal?'

Will seemed to be more interested in getting on with his pizza. His face was weary, as if he was all talked out on the subject.

'OK, just go steady. So long as you don't handle things on your own, and you must promise to tell the police if you find anything... Are you listening to me? You're the one who started this conversation—'

Charlotte's attention was drawn to a student sitting on the other side of the room, alone, eating a sandwich and idly playing with her phone.

'I recognise that woman over there,' she said. 'What a coincidence. I wouldn't have looked twice if it hadn't been for the piercing through the eyebrow. She's the woman you were talking about, isn't she? Your stalker. How bizarre that I should see—'

Will leapt up from his chair as if he'd just been stung by a wasp, sending his cutlery flying onto the floor. He turned round fast, then slumped down angrily in his seat.

'Yes, that's Hollie Wickes,' he said, in a whisper that couldn't contain his fury. 'I warned you about this. I said to look out for her.'

'Steady on, Will. She was as nice as pie when we chatted. She just passed Daisy and me on our parkrun and exchanged a few pleasantries. It was fine; she didn't say anything that bothered me.'

'That's just it,' he fumed. 'That's how this works. She gets under your skin, then you realise there's something going on. It's unnerving, Charlotte, and it's dangerous for me. If she makes an allegation, who do you think they'll believe?'

246 PAUL J. TEAGUE

'She's entitled to get some lunch, Will. She's also entitled to go on a parkrun on Morecambe Promenade—'

'Yes, but it's funny that she should talk to you.'

'She might have spoken to all sorts of people. It's how
parkrun works; you go for a run, and you chat to people you
don't know.'

Will retrieved his cutlery from the floor and placed it
next to his plate.

'I don't feel like eating any more,' he said. 'There's a
knot in my stomach. You might think it's a laugh, but I'm
worried about this.'

Charlotte was about to tell Will he was being paranoid,
but then she thought back to her own uneasiness when
she'd suspected she was being followed in a car through the
city. Someone had just thrown a stone through their
window too. She had every reason to be a little paranoid.
But Will hadn't been chased by Vinnie Mace, nor directly
threatened by him. He didn't even know about the window
yet; she'd save that for later, bearing in mind how this was
playing out.

'You've told your department head about it, so just
follow her advice and make sure there's always somebody
around when you're speaking to her. She's a student and
you've got to live alongside her. It's perfectly reasonable for
her to eat lunch here.'

How stupid of him to make such a fuss. It was way out
of proportion to the situation. At least she couldn't harm
him physically; even Will could defend himself in a fight.

Charlotte continued eating her food. Will could go
hungry, if that was how he wanted to play it. Occasionally
she glanced at Hollie. She seemed to be an ordinary
student. Will had said she was slightly older, but Charlotte
wouldn't have known. She was attractive, had gone easy on

the makeup and was dressed simply, in jeans and a T-shirt. She only stood out because of the eyebrow piercing.

Then it hit her. Hollie was a younger version of herself: same hair colour, same dress sense, and the same physical build she'd had at that age. A surge of heat burned her forehead as another scenario played out in her mind. Had Will encouraged this? Could it be the early stages of an affair which he was trying to snuff out before it grew big enough to bite him?

She dismissed the thought from her head. Sure, things had been difficult in the past year, but any friction was due to Will being over-protective. He cared too much about her to be treading the well-worn path of a mid-life affair with a younger version of his wife.

Charlotte couldn't finish her own food, so she asked a passing waitress for the bill.

'I'll get this,' Will said. 'I went to the cash machine on campus this morning, so I'm flush for cash.'

'Good job,' she replied, 'I only have a pocket full of loose change on me.'

The bill arrived and the waitress placed it on the table in front of Will. He thrust his hand into his back trouser pocket and pulled out two ten-pound notes, a receipt and a computer printout of an image.

While Will sorted out the cash for the bill, Charlotte leaned over to check out the photograph. What an odd thing to have in his pocket. She turned it over, half expecting to see Will's stern passport photo face staring up at her. Instead she got an image of Hollie Wickes, pouting at the camera, her V-necked T-shirt worn suggestively low.

CHAPTER FORTY-ONE

Charlotte couldn't shake off her indignation at Will's lame protests. She'd never in all their years of marriage suspected him of cheating, but now the seeds of doubt were well and truly sown, and they'd begun to germinate. He was quick to declare his innocence, expressing disbelief that the photographs could ever have made it into his pocket. Charlotte had come seeking peace, but all she'd got was the promise of another battle.

She brushed it off; it would have to wait until later. She had no intention of conducting a forensic analysis in the middle of a campus restaurant. She'd done some undignified things in her time, but washing her dirty laundry in public wasn't going to be one of them. They parted with a terse kiss and a promise to sit down and talk it over when they were both back at home that evening. He'd see the broken window then, too. She was dreading it already.

As Charlotte was making her way back to Alexandra Square to visit the library, she spotted Hollie Wickes walking ahead with a group of students. She paused momentarily and considered following them. Her time was short; she needed to get to Morecambe Police Station to give them a formal statement about Sunday's events at the air field, and she was also keen to get a crime number for the broken window. She'd be cutting it fine, but this was too good an opportunity to miss. It was time to turn the tables on this potential stalker and do some lurking in the shadows.

Charlotte looked down, trying not to draw attention to herself, and followed the small group at a safe distance. Alexandra Square was always bustling, and the constant queue outside the bakery provided some temporary cover. They were heading across the square towards the Bowland accommodation. She had a rough recollection of the basic layout from the eighties when Will had been a student there, though she'd never mastered the geography of the place. Back then she'd arrive on the bus at the underpass drop-off. Occasionally they'd save money by using the hitching point, but she'd always had Will as her guide back then.

The small group dispersed, and Hollie darted into a doorway. Charlotte cursed as she saw her taking out a key card. When she'd been a student, the only key you needed was the one for your room; these days everything was like Fort Knox. She scanned for security cameras, not even sure if universities had them. Surely not; students would be in and out of each other's rooms all the time. There must be some privacy policy to prevent it.

Two girls had emerged from a side path and were heading towards the same doorway as Hollie. She watched Hollie go inside, then darted up to the girls as they took out their key cards.

'Hi, I was trying to catch up with that girl who just went

in. She dropped her cash card, and I want to return it to her. Would you let me in please?'

They looked at her, then waved her through. She was becoming more like Nigel every day, using his tricks to get through security doors and deploying white lies to achieve what she wanted.

Charlotte just caught a fire door closing to her left as she entered the hallway. She darted at it, taking a chance that Hollie had gone that way. The corridor was long, with doors on either side. Many of them had been blinged up with the names of the occupants announced in gaudy graphics. She passed one with a poster of a bare-chested Brad Pitt stuck on it. Now that was a door decoration she could get behind. Hollie was ahead of her.

She held herself back, avoiding the automatic sensor lights which luckily were off. It looked like a cleaner was on the floor, judging by the presence of a trolley packed with cleaning fluids, utensils, cellophane wrapped sheets, and a big bag of dirty bed linen dangling from the handle.

Hollie stopped by a door and waved her key card against it. Charlotte ducked behind the trolley as Hollie walked into her room, came straight out again, then walked a little further along the corridor and knocked loudly at somebody else's door. The rooms at the end of the hallway appeared to be set into a recess, because Hollie was no longer visible. Charlotte could hear voices; it sounded like she'd popped over to see a friend. It was a golden opportunity. She jogged along the corridor, setting off the next set of automatic lights, and walked into Hollie's room. She gasped as she realised what she'd just done; if she got caught, she'd have some explaining to do.

The voices of Hollie and her friend were carrying along the corridor, so she decided to push ahead. She wanted to find out what she was dealing with. Was Hollie just an infatuated student, or was there more to it? She scanned the room. The bed was unmade; the cleaner hadn't got this far yet.

For a student's room, it was remarkably bare, with no signs of personalisation such as posters, stickers or pot plants. Hollie had one pin board by her desk, but all it contained was a few receipts, a timetable, some fast food delivery leaflets, and a reading list. On her desk was a blue cardboard folder, with her purse and phone on top of it. If she wasn't breaking into Hollie's room, she'd be tempted to give her a lecture on basic home security.

She could hear them chatting away, so she must still have time. Charlotte pushed the purse and phone to the side and picked up the folder, opened it and checked the contents. There was a tourist map of Morecambe inside and her stomach spasmed as she saw that the small advert for their own guest house was circled in blue ink.

As the familiar sensation of panic rose in her chest, Charlotte hastily put the folder back on the table, placing the purse on top. As she did so, she touched the phone screen, activating it. Hollie must have just been using it, and it hadn't returned to sleep mode. Charlotte felt drips of sweat running down her forehead. She'd never invaded someone's privacy like this before. Activating the camera app, she gasped when she saw the last images taken.

They were of she and Will, eating their meal in the campus restaurant. Hollie had spotted them and had taken photos. She scrolled back through the images, her legs almost giving way when she saw pictures of Will in his lecture earlier in the day. This girl was obsessed, or else they were having an affair. Perhaps it was both.

The voices were still in full flow along the corridor

when something made Charlotte notice that the drawer on Hollie's bedside table was partially open. She put the phone down and opened it up. Stuffed inside were photocopies and scans of newspaper clippings. She'd got copies of the reports into the aftermath of Edward Callow's death, Bruce Craven's body being dug up, the lot. There were also cuttings Charlotte had never seen, of Tiffany and David Irwin at some social functions, clippings from the year 2000 after the disappearance of her family and also printouts of the coverage Nigel had written on the newspaper website, outlining Callie's sudden reappearance.

She froze with fear, sensing an immediate threat. Was this a weird obsession with victims of crimes, or something much more sinister? She didn't get any more time to wonder about it. The fire alarm sounded and doors started to open all along the corridor as the students began an evacuation.

CHAPTER FORTY-TWO

In her panic, Charlotte picked up Hollie's phone and tucked it in her back pocket. Voices in the corridor were getting closer; she had to hide, but there was nowhere to conceal herself. She ducked in behind the open door of Hollie's room, just in the nick of time, as Hollie rushed in to grab some things.

'Bloody fire alarms,' Hollie cursed. 'It'll be those idiots on floor two burning toast under the grills again.'

Charlotte peered around the door as Hollie reached for the things she'd left on her desk. Only then did she realise she'd picked up Hollie's phone, the very thing the student had come back to retrieve.

'Did I leave my phone in your room, Laura?' she asked, picking up her purse and making for the door.

'I don't know,' came a voice from the hallway, 'but we'd better get moving; we're the last out on this floor. It'll be safe, wherever it is.'

The door slammed shut and Charlotte counted to ten, estimating how long it would take them to reach the end of the corridor. She intended to leave the phone on the desk;

she was no thief. But she had an opportunity to clear up her concerns about Will once and for all. This woman could harm her husband's career. She might even wreck their marriage.

The phone was unlocked, so she could search through the photos, text messages and call logs to see if Will was telling the truth. She hated herself for doubting him, but she had to be sure. She'd find a bench somewhere, make some checks without invading Hollie's privacy too much, then hand it in at the library as a lost and found item.

Charlotte moved to the door, opened it cautiously, peered out and stepped into the empty corridor. A student fire warden admonished her when she emerged into the hallway.

'You're almost the last one out; what were you doing? We need to clear the building faster.'

Charlotte's hackles rose, but despite her irritation at the professional clipboard holder, she needed to avoid drawing attention to herself.

'Sorry, I had my noise cancelling headphones on. It won't happen again.'

Head down, she weaved a course among the students who were gathering at the assembly point and made her way towards Alexandra Square. The central, paved area was distinctive, bordered on one side by a row of steps. She sat down and took out Hollie's phone, with every intention of flicking through it then handing it over as lost.

But before she could make a start, her own phone erupted in a frenzy of calls and messages from Nigel.

'Hi Charlotte. Sorry to interrupt your shorthand—'

Charlotte snorted at his remark, despite her state of nervousness. She'd been playing with fire going into Hollie's room.

'There's been a breakthrough with Callie Irwin. She's awake and has been speaking to the police. I got a tip-off, so I'm heading over to the infirmary now. DI Comfort is giving a press briefing. We can't report it yet until we hear it officially, but my source has confirmed it is Callie Irwin. Only it seems she's been living with a different name for years—'

'My God, this just gets worse. It sounds like she was raised by somebody else, or even trafficked or sold. This could be even more dreadful than we thought—'

'It's too early to say. Please don't repeat any of this until they confirm the facts at the briefing. Shall I pick you up and take you to the infirmary?'

'I'm in Lancaster now.'

'I thought you were—'

'My plans changed. It's a long story. I've got the car, so I'll meet you there.'

'There's one other thing, Charlotte, but you must swear to keep this to yourself. This is a police investigation now. You'd be interfering with the course of justice if you shared this information with anybody. Believe me, I'm serious: if you thought the complaint from Quinton Madeley was a problem, that's nothing compared to the police tackling Teddy about interference in an investigation. I won't be able to shield you from that.'

'I'm listening,' Charlotte replied, desperate to hear what he had to say. She had an inkling before he told her.

'Because of that photograph that was left by Callie's bedside, the investigations team think DCI Summers knew what happened to them all those years back. They want to question her. And guess who's just gone AWOL?'

'You're kidding?'

'No, I trust my source. They won't confirm it at the

press briefing, as it's a police matter, but DCI Summers is on the Morecambe Police most wanted list.'

Charlotte's phone vibrated with a text notification. She didn't recognise the number; it was probably some sales-related message.

'Where does this leave Kate? Is she in trouble? She has to be, if Callie has implicated her.'

'She's not helping matters by going to ground. They need to speak to her, but she's disappeared. That won't play well; it looks like she's got something to hide. She of all people will know that.'

'I can't believe Kate will have done anything wrong—'

'We'll talk about it at the infirmary, Charlotte. I'll see you there.'

Nigel ended the call. Charlotte stood up and started walking towards her car. As she walked, she couldn't resist opening the text message. It wasn't what she was expecting. She stopped dead in the middle of Alexandra Square as she read it.

Charlotte, it's Kate. I've got to use a different phone; they're looking for me. Meet me at Sunderland Point ASAP. I have to tell you something now, in case they find me. I'm in danger. I'll be here until 4 pm.

CHAPTER FORTY-THREE

Charlotte didn't bother contacting Nigel, and she forgot all about returning Hollie's phone. Having promised to help Kate Summers, this was the time for her to deliver. She checked her phone and realised she'd have to break the speed limit to get there in time.

Why Sunderland Point? Of course, it was remote. Perhaps she was safer there; they wouldn't be able to track a mobile signal. But she'd been cautious enough to use another phone to make contact. Could it be connected to Brett? That made more sense, given the circumstances. Charlotte had to make the meeting and hear whatever Kate had to tell her.

She ran between the university buildings to get back to her car. There was no time to tell Nigel where she was heading. He'd pick up the new information about Callie, and they could compare notes later. She started the car, trying to remember the route and cursing out loud as she realised she'd have to navigate the city's one-way system just as the schools were finishing for the day. It was at least a forty minute drive at this time of the day and she had to do it in twenty-five. She revved up the car and set off around the road which encircled the campus.

Charlotte was already agitated by the time she reached the intersection with the main route into the city, but after being held up by a stalled car and a painfully slow crawl past the infirmary, her patience had run out. She fought with her conscience over whether to attend the briefing. As a group of secondary school children made their way over the crossing in front of her, she fumbled in her pocket to send Nigel a text. She stopped immediately as she noticed a police car draw up on her right-hand side; a fine for using her phone was all she needed.

Once the lights changed, she took a shortcut, breaking the speed limit but staying alert for youngsters and pedestrians.

DCI Summers was in danger. Callie Irwin was out of her coma and speaking to police. Yet Charlotte knew enough about this screwed-up situation to realise the danger didn't come from the police; it came from Fabian Armstrong, and his tentacles had reached out and drawn her in. Nigel and Will had warned her not to get involved, yet how could she avoid it?

After wending her way through the city, at last she turned onto Morecambe Road and made for Sunderland Point. She checked her mirrors for police cars and spotted it again, the same car she'd thought was following her on her way to meet Will for lunch. Was it the same? She couldn't be certain. It was a common make of car, in navy blue. No, she was being ridiculous; it would take an expert to track her through the traffic of Lancaster on the route she'd just taken.

She braked hard as she suddenly gained on the vehicle ahead, nearly bumping it from behind. It was an elderly driver crawling along, and she'd misjudged her distance. That was a near miss.

Charlotte drove through Overton almost in a trance, obsessing over what Kate might tell her. She checked the clock. Three minutes late.

The land to the side changed to salt marsh as she approached the causeway. The light was fading, the grey skies overhead playing as much of a part as the time of day. High tide couldn't be far off.

She hesitated, full of dread at attempting the crossing on her own. The tide was already lapping the mud-covered causeway. Directly ahead, a road sign warned of fast tides, hidden channels, and quicksand. Recalling how she'd over-reacted when Nigel had stalled the car here, she knew there was still time. She'd leave when the water just covered the track, regardless of whether she'd seen Kate Summers or not.

Another warning sign came into view, one with a photo-graph, showing the causeway covered in water. *Tidal flow can carry a vehicle off the road,* it warned. Kate Summers knew what she was doing; she wouldn't risk her life. Besides, if the worst came to the worst, she'd find Jed. He would give her shelter for the night. She could always spend the night in the pillbox or the car if needed, though she shuddered at the thought of it.

Charlotte looked at the sloshing water ahead and drove on regardless. She'd learnt the lessons of the previous week: drive slowly, don't allow the water to soak the engine, and take your time. At last she reached the car park. There was one other car, which she didn't recognise. Was it Kate's?

She looked around but saw no signs of life. The car had tinted glass, making it impossible to see if anyone was inside. Mindful of the tide, she opened her car door, glancing at her phone. As she got out, Hollie's phone dropped from her pocket onto the ground. She swore under her breath as she picked it up; that was another mess she'd have to sort out. She'd get Will to drop it at lost property on campus when he went into work tomorrow.

Charlotte reached into the car, pulled out an old supermarket bag and put Hollie's phone in it. Leaning over the gear stick, she placed it in the glove compartment, then backed out of the car. She made sure her own phone was secure in her pocket.

There was a sudden movement at her side and a blow to her head. Charlotte hit the ground hard with a groan. The last thing she remembered before blacking out was that she still hadn't been to the police station to give her statement about the parachute jump on Sunday.

CHAPTER FORTY-FOUR

The first thing Charlotte noticed was the taste of water in her mouth, muddy and gritty, its saltiness making her want to throw up. Her hands and legs were tied, but she was sitting up, the seat belt tight across her chest, unable to see anything because of the sack over her head. The hessian was heavy with water, dripping onto her face. She panicked, terrified at not being able to see, as her head throbbed with a constant pounding, oppressive and over-whelming.

Despite her fear, there was a still some level of calmness in her as she worked out what had happened. Somebody had attacked her and they were making sure she would drown. It was difficult to tell how dark it was outside, with no light coming through the sack. She could sense from the sound of water sloshing nearby that the doors of the car were wide open. The tide was up to her ankles, meaning the causeway would be under water by now. Somebody must have moved the car. She felt with her feet for pedals, but there were none. She must have been moved to the passenger side.

Charlotte wriggled her hands and twisted her feet, but it was no good; they were too tightly bound. Shaking her head didn't work either; the saturated sack was too heavy to shake off. Despite the seat belt holding her down, she struggled again, panic rising at the realisation that she was trapped. She'd been in a situation like this before, on the stone jetty in Morecambe when she had tried to rescue Olli. But on that occasion, she'd alerted the RNLI beforehand, so they'd known to look for her. Her arms and legs had been free too. Even though Olli was tied up, at least she'd been able to move. The waves had been more powerful then, splashing angrily all around them, pulling them under the water, working hard to overcome them.

This was different; the water was slower and stealthier, but every bit as powerful. It was gently rocking the car, lulling her into a slow death. The water would rise, the sack would become heavier, the water would flow around her as it filled up the car, and she wouldn't be able to do anything but sit there. She didn't even know where she was on the causeway, but it was bound to be the halfway point, where she'd be damned whichever way she tried to escape, even if it were possible.

The water was at waist level now, making her shiver with the cold. Was it worth screaming? Anybody with any sense would have crossed the causeway well before the tide came in, so nobody would be out there now. Even Jed, who knew these waters, would have left his boat, heading back to his home as soon as the water started to creep in. That's what anybody with a jot of common sense did; people who were not like her.

Who knew where she was? Nobody. She realised how stupid she'd been. Kate Summers couldn't have sent that text. It was a hoax, a trap set to lure her out there. She was stupid; she'd fallen for it hook, line and sinker. And now she would pay the penalty for her stupidity, leaving Olli and Lucia without a mother. After everything they'd been through, this was how it was going to end, slowly drowning as the water rose, with plenty of time to think about how stupid, careless and impetuous she'd been, before spluttering through her last breath.

Nigel would miss her. He might raise the alarm, perhaps wondering where she'd got to after leaving the university campus. He'd be too late though. They probably wouldn't start a serious search until morning. By then, someone would have found her body, one of the Sunderland Point residents, no doubt, or an early morning bird watcher crossing the causeway at the crack of dawn. Would the car even be there in the morning? Perhaps the tide would carry it away; she had no idea how these things worked.

Whichever way she looked at it, there was no way out. She struggled with her ties once again, but she couldn't work her way out of them. The sack wasn't going anywhere either. There was nothing she could do. Her head felt like a thunderstorm was crashing inside it, but as the water began to soak her top, a calm came over her as she resigned herself to her fate. This was it; she was on her own, with no cavalry coming over the hill to rescue her. She thought of Olli and Lucia as the pain in her head overwhelmed her once again and she slipped out of consciousness amid the sound of lapping water.

CHAPTER FORTY-FIVE

Charlotte blinked as a ferocious light shone through the sack. There was the distinctive growl of a diesel engine, then a movement to her side and a voice... no, two voices. They were urgent and frantic, vaguely familiar, but she couldn't place them. She faded out again.

It was dark when she came round. The sack had been removed, and she could hear hushed, urgent conversations to her side.

'Go, just go. You know where to hide. The moment the tide is out, take your car and disappear. She's fine.'

A female voice. Kate Summers. Kate was here. Why couldn't she open her eyes? It was as if they were glued shut. Still her head pounded, dominating everything, dragging her into unconsciousness. As she drifted away again, she realised her hands and legs were now free. She was no longer in the car.

Charlotte awoke to the twittering of the dawn chorus and the welcome sensation of being dry, lying in a bed with cool sheets. She forced her eyes open. This wasn't a hospital; it was a bedroom, decorated in an old-fashioned style.

She turned her head to the side and glanced around at the dark, heavy wooden furniture and the seventies-style curtains. Then she heard steps coming up the stairs.

Charlotte closed her eyes, playing dead, unable to tell if a friend or foe had taken her. The door opened, creaking on its hinges, and the floorboards groaned under heavy footsteps.

'I brought you tea, Charlotte.'

She recognised the voice immediately as Jed's. That made sense. It was his type of house, unmoved by the passage of time, just like the man himself. She pulled herself up in bed, forcing her eyes open once again. The cold had made her stiff. Her hand moved to the back of her head, and she winced as it touched a large bump where she'd been struck.

'How did you get me away?' she asked.

'Here. Have a warm drink. The sea is a cruel master; you were freezing when we found you last night.'

Charlotte took the cup, its warmth spreading through her hands.

'How did you find me?' she asked again.

'You have Brett Allan's sister to thank for saving your life. She left her car at the other end of the causeway to wade through the water. I'm not sure how you know her, but there was no way she was leaving you out there last night. She could have died wading out to you like that.'

So, Kate was there. Had she been following her? Perhaps she hadn't been imagining things.

'Why did you get involved? How did you get me out of there?'

'I had the tractor out to move a boat for a friend, out Heysham way. I'd cut it a bit fine, but I know these waters, and a tractor can stay in the water a lot longer than a car can. Anyway, I almost ran that woman down. It scared the life out of me, seeing her in the water. We found you in the car and got you to safety. You'd have been dead in half an hour with your head slumped like that.'

'Where is Kate now? Can I speak to her?'

'She's gone. All she would say was that she was in terrible danger, but she wouldn't let me phone the police. I couldn't have done it anyway, not with the atrocious signal out here. Once she knew you were OK, she left as soon as the tide was low enough.'

Charlotte slumped back on the pillow, to get some relief against the pain in her head. She could easily lie there for a day while the soreness melted away.

'Oh God, Jed, what have we done? What have we got ourselves into?'

'I tried to tell you. The police should have taken notice of me when I was a kid. They ignored me then, and now there's unfinished business. Things have a habit of playing out, however long it takes.'

A mobile phone rang. Charlotte raised her head from the pillow.

'Is that yours? I thought you couldn't get a signal?'

'No; mine's downstairs on the kitchen table. I found another phone in your pocket. It's a write-off. I left it near the Aga to dry, but the sea water got it, I think.'

Charlotte tried to pull herself up in the bed, but she was too stiff. Sensing her discomfort, Jed moved across the room and passed her the bag which contained Holly Wickes' phone. She took it out; the bag was still damp and the phone case was cold, but it had escaped the worst of the water. The home screen lit up, the battery deadly low but hanging on. It was an incoming phone call rather than a text, and a persistent one at that. The caller identification flashed across the screen of Hollie's device, announcing the identity of her early morning caller. There was no surname, just a first name. *Callie?* it read. Callie Irwin was phoning Hollie Wickes.

**The story continues in Fall From Grace,
available now as an e-book or paperback.**

AUTHOR NOTES

It's so good to be back with my Morecambe Bay characters once again; I've missed them. Charlotte has had barely enough time to recover from her last adventure, and here she is again, right in the heart of the action.

This is a story I have wanted to write for some time. In my previous career as a BBC radio reporter, I was assigned to a special project called The Search whilst working for BBC Radio Humberside. The campaign entailed speaking to the relatives and partners of people who'd gone missing, in the hope the BBC's network of local radio stations could help to locate them. My task was to speak to the sister of a young man in his early twenties who'd gone missing in the Liverpool Docks area, if my memory serves me correctly.

His sister was younger than him, perhaps eighteen years old, and she was both articulate and passionate about his story. I'd turned up to the job expecting it to be a run-of-the-mill interview, but it is an experience which has stayed with me for many years now.

The family had kept his bedroom untouched, convinced he was still alive. He'd last been seen walking on his own in a short sequence of CCTV footage. There was no evidence of foul play; the police thought he'd slipped into the water and his body had been washed away from the shoreline.

Speaking to this young woman was an emotional experience. I realised it must be impossible to get on with your life when you don't know if a loved one is alive or dead.

I was astounded to discover that 180,000 people go missing in the UK each year: that's one every 90 seconds. I'm shocked by those numbers, and every photograph that appears on the missingpeople.org.uk website is a terrible story of sadness, loss, uncertainty and tragedy.

It's actually very hard to disappear. Your mobile phone can be traced, there's CCTV footage everywhere, and your bank card is registered every time you use it. So, how come that many people avoid being found? You only have to watch the TV series *Hunted* to understand that going missing takes some doing these days.

I wanted to reflect all of that in this trilogy. These stories are about the people who are left behind when someone disappears, but we'll also discover what makes people decide to leave in the first place.

I have used some new settings in these stories. Feedback from readers tells me just how important location is in my psychological thrillers. I receive so many emails and social media messages from readers who live in the Morecambe Bay area and love reading about the locations, or from people who used to visit the area and have fond memories of it, often from childhood.

I used to teach at a primary school just along the road from Morecambe Police Station, so I passed it every day for a couple of years on my way to work. Charlotte walks in on a school assembly in the adjoining church. That's based on real life; we used to have an assembly in there once a week.

Sunderland Point is worth a visit too. It really is as remote as I portray in the book, and subject to the tides, but it's a remarkable area steeped in history. Just make sure you take notice of the warning signs that are placed there for your safety.

When Nigel drives the car too fast through a puddle and soaks the engine, that scene is based on my own, recent experience. Fortunately, when it happened to me, I was on a narrow country lane, not on a causeway with a salt marsh at either side of me.

I thought I was stuck for the next hour or so while the engine dried off, but I did exactly what Charlotte does, and although it spluttered at first, the car finally got going.

Wind turbines feature prominently in these books too, less so in book one but increasingly so in books two and three of this trilogy. Believe me, by the time you've finished reading this series, you'll never look at a wind turbine the same way again.

So many elements of the stories in these books are based upon personal experience and observation.

I was a frequent visitor to Lancaster University in the '80s; it was where I started my radio career, working at the student radio station, URB (University Radio Bailrigg).

I know the spines of the university well, having spent time in the library there. As recently as two years ago, I met up with an old friend for lunch in the restaurant where the mysterious photographs of Hollie Wickes appear in Will's back pocket.

The Bay View Weekly is modelled loosely on the local newspaper, The Visitor, though it has more in common with the newspaper I used to buy and read in the nineties than what you'd read in the present day.

It's also worth pointing out that the remark about Charlotte dressing practically for the job, rather than in office attire, is based on my own first-day experience as a radio journalist.

It was the start of a week's work experience with a wonderful BBC reporter called Martin Lewes, whilst at the University of Central Lancashire.

I turned up in a suit and tie wearing my posh black shoes and ended up reporting on a news story about an overgrown footpath somewhere in the Lake District. Naturally, I got covered in mud; after that, I followed Martin's lead and dressed more practically.

As a radio reporter, you never know where you'll end up during the average day.

You may be reporting on a court case, you could be speaking to the Deputy Prime Minister, or you might find yourself shearing sheep or milking cows in a muddy barn.

And yes, I did all of those things and more as a reporter.

Martin Lewes inspired and encouraged me in journalism as much as Nigel Davies supports Charlotte. We need people like that in the world, so thank you Martin. You were the first inspirational port of call in a wonderful radio career which spanned almost two decades.

I must mention the Half Moon Bay Café, which my wife and I discovered while checking out Heysham Port for Truth Be Told.

We visited the area for a day and stumbled across this wonderful café nestled at one end of the bay of the same name.

A dog was lying down in front of the wood burner, and they served the sort of food you'd expect. We had a wonderful time, and I just had to feature this location in the book.

Finally, if you've read the Don't Tell Meg trilogy, which is set in and around Lancaster, Morecambe, Heysham and Blackpool, you may have spotted a familiar name or two.

Pete Bailey, DCI Summers, Steven Terry and Martin Travis all pop up in this story, but play different parts in the Don't Tell Meg series of stories.

As you can tell, I'm not letting Charlotte and her family off the hook in this second trilogy.

Things are about to go from bad to worse, and she has a lot more to deal with before this story concludes in Bound by Blood.

All the loose ends will be tied up in that story, and I promise I will try to give Charlotte the opportunity to get her breath back.

If you're not signed up to my author emails already, you can do so at https://paulteague.net/thrillers.

That's the best way to find out about new releases and special offers, so if you enjoy these stories, I recommend that you register.

In the meantime, get ready to settle down with Fall from Grace and prepare to see DCI Kate Summers as you've never seen her before.

Paul Teague

FREE GIFT

Are you enjoying the second Morecambe Bay Trilogy?
You can now access an exclusive gift showing you many of
the locations used in the book, with many amazing
photographs of Sunderland Point.

Grab your FREE copy of Charlotte's Sunderland Point
Scrapbook ...

This downloadable scrapbook will show you all the key
locations used in the second trilogy.
You'll get to see what Sunderland Point looks like as well as
several other key locations, such as Happy Mount Park,
Hest Bank, Lancaster University and the stone graves at
Heysham.

**To grab your copy head for
https://paulteague.net/SB2 on your PC.**

ALSO BY PAUL J. TEAGUE

Morecambe Bay Trilogy 1

Book 1 - Left For Dead

Book 2 - Circle of Lies

Book 3 - Truth Be Told

Morecambe Bay Trilogy 2

Book 4 - Trust Me Once

Book 5 - Fall From Grace

Book 6 - Bound By Blood

Morecambe Bay Trilogy 3

Book 7 - First To Die

Book 8 - Nothing To Lose

Book 9 - Last To Tell

Note: The Morecambe Bay trilogies are best read in the order shown above.

Don't Tell Meg Trilogy

Features DCI Kate Summers and Steven Terry.

Book 1 - Don't Tell Meg

Book 2 - The Murder Place

Book 3 - The Forgotten Children

Standalone Thrillers

Dead of Night

One Last Chance

No More Secrets

So Many Lies

Two Years After

Friends Who Lie

Now You See Her

ABOUT THE AUTHOR

Hi, I'm Paul Teague, the author of the Morecambe Bay series and the Don't Tell Meg trilogy, as well as several other standalone psychological thrillers such as One Last Chance, Dead of Night and No More Secrets.

I'm a former broadcaster and journalist with the BBC, but I have also worked as a primary school teacher, a disc jockey, a shopkeeper, a waiter and a sales rep.

I've read thrillers all my life, starting with Enid Blyton's Famous Five series as a child, then graduating to James Hadley Chase, Harlan Coben, Linwood Barclay and Mark Edwards.

Let's get connected!
https://paulteague.net

Printed in Great Britain
by Amazon